Sweet
LIKE
Honey

Sweet LIKE Honey

KIM LOUISE

ARABESQUE®

SWEET LIKE HONEY

An Arabesque novel

ISBN-13: 978-0-373-83070-1
ISBN-10:   0-373-83070-X

www.kimanipress.com

Printed in U.S.A.

To the one and only Valencia Dee Battle.
I mean, who else, right?

Acknowledgment

Like a favorite song that I listen to over and over again, I have to thank my RWA chapter, Heartland Writers Group, for being a dedicated and supportive group of writers who continue to inspire me every day. Thanks to my critique group, Dee Ann, Patti and Theresa. Don't know what I'd do without you. To the fabulous readers who buy my books and keep asking for more, you are the center of my writing heart.

An extra-special thanks goes to Mr. CW himself. Creative Director extraordinaire...thank you for naming my character. And just in case you were wondering, any resemblance between you and Honey's ex is purely coincidental and a product of my vivid imagination.... Grins and hugs!

Chapter 1

There comes a time in every woman's life when she looks into the eyes of the man with whom she's shared the most intimate parts of herself and realizes she was meant to spend the rest of her life with him. Fortunately for Honey Ambrose, Cliff Watson was not that man.

He stood in her living room, as he had for the past five years, all six foot three of him, arms folded across his chest in exasperation, eyes soft and intense at the same time. She could barely believe it was true. She wasn't in love with him anymore.

"It's because I'm white, isn't it?"

Honey's patience was running thin. It was time for this back and forth between them to stop. For the first time in their hot and cold relationship, she was the one who would call it quits.

She folded her legs beneath her on her brown Broyhill couch, finally comfortable with the thought of being without him.

"You know that's not the reason. And you're just saying that because it's me doing the breaking up this time."

Cliff opened his mouth to speak, then clamped his lips shut. Her eyes followed the movement. Damn, she would miss kissing that mouth, tonguing his goatee.

"Okay, you're right," he admitted.

He looked like he wanted to sit down beside her, then thought better of it.

"Look, Cliff, I'm just giving you what you've wanted for a long time—your freedom."

"Yeah, but I only wanted it when I knew I couldn't get it."

He rocked a bit, with his long arms still crossed in front of his chest. His glasses caught the soft glare of her floor lamp, reflecting a vulnerability Honey didn't know the man had.

"Thank God, I've come to my senses," Honey said and meant it. The man in front of her had tied her life into emotional knots for so long that she didn't know how to live any differently.

Cliff took a seat next to her and placed a hand on her exposed leg, drew circles around her ankle with his finger. "You know what will change up this whole situation?"

Instead of sending thrills to all parts of her body, the sensation tickled. Honey laughed and pushed his hand away.

"Not gonna happen, Watson."

"I knew that. I knew that."

His head dropped to his chest. "Damn. This really is the end."

"Yeah," Honey said, a twinge of sadness weakening her voice.

He sighed and stretched his long, denim-clad legs out in front of him. "I'm going to miss you."

"How? You live next door."

"I used to live in you."

"Cliff, we'll always be—"

"Nope, not going there," he said, standing quickly. He headed for the door, his skin starting to flush.

"Don't give me that we'll-always-be-friends, I-love-you-like-a-brother crap."

"But it's true."

He opened the door. He was a slim man, but at that moment he looked like he was carrying a thousand pounds. "No it's not. That's why we couldn't make it. With us, it's all or nothing."

A pang of doubt made Honey bolt off the couch. "Cliff…" she began but with no idea of how to finish.

"Don't, baby," he said. "You're doing so well. I'm proud of you. Hold your ground…even if it means letting go of me."

Honey met him at the door, wondering where the strength of her heart was going. The power of her convictions.

Out the door?

She stood at the doorway of her two-story, custom-built home. Her lawn was well manicured, not a blade of grass out of place. No, the only thing out of place was the man walking across her yard and the piece of her heart he took with him.

West Cheyenne was unusually busy for a Monday morning. Cars rode past as though they were on an expressway rather than a residential neighborhood. It wasn't like there were a bunch of kids around. Most of the two-income families in the six-block square of her affluent subdivision were too in love with their independence to be tied down by children. Honey had chosen the neighborhood specifically because of that.

Independence.

Hearing the whoosh and bang of Cliff's door made her question her decision as she realized that even though she no longer wanted a life with him, she didn't want a life alone.

Two more cars sped by. In a hurry for what, Honey wondered. She didn't think she would be in a hurry for anything ever again.

She ran a hand through her crinkly hair and glanced around as a single woman for the first time in five years.

It was a strange feeling, but not as debilitating as she'd envisioned.

A bright sun pushed through thick white clouds. Honey smiled. If she'd known that the end of life as she'd lived it would not kill her, she would have ended her relationship with Cliff a long time ago.

She was eager to begin her new life, but her feet wouldn't move. Her legs had turned to lead, and Cliff's leaving had welded her to the spot. She was still standing stiffly in place when a big truck rolled down the street and backed up into her driveway. It wouldn't have been so bad except for the Dumpster attached to the back end and the fact that the driver of the truck had parked and was getting out of the cab.

He was a short guy, built like a rectangle. The name stitched on his blue company jumpsuit said Charlton.

"Can I help you?" Honey asked, gaining some of the feeling back in her legs.

"I just need a signature," he said, seemingly by rote. He must have said those words ten times a day for years.

"You've got the wrong address," she said.

"Ambrose? Honey Ambrose?"

The expression on his face hadn't changed. It was deadpan. Emotionless. There was no indication at all that he might be at the wrong location.

But Honey had no idea where or how he could have gotten her information. Although her brother, Brax, often accused her of harboring a landfill in her home, she didn't think of her piles and accumulations in that way.

"I'm Honey, but I never ordered a Dumpster."

That put a chink in old Charlton's chain. He stared down at his clipboard, lifted the top sheet and scanned the paper beneath it. When he looked up, his placid expression had been replaced by mild confusion.

"The name on the order is Houston Pace. He live here?"

"Never heard of him."

"Well he's heard of you. This Dumpster's been rented for a week. Paid in full."

A flicker of unease moved through her. Honey shifted her weight. "I don't know what to tell you except there's been a mistake."

Charlton tucked the clipboard under his arm, pulled his keys from the snap back clipped to his belt. "You sure you don't want the bin? This Pace guy put it on a credit card."

Honey glanced back at her house. Hills of inventory and mountains of merchandise choked damn near every room in her home.

"No, thanks," she said, turning back to Charlton.

"Okay," he said and went right back to his truck. He pulled out the same way he pulled in, nice and easy.

Honey went back into her house nice and easy and concerned, wondering why someone was trying to use her name and hoping that there wasn't some identity theft in progress. She made a note to get Roger Sprague, her credit advisor, to look into it for her.

As a matter of fact, she thought, maneuvering from her living room to the dining room amidst boxes, papers and catalogs, she'd call him right now.

Honey picked up the third stack of papers on her dining room table, took out the phone book underneath, then replaced the papers. She flipped to the *S* section, found the number and dialed.

Roger Sprague picked up after the first ring.

"Hey, gorgeous," he said.

"Hey, sweetheart. How've you been?"

"All right, but better now. What's up?"

"What do you know about identity theft?"

He paused. "Everything. Why?"

"I need to know if someone is using my name."

"I'd like to use your name," he said.

"What for?" she asked, but Honey had an idea.

"Honey, ah. Honey!"

"Fresh!" she retorted, but laughed.

"That's me. Okay, on the real. I'll check into it and call you back when—"

"Hold on, Roger," she said as her doorbell rang.

That better not be Cliff, she thought. It couldn't be. She didn't think her heart would be strong if it was.

Honey opened the door and was absolutely right about her heart. It wasn't strong. It was as weak as a wet paper towel—the no-name kind popular in ninety-nine-cent stores. The man standing in front of her was the cause and the effect.

Six five. Had to be. A wonderfully delicious bald head. His onyx eyes sparkled almost as brightly as the diamond-studded earrings in both his ears. In a crisp, copper-colored long-sleeved shirt and deep, bronze-colored linen pants, he had a body a wrestler would do a flying dropkick for and a mouth so luscious and sexy it could stop a convoy.

Honey had her own private heat wave goin' on inside her body.

"Uh, Roger…let me call you back."

"Okay, gorgeous," he said.

Honey pressed the Off button on her phone. The man in front of her had pressed her On button just by standing on her porch.

"May I…help you?" she asked, grateful she'd decided to put on a tank top, sans bra, and her favorite hip-hugging jeans. Her breasts lifted and jutted all on their own, and her hips swerved on autopilot.

"Yeah," he said, his robust voice making Honey tingle in all the sweet places. "You can tell me what happened to the Dumpster I ordered."

Chapter 2

If Honey Ambrose had known when her brother said he was getting her something special for her birthday he'd meant a man, she would have changed from tight jeans into don't-bend-over shorts.

"Excuse me," she said, hoping the tall drink of hot chocolate at her door would repeat himself.

"I'm Houston Pace. Your brother sent me. Happy birthday."

Honey gazed full-on at the delectable morsel of a man. Hershey's Special Dark complexion, eyes that held a wicked sparkle. The studs in his ears were a half carat each, she guessed. And the most dazzlingly sexy smile she'd ever seen up close.

She took one scorching look up and down his body, remembering a silly conversation she'd recently had with her brother Brax about male exotic dancers and thought to herself, *I didn't know strippers had stylists and exquisite taste.*

She couldn't wait.

"Well, come *on* in."

She stepped aside and let him enter. She made just enough room so he could squeeze past her. He smelled good; she knew he would. He just looked like the kind of brother a sister could inhale and get tipsy on. His cologne didn't disappoint—dark, woodsy and sexy as hell.

She closed the door, grateful that she was an early riser. She checked the time on her living room clock: 9:00 a.m. She would not have wanted to be asleep and have missed *this!*

"It's kinda early isn't it?"

"Yeah," he said, looking around her overstuffed living room. Probably trying to figure out how much room he'd have.

"Brax didn't lie. You've got a lot of stuff."

"Yeah, but we can move it," she said, already imagining him naked, sweaty, gyrating. She glanced at his empty hands wondering where his gear was. She'd been to enough strip parties to know the men usually came with a boom box and at least one change of clothes. "Where's your gear?"

"Gear?" he asked. He was walking around the Stonehenge of her living room. Boxes from Wholesale International, Natural Body and Oriental Trading stacked up like monoliths.

"Actually, I hadn't planned on staying long. I don't

want to take too much time out of your Monday. I usually call this kind of visit a look-see."

Honey smiled. She certainly wanted a *look-see.* Getting an eyeful of what he had to offer might get her over the hump of not having Cliff in her life—at least for a while.

"Okay, let me see what I've got for music."

Honey sauntered over to her collection. He stared over her shoulder at Beethoven, Baroque and Bach stacked neatly in a faux wood and glass case embedded in the wall. Appreciation flashed in his eyes.

"Guess somebody likes classical."

"Yes. I'm a classical junkie. But I also like…" she pushed a button on the remote control. The shelf filled with classical music CDs rotated to the next section. "R & B."

"Sweet," he said.

"Just like me," she responded and gave him the half smile and raised eyebrow that had toppled mountains. Well, maybe all it had done was get a few guys to be at her beck and call.

The man returned her soul-searing look with one of his own. Obviously, she wasn't the only mountain toppler in the room.

Okay, that backfired, she thought, feeling a hot cloud of air settle on her body, draping against her skin like a cape. Instead of having a man that would bend to her will, she decided to bend to his.

"Well." Honey cleared her throat. "Let's see what we can find."

She flipped through, James Brown, Will Downing,

Luther Vandross. Too fast. Too sultry. Too mellow. She took another searing look at the man she caught staring at her backside. He needed a sweet, sensual blend of all three. He did or she did.

"Are you looking to trim down your collection?"

"My music?" she asked as her hand slid over the plastic container. Searching.

"No."

"Good. You've got a nice selection. Very…well-rounded."

Was he talking about her CDs or something else?

She threw him another look over her shoulder. "You're good, and you haven't even started."

Finally, she selected something she thought would work, at least for her.

She pressed her index finger against the cool touch screen of her wall-mounted CD player, licked her lips. Exhaled the masculine aroma of Houston's cologne.

The tropical sounds of Shabba Ranks's "Take It Off" sailed through small, high-tech speakers.

She'd forgotten she even liked this song. As a nice distraction from her morning inventory duties, her cup of black coffee forgotten. Thoughts of Cliff vanished. Honey let the music take her hips for a moment. She sashayed to her couch thinking *Shakira ain't got nothin' on this,* and planted herself center stage.

"Take it off," she whispered, totally open to the wonderfully thoughtful birthday gift her brother got her, even if it was off-the-wall and unexpected.

Honey slung her arms against the back of the couch, settled in. Damn, she should have made popcorn.

* * *

Houston helped himself to an eyeful of the woman who looked hotter than two hells and just as sinful. With all that chocolate-chocolate skin showing and a voice deep and smoky like a fire tunnel. Only a few minutes in her presence and Houston felt if he'd stayed any longer, he wouldn't want to leave—ever.

But the way she was looking at him, maybe he should.

"I think you've got me wrong," he said, allowing the music and her response to it sink in.

She frowned, disappointment turning her sensuous features into a soft pucker. "Well, you should have brought your own music. I mean, what kind of stripper doesn't come with his own music?"

Stripper? Houston almost laughed out loud. He'd been called many things. *Stripper* had never been one of them.

She got up from her couch with a huff. Used the remote to rotate and expose another long row of CDs. She must really like her music.

He followed her over. "I'm not—"

The phone interrupted his clarification. She huffed again. "Why don't you see if you can find something?" she said, then headed into the dining area to take her call in private.

The moment she left him alone, Houston leaned against the wall, ran a hand down his face and chuckled.

If Brax only knew. What his sexy little sister really wanted for her birthday was a skin dance.

Then a thought struck him so much in the center of

cold and hot, it gave him a chill. He smiled like the Grinch Who Stole Christmas.

He'd squeezed this little excursion into his schedule as a favor to a good friend. A friend who'd been the catalyst for Houston moving from a consultant with a radio show to debuting a nationally syndicated weekly show on Bravo. With all the loose ends he still had to tie up before *Pickin' Up With Pace* aired on television, he really didn't have time to squeeze in one more thing. Especially not a whole home reorg, even if the home had just been a run-of-the-mill clutter job. But Honey's place needed extra-special attention. He gazed at pile after pile of paper, files and boxes. Brax should have warned him.

To get it done in time, he'd have to clone himself and work around the clock. There was just no way.

But, maybe he could give her something she *really* wanted. How hard could it be to dance to a few songs, strip down to his boxers and make a clutter bug happy? He'd be over and out inside of an hour. Honey would be happy, and he'd get on with his TV life. Plus, the idea of getting naked for Miss Sultry and Sexy didn't exactly rub him the wrong way.

He took a quick scan of Honey's hip-hop music collection and found a track he recognized.

Perfect, he thought, working the CD changer and sliding the disk in. He advanced the selection to the third track, pressed Pause and held the remote ready.

She came out with her cell phone bulging from a front pocket and her Bluetooth technology stuck in her ear. But he couldn't wait. If he did, his nerve might evaporate and he'd be forced to go through a landfill of clutter. His show was too important. He'd do whatever he needed to do to make it successful and to take as much time as he needed to start on the right foot.

No time, he thought and pressed Play.

Actually, this wouldn't be a bad gig. Brax's sister looked like "tic toc ya don't stop" personified. The word *sexy* didn't do her justice at all, although he could start there. Curly auburn hair, eyes so intense they looked feline. Round, moist lips. Curve after curve of pecan skin in the tightest tank and jeans he'd seen in a long time.

Maybe this would work out for the best after all.

Honey had to be careful or her smile would hurt her face. "I don't say this much, but I love you."

"I take it Houston showed up."

"Yes. Thank you! I can't believe you."

The pause on Brax's end of the line surprised her. She waited for him to say something.

"I gotta tell you, I wasn't sure how you'd react."

She stole a glance into the living room, then turned away. "I guess not. I mean, who would have thought?"

The moment she stepped back into the living room, the smoldering look in Houston's eyes made her stop short. The music started, and her heart flipped. So much sensuality and determination in his eyes, she couldn't move. The only thing she could do is stand and be hungry.

Usher's "Seduction" drifted rhythmically toward her, the beat familiar and long overdue. She smiled even more and prepared for the show. She retook her seat and forgot her brother was on the line until

Houston had started unbuttoning his shirt and Brax said, "...straighten up that mess you call a house."

"What?" she asked, noting something amiss in Brax's conversation, but keeping a *good lookin' out* on the man who mesmerized her with every button freed, ever hip sway, every penetrating gaze.

She would have undone a button of her clothing, if she'd had any buttons.

"So when he gets finished organizing everything, call me. I want to make sure he's done my sister right."

Oh, he's doin' me right, she thought. Then her mind slid back a few words.

"Do what now?"

"I know Houston's a big-time professional organizer, got his own show now, but I want to make sure he does exactly as I asked and not a halfhearted job."

Each word her brother spoke dropped like a brick in her mind. She didn't know what tore at her more—the fact that the guy was a neat freak or the cocoa-brown six-pack slowly being revealed underneath a copper-colored shirt.

She could only imagine that the expression on her face revealed how much she wanted to reach out and touch all that fine, sexy skin he teased her with.

He licked his lips. "Tell 'em you'll call 'em back, baby." His deep voice stirred her. Made her pinch her thighs together and press into the throb there.

"I gotta call you back," she said. Honey switched off her phone and settled back.

Houston smiled with pretty white teeth. *Whew, delicious,* she thought.

Mister Sexy Moves pulled his undershirt up and out of his pants, slid the corners left right, matched the movement with his hips, then turned around and leaned back.

He didn't have to say a word. She pulled off the bright white tank, gave it a quick fold and laid it beside her.

He flexed his muscles in all the right places and in all the right ways, like mighty ripples moving down his body from his neck to his hips. When the motion reached his waist, he undulated his hips making an *S* in the air, as if the air were her body and he couldn't get deep enough.

He undid his belt, slid the smooth calfskin leather out of the loops nice and easy. Usher sang "Seduction," Houston made that *S* with his torso, Honey pressed her thighs tighter, throbbed harder, got nice and wet.

"Umm," he said, watching her. He slid his pants down his legs and stepped out of them.

"My, my, my," Honey said, despite herself. Brotherman had muscle-thick thighs and was fillin' out his black boxer briefs like nobody's business. Honey considered the thought of making it *her* business.

He reacted to her reaction. Touching himself, his arms, his chest, sliding them down, framing the package, licking his lips, staring at her hotly. Breathing deep.

Honey responded in kind, squirming in her seat, biting her bottom lip, sliding a finger against an erect nipple. Her body was so hot, so tense, that she actually considered gettin' her a little somethin' somethin' from this man.

He stepped closer, close enough to touch. Every

movement of his hips now matched a drumbeat, a bass line. On point and in time. He held his arms out to his sides. He was magnificent. So fine. Corded brown muscle and sinew, an erotic offering moving for her. Not even Cliff had treated her to such a display. Houston had only been in her house five minutes and already...

He mouthed the last few words, licked his lips again, smiled. *Seduction.*

Honey got up slowly from the couch. She gathered Houston's clothes. He came toward her, daring her to touch him. When she backed away, closer to the door, he took her hand and pressed it against his chest. Her clit jumped, and she felt as if she'd just experienced the world's fastest orgasm. His muscles rippled and bulged, and he had the roundest backside any woman would be proud to call her man's own.

She gasped, her need building hot and tight. *Keep it together, girl.* Keep...it...together.

She continued to back up. He kept coming toward her. When she reached the door, she twisted the knob behind her back, moved her hand away from Houston's soft skin and hard muscle, swung the door open and regained her senses.

"Organize this!" she ordered and tossed his designer clothes outside.

"What?" he said, blinking like he didn't understand.

"I know you heard me—now get out before I call the police."

He had the nerve to look hurt. "Damn, baby. That's cold."

Honey held the door wider, kept her appreciation of

his gorgeous body in check, but took one more look since she knew it would be the last one she got of Houston Pace. '

"Get ta steppin'," she said, flicking her wrist toward the street.

"I promised your brother—" he said.

"Out!" she shouted and slammed the door behind him the moment he stepped outside.

She couldn't wait to tell her brother, and she would give him a big ol' piece of her mind. He better not ever send some crazy organizing stripper to her house. And if he did, Houston Pace would get escorted away from her house by Cheyenne, Wyoming's finest.

Imagine, he tried to take advantage of me. What an opportunist. A fine opportunist, but still an opportunist.

Well that had better be the last time opportunity came knocking at her door. Or else. Next time, she wouldn't be so nice.

Chapter 3

Brax had been blowin' up Houston's iPhone all evening. Houston knew better than to take a call from Brax so soon after the disaster, while he was still seething with anger. Brax was a stomp down friend till the end. But if you messed with him… Houston was no cream puff himself, but he sure didn't want to tussle with Brax right now. He'd give Brax time to cool down and himself time to come up with a plan. He owed his friend that much.

Houston drove his SUV down the winding Cheyenne streets, taking the scenic route back to Honey's house, mindful of Brax Ambrose.

A shipping mix-up left one of Brax's clients with too much merchandise and not enough space. Brax saw what kind of bind he was in and suggested that an expert could help them. Neither Brax nor Houston knew at the time that the man was also an executive at the Bravo TV network. And when the Fab Five taped the last show of their highly successful series, Bravo was looking for just the right replacement. Houston Pace's name had floated right up to the top of the list. The rest, Houston hoped, would be network history.

His mind was already turning with book deals, DVD sales, movie cameos and national speaking tours. The show was just the first stop on a long journey he wanted to take. But before he'd allow himself to think about those things any further, he had to focus on the only favor Brax had asked—help his sister out.

Standing outside Honey's house in nothing but his underwear had brought Houston crashing to his senses. He had to do right by her or the universe wouldn't do right by his show.

So, as his phone rang again for the tenth time that evening, Houston answered it and prepared to face the wrath of Brax.

"What's up, man?"

"Negro, are you crazy? I mean tell me you have lost you GD mind. Maybe then I'll halfway understand and spare your life."

"Whoa, whoa. Hold on, man. You're right. I lost my mind for a minute. But on the real, why didn't you tell me your sister was that fine?"

First silence. And then, "You must want me to beat you all the way down."

"Nah, man. Nothing like that. I'm just sayin'…with

all that woman comin' at me, I lost it. I went nuts. Now the truth is, she assumed—for reasons I really don't want to know—that you had hired a stripper. So I thought, why not give her what she wants for her birthday instead of what you want her to have?"

"Pace—"

"Never mind. I squashed that. Matter of fact, I'm in her driveway right now. I'm just waiting on, uh…some assistants, and we're gonna get to work. I swear. I owe you, man. I know that. And I'm gonna make this right. Aight?"

Silence.

Two Cheyenne police cars pulled up. One parked in front of Honey's house. The other parked directly behind Houston's car.

Houston put on his sunglasses and took a deep breath. "Gotta go," he said, snapping his phone closed. The two officers walked beside his car and stopped at the driver's door. Houston got out and straightened his shirt. It was time to stop messing around. He had work to do.

"What you got for me, Daddy?" Honey asked of the tall, brown drink of tequila standing in her kitchen.

"Everything you like," he said, with a voice as soft and tempting as warm butter.

Honey gave Tony Jara her best thank-you eyes and her I-really-appreciate-this-more-than-you'll-ever-know smile. "You know where everything goes, sweetie."

"Hmph," he said, taking two weeks' worth of steak, chicken and lamb dinners out of his bag and placing them on her Formica counter. "I've been trying to tell you that for weeks."

She chuckled and smiled even more sweetly. "You know I appreciate you," she said, giving him a mild pat on his behind. As behinds went, Honey thought Tony had the best around until this morning. That Houston Pace psycho may have the roundest, firmest, most quarter-bouncing butt she'd ever seen. She picked up one of Tony's recipe cards and fanned with it. He glanced at her and laughed.

"What?" she asked.

"That's about the best workout that card is going to get."

"I told you, sweetie. As long as I have you, I don't need recipe cards."

He put the last of her ready-made dinners in the freezer. Tony sure could cook. She really was grateful that he took care of her the way he did, with nothing but sweet and harmless flirtation for his trouble.

He moved away from the refrigerator and across the kitchen to where she stood next to the wine rack. He got close. Real close. Close enough for her to smell onions, basil and oregano. He truly lived his life as a cook.

"One day, you won't have me to cook for you."

"Don't be silly," she said, stepping closer. "You'll always take care of me."

He bent down slowly. Honey felt a little jump in her heart, a spark in her nerves. Tony planted a quick kiss against her cheek, then stood back looking at her with handsome Mexican eyes.

He was a good man. With Cliff gone, Honey might

be in the market for a good man. But would Tony understand her the way Cliff does…did?

"Tony—"

The doorbell made them both step back. They shook each other off like they'd been under a stupid spell.

"I'll be right back," Honey said, then headed into her living room.

Talk about saved by the bell, she thought. When she opened the door, she discovered she hadn't been saved at all. Her heart started pop-locking in her chest. The handsome annoyance was back. Thankfully, he was not alone. Two Cheyenne police officers were with him. She didn't have to call them after all. But what in the world was he doing around her place that was so suspicious that it had compelled a neighbor to call the po-pos?

She checked out the name tag of the nearest officer. She was a big woman. The authority in her face made Honey believe that Officer Brandt-Cole was just the latest in an assembly line of cops. Probably born with a badge pinned to her chest. Just the kind of law enforcement officer who would keep Houston in check.

"Whatever he's done, I'd like to press full charges."

Officer Brandt-Cole slid Houston a look of impatience. The other officer, a much shorter and more amiable-looking woman, crossed bulky arms against a double D chest.

"Good evening, Honey," Houston said. His voice sounded syrupy and self-righteous. The pop-locking turned into the running man.

Houston stepped forward, turned the sweet mouth of his into a smile. "Since you threatened to call the cops on me, I thought I'd save you the trouble. This is Sara and Valerie."

Honey wrestled back the expletive fighting for freedom at the tip of her tongue. She crossed her arms over her size E chest and emotionally dug in her heels. "What do you want?"

"To make your life better."

Now her heart just melted. "If you're worried about Brax—"

"I'm not," he said. "But what I am worried about—"

"What's going on?" Tony asked, coming out of the kitchen. He stood beside Honey like a guard dog. The moment Houston saw Tony, Houston's right eyebrow went up and his jaw tightened. Honey was even more thankful for her friend's presence than usual. The backup felt good.

"I'm sorry, you were saying?" she asked.

Houston took a deep breath. He ignored the two cops and Tony and focused directly on her. "We need to talk."

"She can hear you just fine," Tony said.

Houston looked annoyed. "Man, you don't want none of this. Trust me."

Tony stepped forward. "What the hell?"

That's when the two cops finally did something besides flank Houston like a couple of bookends. They stepped between Houston and Tony. From bookends to barriers.

"Is all this really necessary?" Honey asked. The idea of police at her house was starting to turn her stomach. And she was all out of patience for Mr. Houston Pace.

"Give me five minutes," he said, then looked at

Tony as if to say "Leap, frog." Tony was not backing down, and neither was Honey…at first.

"What if I say he's trespassing, Officer Brandt-Cole?"

"We'll make sure he leaves your property," the other officer said.

Obviously Brandt-Cole is the muscle, Honey thought.

Before The War on Stupidity raged any further smack dab on her front porch, Honey offered a truce.

She stuck out a defiant hip, crossed her arms tighter over her chest. "Three and a *half* minutes."

"Done," Houston said.

Houston's eyes softened, a sweet, brown thank-you. That softened her.

"Okay, sweetie," she said to Tony. She stood on her tiptoes, put her hands on his shoulders, and kissed his cheek. "Thanks for…everything."

"No problem, baby. You sure you want to be alone with this dude?"

Honey laughed inside. She knew Tony, who was a one-hundred-percent, USDA, Grade A chuck wagon cowboy, had just given Houston the ultimate insult by calling him a *dude*.

"I'll be fine. I just need to know when you're gonna come see me again."

"I got some ropin' to do in Alliance. I'll be back after that." He planted a kiss on her forehead. It was nice.

Honey watched Tony head out the door. The officers followed behind him. Houston stepped inside, smelling good again. She closed the door behind him and turned to see impatience puckering Houston's face like a whiskey sour.

"Thank you," he said.

"What's up with you bringing the cops to my house?"

"I just thought if I brought them, you'd be more inclined to hear me out."

"That's some craziness."

"Yet, here I am," he said, speaking with a confidence she found annoying as all get out and sexy as hell.

"Three minutes fifteen seconds left," she said, starting the countdown.

"Does my name ring a bell with you?"

She checked an imaginary watch. "Three minutes."

"I've been on *Good Morning America,* TV One, *The View*—"

"Oprah?"

His face fell a bit. "Not yet."

"Two minutes," she said.

"I don't have to rely on other people's television shows now. I have my own, starting in a month."

Honey wondered if she was supposed to be impressed. She'd had her own show for years.

"I wouldn't have that show, at least so soon, if it weren't for Brax. I owe him big—"

"One minute."

"And I told him he could have anything except my firstborn and he asked for this."

"Thirty seconds."

"I owe him…everything. And he's concerned that your home is…" Houston looked around, disapproval riding his Nicholas Gonzalez features. "Getting out of hand. Now, I may not be a lot of things, but there's one thing I am and that's a man of my word."

Unlike *some* people, she thought, who say they'll love you forever and then skip out after five years just because you won't give up the booty. Love has got to run deeper than that.

"Honey?"

"What?" she asked, shaking off her anger at Cliff.

"Let me do what I do. I promise you won't regret it."

Damn if this man didn't look sincere. He stood there all business in a tan designer suit. Part player, part pit bull, part puppy dog. Hell, if she looked into his eyes too long, she'd probably be the puppy licking his face. All those clothes didn't do him any good. All she could see was brown skin and muscles. So she turned away.

Suddenly she saw her living room and dining room the way he must see it. Clutter, clutter and more clutter. Hills and mountains of it. And it didn't stop there. The towers of stuff followed her each evening up her stairs and onto the second floor of her home. What was wrong with her? What rational person would live in this state of disarray?

"Do you have a business card?" she asked.

"Yes," he said, reaching into the front pocket of his jacket, "but I'd rather give you this."

He pulled out a sleek, black pen and handed it to her. "It's a flash drive. There's a presentation about me, my business and more than you ever cared to know about organizing your life. There are links to contact me within the presentation."

"Thanks," she said, wishing she'd thought of that idea for her own business.

"I'm at the Historic Plains Hotel. If you really don't want my services, please let me know as soon as possible. That will give me a chance to fly to L.A. and finish the preparations for my show early."

"Sounds reasonable," she said.

Houston wiped an imaginary layer of sweat from his forehead, smiled that clit-wetting smile of his and said, "Whew!"

"Whatever. I'll be in touch."

He headed to the door. She was right behind him leaning into his woodsy scent. He opened the door and paused before exiting. "Thanks for the three minutes."

"And thirty seconds."

"Yes. Can't forget that."

Their eyes caught and held. The moment was sensual, juicy, hot. Images of him dancing rose up fine and funky in her mind. Tickled her body just like fingers. She had to get him out of her place immediately. If not, she'd put "Seduction" on and this time undress for him.

He left her with a look so sultry that she had to stop herself from stopping him.

"Have a good night," he said.

And the voice matches those sexy eyes.

She sighed, leaning against the door when he left, thinking she was going to be her best customer this evening and headed for her goody drawer. She had a new product she wanted to try immediately.

Chapter 4

"What's the status?"

Houston crossed his fingers behind his back. He'd come out to Brax Ambrose's ranch in Shoresville, Nebraska, to spend the day with one of his buddies.

"Like I said, man. After assessing the scope and magnitude of—"

"Spare me," the big man said, raising a thick and callused hand. "Details, I don't need. A sister with a clear head is a requirement. Especially if I'm living so close now."

Houston and Brax became friends when they both were living in Savannah, Georgia. Just kinda stumbled into each other one day at a back-of-the-bar poker game. When it got down to heads-up play, only Houston and Brax remained. After an hour of back-

and-forth play, Houston won big. Both men left the table with mutual respect. They spent another forty-five minutes drinking cognac and trading poker stories. They'd been friends ever since.

Houston thought he might hurt his neck taking in all of the land that belonged to his friend. Endless waves of rolling grassy hills, trees and pasture. The expanse was more than impressive. "B, this is a long way from double down at Smokey's. How in the hell—"

"Man, I told you. Her name is Ariana," he said.

Houston laughed. Brax joined him. "What is it about a woman?" Houston asked. "I mean, really? Women are coming up, but for the most part, it's still a man's world. We own everything."

"But it don't mean nothing—" Brax began.

"Without a woman or a girl. And if you tell *any*one I said that, I'll sic Sweet Pea on you."

"No worries. If your crazy cousin comes within ten feet of me, well, just let me say Ari is *real* good with a shotgun."

They laughed at that.

Brax tipped his hat back against his forehead. Stared into a cloudless sky. "I gotta put the truth in the river, that woman has done something. She really made me believe."

The big man didn't have to say any more. Houston knew his friend was trying to come up with the most manly, chest-pounding way to say, "I'm head over heels for this little golden-haired gal and there's nothing in the world I would deny her."

"So, what's up with you? How many women callin' you *Daddy* in the midnight hour?" Brax asked.

Houston felt his head go slack, his chest deflate. "I cut everybody loose. Not that I had that many."

"No. Not that."

"I just need to make a fresh start with this TV thing, you feel me?"

"Um."

"There were a couple girls I was seein', you know. For a good time, some laughs, booty calls, whenever. But when it came time to make a move, a serious move, I couldn't see any of them fitting into my new life. Hell, I don't even know if I'm gonna fit into it."

"Man, you were born for this."

Houston pulled the reins on his horse, who'd stopped to put the chomp on a nice-sized bush.

"So, you gonna hook my sister up or what?"

Houston heard the question, but felt the concern. "Man, I've seen her place. Nothin' that a few storage boxes in a spare bedroom can't fix."

"Have you seen her spare bedroom?"

"Damn," Houston said. "That's not your everyday pack rat."

"Don't get me wrong. My sister ain't crazy, just a little lost at times. And I think her junk pile is an expression of that."

It's not clutter that messes up people's lives, Houston thought. *People's lives are messed up, usually by other people, and clutter is a warning sign.* In most cases, a cry for help. Sometimes, the mess outside wasn't half as bad as the mess inside.

Houston considered his work. He was proud of the fact that his organizing business went deeper than just making things neat. He tried to get to the heart of why things got so out of hand in the first place and then provided his customers with tools to prevent their lives from reverting back to their state of disarray.

"The ball's in her court, man. I've done all I could do."

"You sure about that?"

"Uh, yeah."

"What happened to your rep? Back in the day, you claimed you could get any woman to do anything you wanted. Now, you're talkin' 'bout you've done all you could do. What happened to you, man? I thought you were the Mack Daddy?"

"That was game. This is business."

"You're kidding me, right? Negro, if I had said that to you, you would have asked me, 'What's the difference?'"

"See, that's why I don't have friends. After a while, they think they know me."

Brax was right. There was a time in Houston's life where he thought his looks and charm were his ticket to anywhere he wanted to go, especially if that meant between a woman's thighs. Getting serious about his business had forced him to get serious about other things in his life, as well, and he realized that his Mack Daddy lifestyle wasn't doing a thing for him. And he'd reached a point where he saw foolishness like that as a waste of time and a potential threat to his success. No one, including himself, would mess up his chance now.

They finished out their day riding the vast range of Brax's ranch, the Sugar Trail, on horseback.

Before going inside for what Brax called supper, a delayed thought struck Houston. "*Put the truth in the river?* That just hit me! Man, you truly have changed."

Houston got down from the horse, vowing never to let a woman change him so completely.

Chapter 5

She could have him. Any time. Any way. Any where. Any place. Any how. Pablo. The gardener. How clichéd was that?

Honey stared out her front window at a man so handsome, she had wet daydreams about him every time he came to prune a bush. Trim a hedge. Get her roses right. Keep her yard tight. She always drank lemonade when she watched him. The tart kind, just barely sweetened. She liked it that way, preferring the bitter taste of the lemon to the sugar-water kind. And the sour fruit seemed to go well with Pablo's physique, which he hid under T-shirts that were way too big.

Of course, an hour into his work and the T-shirt always came off, revealing a tight set of biceps, triceps, granite pecs and abs that were simply lickalicious.

And the man had some of everything in him. African-American, Native-American, Mexican-American, with a pinch of Italian-American mixed in. But to Honey, he looked like a homeboy from around the way. Half a step up from a thug and just as dangerous. And the things he did to her yard...the brotha had some kinda hands.

Whew! she said, sliding the ice-cold glass across her hot forehead. *Nothin' in the world like a hard-workin' man!*

For a brief and silly moment, Honey thought about Cliff and had the nerve to glance next door at his front yard. She half expected to see him there, keeping a jealous eye on Pablo like he usually did, sensing the turmoil taking place inside her.

Now is the time for girlfriends, she thought, prying herself away from the window and the panoramic view of Pablo's muscles. She could hear the conversation now...

"Girl, I had a stripper in my place yesterday."

"What?"

"Yeah, girl. A fine one, too. I can barely remember his name. Houston, or some city. But anyway, he came up in here, put on some Usher and went for what he knew."

"No!"

"*Yes!* And this Mr. Mister was fine. Okay, when I say fine, I mean hot-flash, wet-panties, I-gotta-touch-myself, how-long-is-his-package kinda fine."

"Damn..."

But there was no girlfriend to call. Honey didn't get along too well with women. They all went off on some jealousy trip. Like Honey could help the way she looked. Sexy eyes, small waist and more pla-*dow,* and ka-dunk-a-dunk than three black women from the South.

And she loved every part of herself. Loved to watch the way men watched her. Hell, yeah. She got off on it. Problem was, her friends' men got off on it, too, and there would always be an argument. A "hell no, I don't want your man, he's lookin' at *me,* girl, listen, you man called me last night" kinda argument. Always ugly. And always left her without friends.

For the past five years, her best friend had been Cliff. But there was no way she could call him and tell him that although she wouldn't give it up to him in five years, a stranger had come into her home and in five minutes, she was ready to drop it 'cause it was so damn hot.

Honey drank most of her lemonade on the way from her living room to her work area—state-of-the-art computer, two long worktables and a digital movie camera on a tripod. She'd gone to the window to watch for the mail carrier. Honey could usually set her LCD by her. Ten thirty-five every morning. Her neighborhood got one of the first runs in the area. Monday was new product day. After doing research Monday and Tuesday, Honey would place her toy orders from wholesalers on Wednesday. Who knew the finest pleasure-makers came from Taiwan?

Honey stepped around a case of motion lotion, stepped over a box of extra-large, glow-in-the-dark, chocolate-flavored condoms and picked up a stack of Do It To It finger vibes from her chair and plopped down. She placed the vibes beside a product she was testing—The Moan Maker. So far it had done little more than coax a small whimper, but she was going to give it one more try before she wrote her review.

Anyway, she forced her mind away from Houston Pace and his home invasion and opened her topic file. She still hadn't selected a subject for this week's show and she wanted to get started with an outline of the broadcast.

Creating your own erotic board games.

The do's and don'ts of remote control vibes.

Pleasure toys that double as practical devices like cell phones.

She had so many possibilities. Usually, she was quick about her selection. Inspiration typically came from her latest shipment and something new she'd discovered. But the only something new that occupied her mind for the past few hours was the image of the gorgeous brown muscle-thick body, hips rolling slow and sensually in her living room, grinding, calling to her…se-duc-tion.

More lemonade! she thought and headed for the kitchen.

Before she got to the refrigerator, she stopped and stared at the pen on her dining room table. Sleek, elegant, well-designed—just like the man. Instead of a glass of lemonade, she picked up her cell phone and dialed.

"No, no, no, no, no, no, no, no. You did *not* ask me over here to tell me that."

"I had to. My body is driving me crazy."

The two of them sat in Honey's living room. Her big-screen TV was tuned to the blues music station. Shameeka Copeland's big gritty voice belted out the story of a woman on a mission. Honey had cleared a space on a TV tray and placed the just-delivered order of lettuce wraps from P.F. Chang's between them, but even Cliff's favorite music and most loved food hadn't persuaded him to give her the advice she needed.

He got up and did what he was most famous for…he paced. This time with his bat. Cliff had a 1960s baseball bat that he carried around whenever he had an important decision to make. He'd told her when they first started dating that it made him think better. Honey thought it was just a phallic representation of—

"No *way!*" he said, stopping abruptly. "Tell me I haven't just spent five years priming the pump so that another man, some cat you've known for all of what…five minutes, can come drink all he wants. Hell no!"

"So…you don't think I should sleep with him?" Honey started on her second lettuce wrap. Nothing wrong with her appetite. As a matter of fact, it was better than ever. She couldn't tell if it was because she was excited or confused. Either way, Cliff better dig in or there'd be nothing left but sweet brown sauce.

"I can't believe this." Left side of the room.

"I can't believe this is happening." Right side of the room.

He started laughing and looking up at the ceiling with his arms wide. "I mean, you gotta be kidding me here. We just broke up!"

"Cliff—"

"I tucked tail outta here, what? Forty-eight hours ago?"

"Cliff?"

"And you have the audacity to—"

"Cliff!" Honey said, with a mouth full of food.

"What?" he said, calmly, as if he just realized he wasn't alone.

"I need you to be my friend." Surprisingly, her voice was shaky. She didn't like seeing him in pain. Or upset about anything. Least of all, about her or them. If she didn't have Cliff, she didn't have anything. It was still too early to tell about her relationship with her brothers. Even though they were blood kin, they'd only met each other three years ago. She was still trying to digest that development.

If her sudden need to be with a man was going to jeopardize her relationship with her one and only friend, well then, she just wouldn't do it. It wasn't worth it.

"Damn," he said and sat down next to her on the couch.

"What?"

"That look. I'm listening to you tell me that after all these years, it wasn't that you didn't want to have sex, you just didn't want to have sex with *me*. And even though that hurts like hell, the only thing I can think when you look at me like that is how beautiful you are."

"Cliff…"

"No. Don't be sweet. Be hard. Otherwise, I'll fall in love with you again, and I've already started unloving you."

Honey smiled. She could never unlove Cliff. With his white Malcolm X face, his long, untucked cotton shirts, his faded jeans, loafers and bat, he had this California-Bay Area vibe that she couldn't do without. She was emotion; he was intellect. They fit so well together; they were the life of parties and he was the party of her life. Whenever her gut threatened to override her mind, Cliff kept her sensible.

He made himself a lettuce wrap and took a bite. She gave him time. Knew he needed it and respected him for taking it.

"Okay. Here's the deal. No sleeping with the stripper."

Honey's hopes sank. "What? I thought you'd want me to finally take the plunge."

"What I want is immaterial at the moment. But what makes sense is for you to hold off. This could be residual stuff from you and me. As a matter of fact, it probably is. Another factor is, I'm the only man you've seen naked in five years, so naturally, seeing someone else strip might have undue influence."

He finished his first wrap and hurriedly made another while Honey reflected.

"What about his deal with Brax?"

"What about it? For all you know, he's a con artist whose done a number on your brother and what he really does is case people's homes so he can come back and rip them off."

"No. I checked him out. He's legit. And not just legit. He's like an organizing guru. He's got books. DVDs. A Web site. He's the real deal."

Cliff wiped his mouth and sat back against the couch. "So, what do *you* think about his deal with Brax?"

"I think it's raw. And I think it's wrong for my brother

to do something like that without checking with me first."

"Hmm," Cliff said. He rolled his bat with his fingers. The imprint mark twirled around and back around.

"What, hmm?"

"You don't really want to give it up do you?"

"I said I did."

"I know you did. But you're lying. This isn't about that at all. This is about you still afraid of sex, but finally meeting someone who challenges that fear in a real way."

"Whatever. Like you said. I only met him for five minutes."

"Sometimes, that's all it takes," Cliff said. His voice was solemn. Closed.

He stood. Kept his bat by his side and low to the ground.

"Cliff—"

"Don't worry," he said. "You're still my girl. It's just that pretty soon, I won't be craving for you to be my woman."

Honey nodded. Licked some of the soy sauce from her fingers.

Cliff shook his head and kept his eyes on her mouth. "You don't even realize what you do to men, do you?"

He turned to the door before she could respond.

"Where're you going?" she asked, standing and walking behind him.

"Somewhere to get laid," he said. His voice sounded strong and determined.

"You know, Jenny Felts has been after you for two years."

Cliff stared across the street and two houses down where Jenny Felts, senior partner of Franklin, Peters, Moore and Felts, kept a trim yard on her tidy and humongous home.

"That she has."

"Maybe you should pay her a visit."

No sooner did Honey say the words than Jenny's PT Cruiser came down the street and turned into her driveway.

Honey smiled. So did Cliff.

He bent down, kissed her on the cheek and lingered near her ear. "Whatever you do, do it with your heart. Everything else is BS."

"Thank you," she said.

Honey watched Cliff for a few moments and chuckled when he called, "Jenny!" and skipped off with his bat.

She closed the door and scrutinized her home for the first time in years.

It was a disaster. Every surface was choked with products, or orders, or returns, or catalogs. For a long moment, Honey felt suffocated, like she couldn't breathe.

She didn't know if she could stand to have Houston all over her home, in her things, sorting stuff, touching belongings. But if he could just get the living room, dining room and her work area under control, it might be enough to give her incentive to tackle the rest of her house…eventually. And it would also get Brax off both of their backs.

Honey headed back to the phone on the kitchen wall—the only one she could find at the time. She had another phone call to make.

Chapter 6

"Look, you don't want to do this and neither do I. Frankly, the sooner I get out of Cheyenne, the better. I can't get to L.A. fast enough. We've already lost a day. If we start now, we can be done with sorting by evening."

He was being unreasonable. Obviously, the clients he was used to having were stay-at-home mothers or something. People who didn't have inventories to keep track of or orders to fill. There had to be a way they both could get what they wanted.

"Houston, instead of taking everything out of my living room, dining room and work area, why don't we dedicate one day to each room."

"No offense, but I'm not trying to be here a whole week."

"When do you absolutely have to be in L.A.?"

"December 1."

"Cool. That gives us an entire month. I'm sure it won't take that long for what we need to do."

A flicker lit up his eyes and Honey smiled, first inside and then, no longer able to contain it, outside, too.

"I really am sorry for taking advantage of a misunderstanding."

"No harm. But to make it up to me, you gotta make this good. I wanna see some organizing, then."

"Oh, don't worry." He smiled that heartbreaking smile of his. "I got this."

"Told you, I'll make it good for you."

Their eyes came back to each other and lingered. Heat rose inside her, from her toes to the top of her head. Almost made her dizzy.

There was something special that happens to a woman when she's near a fine man. Especially one whose eyes are looking at you and telling you he's feelin' you, too.

She liked Houston's eyes. They were vibrant and lit up when they looked at her. They smiled just as pleasantly as any mouth. Especially one as sensuous as his.

She automatically started checking him out to see what else she liked about him besides his face. Tupac's eyes. Denzel's shoulders. LL's arms. Fifty's abs. Boris's hips and thighs. Emmitt's glutes.

But the part of him that fascinated her were his hands. She was a hands woman. A man that takes care of his hands will take care of his woman. Clean, clipped nails. Smooth cuticles. Without a hint of ash in sight. Hands without calluses that she could imagine touching her on all her soft places and feeling good.

Honey always imagined herself with someone like Cliff, who worked in an office. The worst possible thing that could happen to his hands was a paper cut.

Oooh, Lord, she thought and stepped back a bit from the heat that pulled like a magnet.

She leaned against the wall. "So, what, do I go away now? Should I take my laptop and check into a hotel room?"

Houston smirked. So damn sexy. "Uh, no. That only happens on TV."

"I thought you were a big-time TV star."

"It's comin'. In the meantime, we're gonna do this the way everybody else does it. I'll make a visual assessment, we'll talk for a while and then both of us will sort and purge."

"Ugh. That doesn't sound like fun."

"Baby, in my world, everything is fun. I have a motto—if it ain't fun, don't do it."

Houston grinned a little then. "I have another motto, too."

"Yeah?" Honey stuck out a hip, planted her hand against it.

"Yeah, it's…oh, hell. I thought I'd come up with something clever."

Truth was, the only words that wanted to come out of Houston's mouth were, *Let me make love to you.*

Brax's sister had the kind of body that clothes offended. It was simply a disgrace to cover up something that voluptuous. Houston had to find something serious to focus on. Otherwise, he'd be grinding his hips and trying to take his shirt off again. "So, Honey Ambrose…what do you do?"

"I sell sex toys."

Houston gulped and his body felt like he'd been swallowed by a fire-breathing dragon. "Sex…"

"Toys. Uh-huh," she said, reaching over and grabbing the largest dildo he'd ever seen.

He did a double take of all the boxes of all sizes and shapes taking up every available space in her living room, dining room and work area. "So all this…" he said, ordering his imagination to power down from its quick flicker into overdrive.

"I'm surprised Brax didn't tell you. It's called Fulfillment."

Despite himself, Houston became intensely curious about what was in each and every one of the boxes taking over the downstairs of Honey's house.

He picked up a black shiny box about the size of a shoe box. Shook it. Not too heavy.

"Who are you selling these things to?" he asked, putting the box back.

"Anyone that wants them and can pay."

The thought that someone had to resort to artificial stimulation saddened Houston. "Lonely housewives, huh?" he said, trying to make light of the fact that he was surrounded by containers of imitation male members and who knows what else.

"No. Are you kidding? If lonely housewives were my only customers, I couldn't afford to live here."

"Umm," he said, suddenly wondering if she was her own customer.

Houston clapped his hands and rubbed his palms together. "So, how about a tour. I'd like to see what I'm workin' with here."

Honey finally put that darn dildo in an overflowing drawer in her desk. "Okay. You've already seen the living room." She pointed to the left. "This is my dining room." She pointed across to the right. "This is my work area."

She stared at him expectantly.

"Don't stop now," he said, eager to learn more about this sexy woman who sold sex toys for a living. "Show me everything."

She hesitated for a moment and looked like she was about to protest, but then she forced a curt smile. "Right this way, Mr. Pace."

Houston held his breath. Folks with clutter sometimes had untidy kitchens, untidy being a pleasant way to describe nasty. He was pleased to see that her kitchen wasn't that bad. Not dirty. Just junky.

"This is the kitchen," she said, extending her arm in a gesture like Vanna White or the models on *The Price Is Right*. His only concern was the amount of paper and clutter in the room.

"I take it you don't cook," he said.

"Why do you say that?" she asked.

"Because if you ever turned on the stove, this whole room would go up in flames."

"Whatever!"

"So the last thing you cooked in here was…"

"Microwave popcorn!"

He smiled. "You say it with such conviction."

"Darn right."

Look at this, Houston thought. The woman even stamped her foot. And on top of that, her breasts jiggled a little when she did it. He was going to enjoy repaying this debt after all.

"How about the upstairs?" he said.

Honey's eyes softened. She bit her bottom lip, and then said, "Come on."

The upstairs was just as warm and inviting as the downstairs and just as overrun with clutter. The true nature of her home—the vibrancy, strength and potential of it—seemed desperate to be revealed. So many possibilities. This home had an identity despite being cluttered with junk. These were his last days as an independent contractor, and this was the kind of project he could really get into. A total transformation. He'd be exhausted, but he'd be *the man* if he could pull it off.

"You sure you just want to confine this to the downstairs?" Houston heard himself say the words and wondered why, no matter what they talked about, it seemed like they were talking about sex.

"Yes," she said, and gave him a quick tour of the upstairs.

The upstairs wasn't as cluttered as the downstairs. Houston admired the homey atmosphere and the casual feel of the open floor plan. His favorite was her bedroom, with a vaulted ceiling and a separate living space. Truly a spa-like master suite. She'd kept most of the clutter out of her sleeping area. Good. That was a sign that she wasn't completely lost to her untidiness. Just needed some coaching and direction. That he could do.

"So," she said, looking like something that needed to be served up on a plate with whipped cream, chocolate, some of that flavored oil she probably sells and about five condoms. "What's next?"

"Next," Houston said, "we talk."

They headed for the staircase. "Bor-ing," Honey said.

He took in the full view of her hips rolling against her backside on the way down to the first floor. "Do you have something else in mind?" he dared to ask, feeling cocky.

"Yes. Food. I'm starving. Can I nuke you something?"

Houston chuckled, fingered the elaborate woodwork on the staircase railing. "Sure."

While Honey took cellophane-wrapped containers from the refrigerator and popped the contents into the microwave, Houston started his favorite part of the organization process—finding out why people were disorganized in the first place.

"So, how bad am I?" she asked.

"Bad," he said, truthfully.

"But you see this kinda stuff all the time, right?"

"Actually, most of my clients have one or two, sometimes three rooms that need my attention. You could use my help from top to bottom."

She nodded, but Houston detected a hint of disappointment in her eyes.

"You have a basement?"

When her eyes widened, Houston decided he didn't want to know the answer. "Never mind," he said. "Let's just stick to the downstairs."

"Sounds good to me."

While Honey gave her microwave a workout, Houston surveyed her work area and thanked the universe that all he had to do was three rooms downstairs. And they weren't individual rooms. It was actually one large space barely separated by angles and architecture but no real walls. He prided himself on not only his organizational skills, but his ability to get things done quickly. Honey's inventory would be an interesting challenge.

"Do you mind if I use you as a case study?"

"Me?" she called from the kitchen.

"Your space. This project. I've been kicking around ideas for a third book and organizing a business might make an interesting chapter."

"Well, sure. Yeah. I guess. I like the idea of being in a book. And talk about exposure," she said, timing her comment just right as she stepped out of the kitchen, breasts first, followed by a smile and two plates.

It was going to be hard to keep his mind off of those delightfully perky double D's in order to get her organized, but a man had to do what a man had to do.

"So, basically," he started, then the full aroma of the meal lulled him like a sweet dream and brought a growl from his stomach. "What is that? Who made it? And where can I get some more?"

"You haven't even tasted it yet."

She put the plates on the table. Side by side. There was no sitting across from each other meeting-style. This was close. Intimate. Familiar.

"I have an unusually sensitive nose."

"Most men don't," she said, taking a seat, her eyes dancing, coaxing him to do the same. He did so eagerly.

"My sense of smell is probably better than yours," he said.

"Really?" she opened her napkin, slid it across her lap. Lucky napkin.

"I'm especially good with food. I can usually tell what's in something, spices and herbs, just by smelling it. And it's not just the spices. It's amounts and how they've blended together. One whiff, and I can tell whether I'm going to enjoy something before I..." he smiled at her. He couldn't help it. "Taste it."

She slid her tongue slowly across her lips. He saw the movie playing in her eyes. She didn't have to say a thing. She was doing the same thing he was. Imagining them together. Entangled. Entwined. A delicious and sexy taste fest.

She slid a piece of the chili rellenos into her mouth and pulled the fork out slowly with a soft moan. "Ummmm. That's so good." Her voice was softer, preoccupied with feeling. Laced with pleasure.

Houston got his own forkful and prepared for some moaning of his own.

"Wait!" she said, when the fork was less than an inch from his mouth. "What will it taste like?"

Houston closed his eyes. He exhaled the aromas of the chili rellenos but focused on Honey. "Sweet roasted tomatoes, cumin, simmered ranchero."

Honey licked her lips.

"Dipped in—"

"Hey, baby girl…" The man's voice not only broke Houston's concentration, but set his teeth, on edge.

His temple throbbed, and he shot a hot glare at the man who dared to disturb his groove.

The man, who reminded Houston of Lurch from *The Addams Family,* completely ignored him. Honey wiped her mouth with the red linen napkin and stood.

"Excuse me for a second," she said and took her voluptuous body, especially those rolling hips, over to the man standing in the doorway who hadn't even bothered to knock.

"She's all finished. I can show you what I did with the side slope if you like."

"No, sweetie. I trust you. I know you hooked me up. I just pulled some chili rellenos out. Are you hungry?"

"I'm starving, and I have a meat lover's pizza at home calling my name. I will take a glass of ice water, though."

The man came in dripping sweat. He was shirtless. Obviously trying to impress. *Get your water and get out* reverberated in Houston's head like a bad echo.

"Pablo, this is Houston. He's helping me get organized."

"Hey, man," Pablo said, extending a hand. Houston took it. They shook briefly.

"What's up?" Houston said.

Honey smiled from man to man. "I'll be right back."

The moment she disappeared into the kitchen, Pablo stepped closer to the dining room table. "You know what, that looks good."

Before Houston could say, "Back off, bro," Pablo

had reached over and taken a bite of Honey's rellenos from her fork.

"Not bad," he said, smacking.

He was still smacking and picking his teeth when Honey came back with the water.

"I hope you don't mind. I helped myself."

Honey's whole body went sweet; Houston's went rigid. "Now, you know you can have anything I got."

The gardener gave her a look. All the way up and all the way down. Funny. It wasn't carnal. Just appreciative. Houston shoved an onion into his mouth before he said something stupid like, "Shit. I was almost in there, then here you come!"

Pablo downed a sixteen-ounce glass of water in less than five seconds. He burped into his fist and handed the empty glass back to Honey.

"Thanks," he said.

Honey kissed the side of his sweaty cheek. Houston's hopes disintegrated.

"Anytime," she responded with that voice she'd just used with Houston.

"See you in two weeks," Pablo said.

"If I don't see you first."

The moment the man was out the door, Houston's curiosity got the best of him. "Friend?"

"He's mostly my landscaper, but yeah, he's a friend, too."

Houston groaned. He knew exactly what kind of *friend* Pablo was. Probably didn't charge her a dime for all the work he did. Or if he did charge her, it was only a dime.

Honey slid into the chair next to him nice and easy. Her red skirt slid up against the leather seat exposing a perfect thigh. He imagined the words You Want This stamped and flashing golden against chocolate brown skin.

"So, what's next? Will you start today? And don't shortchange me. I want it all."

Before it was over with, he had plans to experience it all—with her. She looked like a woman who liked to…party. Houston had been cooped up in his hotel suite for too long. It was time for him to come out and play.

"You want it all. You'll have it all."

"Really?"

He bowed slightly. "Your wish is my command."

"Thank, Houston. I'm starting to think this will be a good thing after all."

Her smile brightened and Houston managed to keep his eyes on her eyes. "How about some dessert?" Honey asked, cleaning up their dishes.

In his mind, her clothes fell away, and Houston was treating himself to one luscious gulp of woman before taking off for the big time. What a way to celebrate, he thought.

"Dessert sounds good. It sounds real good. Whadaya got?"

She stood, gathered plates and forks. "Just about anything you can imagine."

Chapter 7

What the hell am I doing? Honey wondered. She'd flirted with Houston as though she were ready to invite him into her bed. She'd thought about it. Lord knew, she'd thought about it. Her imagination had run wild. She'd awakened that morning with her hand between her legs, her fingers shriveled and damp. Must've been a hell of a dream. She took a warm shower, wanted to prolong the feeling. Not ready to give it up to a dry day of inventory and sorting.

Houston, all night long. It had only been twenty-four hours and it felt like her personal space lacked something...some*one*.

No shortcuts, she'd insisted. At the time, it sounded like a great idea. Like that next drink to keep the buzz going. Honey wanted to keep Houston around for as long as possible. Although he agreed, his concession sounded weak. His intention was to put in as little time as possible and get as much done as possible. The fact that he'd shown up first with a Dumpster instead of boxes and sorting bins told her that.

So now, here she was primping in front of her big mirror—the one so large and heavy, she had to lean it against the wall—just to make sure her sexy self, was supersexy.

She turned, twisted. Looked at herself from every angle and liked what she saw. She was one of her favorite customers, paying herself often in the lingerie, sexy tops and shoes that she sold in limited quantities. The main reason she kept her clothing products at all was because she could buy the clothes for herself at such low prices— six dollars for a twenty-five-dollar blouse, ten dollars for a fifty-dollar pair of shoes—but her customers didn't care nearly as much about the clothing as they did about her gadget-of-the-month specials. Even at fifty percent off, Honey still cleaned up. She was thinking about investing in a new product. Music to get your sex on to. She'd found a warehouse that distributed compilations at less than wholesale prices. The Internet was a beautiful thing. After checking her image one more time, she decided she was, too.

She'd recently gotten into the bed-head style and had started wearing her hair in a shake-and-go chunky fro. She'd stopped wearing eye shadow and now just used a coal-black eyeliner and mascara. Now blush. Mineralized powder for a foundation. Her last makeup touch was earth-brown lipstick that kept its moisture all day.

Her top was a charcoal lace crop that she wore a size too small and coordinated with a pair of House of Deréon gray jeans. The perfect outfit to accentuate the French manicure she wore on her fingers and toes.

Houston didn't stand a chance.

At least that's what she thought until he rang the doorbell and she opened the door. Then she realized that he'd dressed to impress, too, in a muscle shirt and linen pants that looked like he'd just stepped down from a New York billboard.

"Damn," they both said at the same time.

Girl, what were *you thinking?* Honey kept her cool, even as the muscles in her thighs fought to spring open like hinges and wrap around Houston's waist.

"Come in," she said and put an emergency call in to God. "Lord, if you just get me through this..."

"So, are you ready to get started?" she asked, eagerly. "I put my work clothes on today." She lied. She'd squeezed into her I'm Too Sexy clothes hoping to make an impression. Judging by the way Houston's eyes locked onto her body, then went smoky and heavy-lidded the moment he stepped into her house, she'd say mission accomplished.

"Where are your boxes and bins and helpers?"

"My boxes and bins are in my SUV. I have industrial-size trash cans and a Dumpster arriving tomorrow. As for a helper, I usually go it alone, but for this, I've got my cousin, Paul, on standby and speed dial."

"So, what's up today, then?" Honey asked, disappointed. She expected to see Houston at work, maybe getting a little sweaty, but now he sounded like today would be different.

"Today, I just want to get a feel for the job, or rather what *you* feel about the job."

"I feel good about it, I guess."

Honey wrapped her arms around herself, fighting off a chill of discomfort.

"Good. Hold on to that feeling. Now, last night at the hotel I—"

"You're staying at a hotel?"

"Yes."

"You don't live in Cheyenne?"

"No. I'm from Savannah. I flew in. It's part of the favor."

Honey stiffened, riddled with disbelief. "I'm going to kill Brax."

"Oh no you don't. If he can get me a television show, who knows what else he can do? We need that brotha alive."

Houston was obviously trying to crack a joke. Honey was not amused. "But to fly in just for this…"

"It's not a problem. For real. With the money they're paying me for this thing, I could have flown in to Cheyenne ten times and stayed in a penthouse suite every time. Besides, from what I can tell, you're worth every dime."

Honey's whole body warmed and felt ready to serve. *Just heat and eat,* her mind said, already in a bedroom mood.

"Thank you," she said, smiling with the words, trying to reflect some of that warmth back.

"No prob. So, anyway, I was in my room and had an outrageous idea. I want to run it past you before we get started. If you like it, it changes the whole project."

"Okay, lay it on me."

The sentiments *Wouldn't I like to* and *Just you wait* flashed in Houston's eyes.

"Why don't we compartmentalize your computer space? That way, your work area is all in one place instead of three places with inventory sprawling everywhere in between. I'll make the entire west wall an assembly, packing and shipping area. You'll be able to fill orders in half the time."

"Okay. You're talking about more than just organizing. In corporate America, they call that restructuring. That's why I left to do my own thing."

"In this case, I think restructuring is good."

"Why don't we just stick to boxes and bins for now? I'm not ready for anything that drastic."

She said she wanted the full treatment. Then when he came with the bomb idea, she batted it down. Oh, well. Her loss. And to be honest, it would get him to L.A. quicker. But why didn't that give him any peace of mind?

"Cool," he said. But was it cool? He was disappointed, and he shouldn't have been. "I'll go out to my truck and get the boxes and bins."

He headed outside thinking that he only needed sorting bins. Honey had enough boxes to organize her house and three other people's places.

Keep. Toss. Sell. Give away. Piece of cake. He'd be done before the end of the week.

* * *

By the end of the evening, Houston wondered if God was trying to punish him for something he couldn't remember doing. The more they got into her inventory, the more it seemed to expand. He thought he might never be finished.

Houston blew out a breath of exasperation. He stared at the pile of funny-shaped gadgets, grief curling like a fist in his stomach. "Tell me again. I need to hear you say it. You ordered these five years ago. You got a great discount. So far, you've had three orders for them. One of those orders was returned."

"Yes, but I'm going to repackage the whole product. Nipple Genies are coming back. I know it. I just need to find a marketing angle."

"When?"

"When I get around to it."

"Honey. It's been *five* years."

She turned the high-tech pasties in her hand. "So, what are you saying?"

"What do I need to say besides, throw these things away?"

"I can't. That would be too much of a waste."

It had been like that all evening. The woman didn't want to part with a thing. She only wanted to move it from one location to another.

"Okay. This is like pushing dust."

"What?"

"You heard me. This is not shuffleboard. Now, you've got so much stuff in your Keep pile, it hardly justifies me being here."

He was dealing with a woman who was obviously not ready to let go of her past. Not to mention the fact that most of the stuff she wanted to hold on to was the *real* waste of space.

"Okay, these," he said, holding up a giant Ziploc sack of silver balls. "What the heck are these?"

The delight in Honey's smile told him that not only did she know what they were, she knew exactly how to use them. "Ben-wahs," she said. "A woman inserts them into her V-jay-jay, touches them with a vibrator and…they dance!"

"You've got to be kidding."

"Not even a little bit, sweetie."

Houston shook his head and looked away. "What kind of woman needs metal dancing in her—"

"What's that?" Honey asked.

"Nothing. I'm just mumbling. Is that a hot seller?"

"You better believe it!"

Houston grunted. Either Honey was exaggerating, or there were a mess of lonely, desperate women out there.

Honey fingered the bag gingerly, sweetly, with reverent affection. "Don't knock it till you've tried it."

"I don't need to. I have my own set, right here."

He patted the crotch of his pants. Not in an obscure, vulgar way. In the same way one would pat a wallet in a back pocket, or keys in the front.

The flicker of appreciation in her eyes told him that Honey didn't seem to mind.

Get your work done, buddy. Business before *pleasure.* Houston clapped his hands together. "Okay.

Why don't we do this? Let's separate the bestsellers from everything else."

Honey hesitated, but only for a moment. "Sounds good," she said.

In less than an hour, the two of them had Honey's living room, dining room and work area assigned to categories—fast-moving, top sellers, medium- to slow-movers and no movers. Surprisingly, Honey had very few top sellers.

"What's wrong with this picture?" Houston asked.

"Nothing. Don't let this sorting fool you. The top sellers might be the smallest pile, but they represent ninety percent of my profit. And don't get it twisted. I make big money. I struggle to keep these items in stock. But that's a good thing."

"What would be a good thing is if you got rid of all of these low and no sellers, or at least reduced your inventory. That way you'd have more room for your top sellers and you'd have the space to keep them in stock."

Honey had to admit that seeing her inventory all laid out like this instead of in pile after mountainous pile gave her a brand-new perspective. Part of the reason that she didn't order more wands, bullets and c-rings was that she had so much other stuff. She'd thought for sure that her hand-helpers and sex machines would take off. But all they'd ended up doing was taking up room. Houston was right.

Her emotions played on her face like a movie. Houston was so tempted to do the part of his job that he loved, even beyond sorting, purging, reorganizing. He loved getting inside people's heads and uncovering what made them so messy in the first place. He'd discovered early in his career that most folks had issues, internal issues that were often manifested in external ways. The most obvious was their home.

Her body and everything about her—from her sexy hair to the way she stood, the way she strutted, the way her clothes caressed her like hands, even the sound of her voice—said confident, all-the-way woman. A keep-your-head-to-the-sky, always-have-your-own-money, my-body-is-kickin' kinda woman. But her eyes told a different story. There was something soft and fragile underneath the diva exterior. She was a woman who wanted something besides flirtation. Decorative frosting, but the cake underneath was much, much softer and sweeter.

Houston's mouth watered at the thought. He definitely had a sweet tooth.

Thinking back to the task at hand, maybe if he got her to open up a little and talk some about her business, why she chose it, he'd uncover a piece of what she seemed dead set against showing him—her real self.

"What would you say to a dinnner break? Let me take you someplace," he suggested.

"You're not from around here, remember? I should take you someplace."

"How about a compromise? You pick the place, and I'll drive. You give me directions, and I'll pay."

Honey smiled. Houston liked her smile. Sexy as hell. "I like that compromise."

Houston stood up from where he'd been parked on the floor for the last half hour sifting through all the merchandise. Honey headed toward the stairs. "I'll just get my purse."

As much as Houston loved sex, he realized that Honey was cocooned in it. She needed to be away from this, far away. He wanted to separate her from her erotic clutter. Cut the umbilical cord. Surrounded by it, it was easy for her to defend. Getting away from it might give her some objectivity and detachment.

Chapter 8

She strutted down the stairs; Houston was riveted where he stood. She looked stunning. What had she done? She had on the same clothes. She must have done something to her hair, her makeup. She must have put on a push-up bra, took the belt in on her skirt, applied another coat of polish on her nails. Why did she look ten times sexier now than she did when they were on the floor together touching and arranging all her toys?

Houston shook his head to break the spell. It had to be the surge of testosterone that accompanied that victory he just won. It puffed out his chest. Made him remember his younger days when he was always beefin' with somebody, and those beefs made him feel like a man until a bullet in the leg put him down one day and he wondered if he'd ever get back up.

So now, he fought with things instead of people, even though it often seemed like things were a lot harder to put in their place because of the people attached to them.

His veins were so hot looking at Honey that he would have sworn his blood had been replaced with Red Devil Hot Sauce.

Honey's chest heaved. She breathed heavily like a woman on the verge of a strong orgasm. She stopped before reaching the bottom step.

"We don't have to go out." She placed a hand against soft brown cleavage. "We could stay in."

And here's my reward, he thought. *Laid out on a platter.* All he had to do was reach out and—

The hard knock at the door set Houston's teeth on edge. Bad timing, he thought angrily as his jaw tightened.

Mixing business, pleasure and a favor couldn't be good, could it? A moment ago, he didn't care, but rational thought snuck into his brain right behind that knock. Damn it all.

"I won't answer it," Honey said.

"Okay," Houston responded. "Then I will."

He opened the door and was greeted by the most pained grimace he'd ever seen. The face belonged to a man who was built like Paul Bunyon. He was a few inches from having to duck to get into the house. The man was obviously surprised to see Houston at the door.

"Where's Honey?" he asked.

"Where're your manners?" Houston responded. Big and untrained. Who was this guy?

"Hey, Bill," Honey said, coming to stand next to Houston.

"I'm not early," he said. He'd completely ignored Houston, his eyes fastened on Honey like Velcro.

"No, sweetie. You're right on time, as usual. It's me. I'm sorry. I forgot today was our day. My friend Houston is helping me right now. Let's skip this week, okay?"

"You sure you don't need me?"

"Not today. But you'll come back next week, right?"

The big man nodded slowly, obviously broken in half by Honey's words. The woman says, "No, you can't come in," and it's just like choppin' down a tree. Houston fought the silly urge to hold Honey back so the tree wouldn't fall on her.

A second passed and Honey flashed that sexy smile at Bill. That brought him up some. Made him taller. "I'll be back next week," he said.

Honey stepped forward, stood on tiptoe. On command, Bill bent down. Honey planted a quick smack on his check. "Thanks, sweetie."

When the man turned and walked off the porch, Houston knew he had no right to look at Honey the way he did and allow the questions to run through his mind the way they were. "Who was that? Why does your place seem like man central? How many men do you have? No, really, who *was* that?"

Step off, bro. This ain't your woman, his mind said. But his curiosity and his testosterone wouldn't listen. Before he could open his mouth and say something he had no business saying, she beat him to the punch.

"He's my box opener. He helps me with my weekly shipments."

"Box opener, cook, landscaper. What do you do for

yourself?" Houston asked, trying to make his question sound like a joke.

A smirk crawled across her face. She folded her bottom lip in and bit it.

Houston cut off the X-rated image before it got going good in his mind. "Never mind. Let's go get dinner. Or ice cream. Shall we get ice cream? I feel the need to be cooled down."

"Come on," Honey said, eyes dancing. "I know the perfect place."

I bet you do, Houston thought, keeping a close eye on her perfectly formed hips and following Honey out the door. He didn't wish to be just another number on an assembly line of men, but damn, there was just something about her. Not wanting to turn into a sniffing punk, Houston decided he'd use all of his strength to keep his mind on business. *Business.*

Honey had been flirting with men since she'd turned nineteen. She'd made an art of it. Loved every cat-and-mouse dance of it. Loved seeing the power and effect a bright smile, a carefully timed phrase or the turn of her ample hip could do to steal men's attention. Since the moment Houston Pace stepped into her house, all of her experience as a world-class flirt had flown right out the bay window. Of all the men she'd ever met, Houston was the one she wanted to flirt with the most.

His soul-deep eyes, his dangerous smile, a thick, ripping body that wouldn't quit for days. He had the kind of looks that made Honey want to hold her stuff the way she'd seen men do. Just checkin', she thought.

To make sure she was still all there and not melted away by the heat of his allure. Her years of celibacy were over. Honey could actually picture herself with this man. Naked and open all the way. To hell with saving herself.

It was time.

Over the years, more men than she could count had tried to get into her bed. She couldn't understand why, when she'd been very clear that she'd much rather take Houston upstairs than take him out to dinner, he'd refused and chosen eating food over, well, eating her.

That was something new.

"See. You can't believe it yourself."

Honey sat up straighter in her chair. She didn't think she could push her breasts out any farther, but she tried. "I'm sorry. I missed that."

"I was talking about your customers. I can't believe there are enough people out there who would buy your…toys…enough to keep you living the life you obviously live. Do you get alimony or something?"

"No."

Houston's eyebrows went up. "Child support?"

"No," she responded. "Never married. No kids."

"Really?"

"Don't act so surprised. And for the record, I don't have customers. I have clients. Most of the people who order from me are repeat clients. More than half with standing orders."

"You have got to be—"

"I also have clubs. Friends who go in together and order in bulk. Lotions, stimulation enhancers, condoms."

The shocked expression on Houston's face never changed. "What? I can get you a carton of condoms for less than a third of what you pay for them going to the drugstore."

"Trojans?" he asked.

"Trojans, LifeStyles, Paradise, MaxPro. Whatever you want."

"You sound like a drug dealer."

Honey laughed. "Funny."

"No, it's not. Maybe I've stumbled on to something. Using these *devices*...I guess it's like a drug. People try it. For a joke or just because they don't know any better, and they get hooked. They can't stop. So they keep placing orders because it's in their system now. And they can't shake it."

"Sweetie, you're obviously uninitiated in the ways of sex play."

"Stop right there. I know my way around a bedroom. More importantly, around a woman's body. And I know that if the man is doin' the woman right, and vice versa, you don't need accessories in your bed."

"Yep," Honey said. "Just like I thought. You're a virgin."

"When it comes to that, I'll always be a virgin. Not even. I got game, baby. I don't need nothin' else."

"You're just afraid that you might like it?"

"Stop talkin' crazy. I know I don't need it. And any woman I'm with doesn't need it, either. I take *care* of mine."

"Is that right?"

"Yeah, it is."

"So, you think that no woman you've ever been with has had a battery-operated friend on the side?"

"Exactly. Look, men and women were born with all the equipment they need to get the job done. Anything else is cheating."

As soon as he said the word *cheating,* he looked away from Honey and reached for the milk shake he'd been drinking. He couldn't hide the pain, though. A brief hot flicker of it flashed in his eyes.

And he's trying to dissect my *psychology,* Honey thought. He had no idea how much of his own he'd revealed with the last sentence.

So, the man had been cheated on. Honey even dipped into Freud a bit and considered that maybe Houston's mother had cheated on his father and that's why the thought of even a toy going into a woman instead of a penis turned him off.

The sight of the quick pain in Houston's eyes hurt Honey's soul. She wanted to help him shake off any demons that came with that pain. Another, less altruistic thought, entered her mind, as well. If she could free Houston of his demons, maybe he could free her of hers.

"Let me ask a question," she started, not wanting to waste a second. "Have you ever brought whipped cream, chocolate or flavored oils into your bedroom?"

"Of course. Along with pineapple slices, tequila and eatable undies."

"And?"

"And that's different."

"It's not part of the original equipment. That's your argument, right?"

"Yes, but—"

"How about pornos? Ever watch 'em?"

"That's really different. I'm getting off by watching what a woman was born with."

"But it's extra. It's simulation coming from a source other than that God-made organ of yours. Or the cojones you made it a point to tell me you have."

"That's not the same at all."

"Sure it is. The device you're using is a television. It's not a dildo or a butt plug. But it's something other than your body or a woman's physical body getting you off."

Houston shook his head furiously. "You can't sit here and say—"

"Do you jack off?"

Houston stopped shaking his head, then stared at her. "Of course. Don't you?"

"Every chance I get," she said. "As a matter of fact…" she started, then opened her palm to reveal the small remote control she'd fished out of her purse a few moments ago.

"What's that?" he asked, but the lust on his face told her he had an idea.

Honey increased the speed on the tiny vibrator in her underwear from Level One to Level Six. She rolled her hips with the sensation until the rapid vibrations hit her spot just right.

"It's the answer to my prayers, Houston. Since the moment I saw you." Honey panted, struggling to speak coherently through the sensations, "All I've wanted to do was come…hard. Oh—" she gripped the edge of the table with both hands and held on "—so hard."

Houston licked his lips and stared at her in amazement.

Houston took the control from her hand. Honey closed her eyes, bit her lip, rolled her hips. "Ah, uh," she said as the intensity built. Knowing that the remote was in Houston's hands made her so wet, she thought she might slide out of the chair. "There are four more…levels…uh-uh. Take me up, Houston," she whispered. "Make me come, please."

She couldn't believe she was doing this in a public place.

When she opened her eyes, Houston's finger was so close to the button Honey had to stop herself from begging loudly. "Please," she hissed.

Houston took a deep breath and gave her back the remote control. "Sorry," he said. "If you want me to get you off, it's going to be with my own equipment."

"Agh!" Honey groaned. "They say…" she said, snatching the remote "…if you want something…done right…" She slid the level all the way up. The vibration was so acute, she didn't think she could stand it much longer. So fast, she thought her thong would catch fire. "You have to…do it…your…self!"

Then she came harder than she had in weeks.

Chapter 9

"You have got to be kidding. Tell me again and this time, don't skip over anything juicy."

Houston sat at his aunt's kitchen table with his cousin. They'd started catching up on old times, times when Houston spent summers there and he and his cousin were best friends. They'd spent the morning covering new ground, but Houston was not about to go into pant-by-pant details. "Paul—"

"Sweet Pea," his cousin insisted. If the man was any more flamboyant, he wouldn't need a sex change operation; he'd just sprout breasts and his manhood would vanish into thin air. But Houston believed family was family. You loved them, whatever. As long as they didn't cause too much drama.

Paul/Sweet Pea was as loyal as they came. He never

started trouble, nor was he ever in the middle of it. In fact, Paul was so low-key, Houston had taken it upon himself to be the voice in his cousin's head, urging him to get out, do things, experience the world. The man had an eye and flair for design that Houston could only dream of and read about in books. Houston was good, but his cousin was the best. Talk about someone who deserved his own television show.

Maybe Paul did deserve a few more details. "She came, all right? Haven't you ever seen a woman come before?"

For a moment, Houston's memory of Honey's public orgasm made him forget who he was speaking to. Then the harsh look of incredulity crossed Paul's face.

"Sorry," Houston said.

"Okay, cuz, run this down again. She's fine?"

"Yeah."

"Built like a brick house on steroids?"

"Yeah."

"Single?"

"Yep."

"And she's servin' it up like Denny's after the lawsuit?"

"Exactly."

"And you ain't been in it?"

"Right."

"Man, you're gay. Welcome to the club!"

Paul's eyes welled up with laughter. Houston let go a long breath. Becomin' a do-right man was hard work. Last night, during Honey's triple-decker orgasm, he'd been hard enough to cut diamonds. He couldn't believe how fast and how tight he'd gotten. The missile his penis had turned into was seeking Honey's heat in the worst way. He woke up in the same condition and hadn't calmed down all day.

"Can't a brother change his ways and become a gentleman?"

"Some. Not you." Paul's slow eye, the one that wandered all on its own sometimes, zeroed in on him. "If you have to assert it, it means—"

"Cut the crap, Paul. I told you because I need some perspective here."

"Cuz, there's only one perspective when it comes to free booty."

"What's that?"

"Got Jimmys?"

Jimmys, condoms, rubbers, hats. Houston had them all by the truckload. In the past, he would have been on Honey's Internet discount on condoms so fast, it would have made her clit spin. But when he got the television deal, he made an important promise to himself—sworn it on a bible. No more babes.

He'd dated women like Honey since he was fourteen and had started getting hair on his face. That's when he realized that his looks could get him just about anything he wanted, and what he'd wanted for years was women, lots of them. The kind with long weaved hair, double D's and toned waists. The ability to complete a sentence, express a coherent thought or carry on a decent conversation was optional. As long as they gave him his propers when he came home, he hadn't given a damn what any woman had to say—

except, "Yes, Daddy. Give me some more, Daddy. Do me hard. Make me come, Papa."

Stupid.

He couldn't believe he'd been that kind of man. Well…yes he could.

But no more. He was stronger than his weakness for fine trim. Stronger than his fixation for the deadly combination of T & A. He had to over a new leaf for the job. An entire leaf. Not just the stem or the tip of the stem.

"Cuz!"

Houston started. "What?"

"Well, never *mind*. You look like you've got more than enough to occupy that smooth head of yours to worry about what *I'm* saying."

"Sorry, I kinda zoned out. What were you sayin'?"

"I said if you need some backup, I got you. If you need an extra set of hands or an eye for new design, I got you there, too."

Houston swallowed slowly, realizing that what he really needed was a chaperone.

Honey could barely breathe, but she knocked on the door anyway, hoping she could get inside before she started gasping.

Cliff came to the door, expressionless, and stared, his hard black eyes unblinking. Without a word, he stepped away and headed into his living room. Honey walked through his door and followed him. He leaned against the wall, barely visible beneath his massive painting by Romare Bearden.

He clasped his hands in front of him. His long arms

dangled in an accusatory position over his private parts as if he'd been wounded there and was covering up as a precautionary measure.

He opened his mouth to speak, then closed it again. His eyes looked tired. Missing sleep. Tired and undancing. But still, they looked at her and knew...everything.

Holding his gaze, she knew. He couldn't look at her fully. That would force him to see the almost-dress that she wore just for Houston. The dress she wanted an opinion on. And she might have to deal with the question she'd come to ask. *Why won't he sleep with me?*

"Cliff—"

"Get some friends," he said. Now he looked worn and puppy doggish. His mouth was tense. Had he started smoking again?

"I have a friend," she insisted, stepping closer.

Cliff turned away and pounded his fist against the wall. Hid his head there. "Damn it, Honey. I don't know if I can be your friend right now."

She moved closer. "I don't have anybody else, Cliff. Please."

Honey didn't think his sigh would ever end. One more pound of his fist and his head drooped lower. "He'll like it, baby," he said. "I sure as hell do."

With her confidence bolstered, Honey rushed over to give Cliff a hug. He turned right on cue, as if they'd timed and rehearsed the whole thing.

"Oh, God, Honey. I love you so much."

He ran his hands up and down her arms. Faster and faster, as if he were trying to make sure she was real or really in his arms.

"I need your help, baby," he whispered.

The words came out dry and misty, like smoke.

"Anything," Honey responded, leaning against him. Afraid of his request.

"I need you to help me get over you, 'cause I can't do it on my own."

A wave of raw emotion rose up inside Honey and she burst into tears. Cliff held on to her tightly, and they stayed that way for a long while.

When Honey let go, she let go for good and knew that many days would pass before she and Cliff would see each other again.

What would she do to keep herself together?

"I got an assignment. A long one. Travel writing in Burma. Can't wait."

"When are you leaving?" she asked.

"Couple of weeks. Maybe a month."

"I can't see you before you go?"

They held each other in the middle of Cliff's sparsely decorated living room. He laid his head gently down on hers. Squeezed tighter. "No."

This time, Cliff's sigh didn't last quite as long as Honey's.

Okay. Be cool. She's not the only woman in the world, although she just might be the finest. Everything is everything. I'm just going to go inside. Sort. Separate. Get the hell out of Dodge. Right? Right.

Houston got out of his SUV on a beautiful Wyoming day. Walked up to the front door, rang the doorbell and waited.

No problem, junior. You got this. Push that coming-in-public incident right out of your head. Forget everything Paul said. Besides, this is just the last stop on the road to TV fame and fortune… "Damn."

He folded in his bottom lip and willed himself not to get hard. "Did I say that out loud?"

Honey licked her lips. "Yes, you did." She stepped aside. "Come in."

Suddenly, Houston's clothes felt too tight, too constricting, and he wanted out of them. Fast. Adrenaline exploded inside his body as he imagined all the ways he could take her. Tune her body like a piano. Make beautiful sex sounds come out of it. Forget the work space. She had a space he'd like to work right between her—

"Are you coming?" she asked.

In more ways than one. He still hadn't moved. He knew better. At this stage of the game, asking him in was like inviting a vampire into her home. Once that was done, the dark creature had free rein. The monster has carte blanche over your soul. Is that what Honey wanted? With her smooth skin, lush lips and wide hips, she looked like that's what she wanted…bad.

"Okay," he said, stepped inside and turned to watch while she closed the door behind him. He forgot all about clutter.

"Honey, I'm going to say something here. If I'm outta line, tell me. I'm getting some serious vibes from you. Like you want something other than my organizational skills. Am I blowing up the wrong skirt?"

She shifted, jutted a sexy hip out to the side. "Not at all."

"Whoo…" he said, both relieved and saddened by his bad timing.

"What?"

"It's just that…even a month ago…why couldn't…"

"My brother said you were straight and single. He wasn't wrong, was he?"

"Nah. He got that right."

"I'm pretty sure I look sexy as hell in this dress, so I don't think it's me that's makin' you hesitate."

Houston heard the frustration in her voice. He also heard the pride. He was drawn to highly confident women like helium to the sky. Always seeking it, pointed toward it, moving toward it.

Only heaven knew what came over him then. It seemed like the most natural thing in the world, so he didn't fight the urge. Instead, he stepped straight to her, put his arms around her and held her softly against his chest.

Heat from her body infused his. "It's definitely not you. You are, without any kinda doubt, the sexiest, baddest, hottest, most desirable woman I've ever met in my *life*."

"Um," she moaned and hugged him right back. "So…let's do this."

Damn it! he reprimanded himself. Why did he feel compelled to be honest with this woman? It sure would make it a lot easier if he could just lie. Tell her he was gay, or impotent, or married, or asexual. But he was none of those things. He was just ambitious, and his new L.A. life would have to shake out a little more solidly before he took on anything as ambitious as a woman. It just wasn't in his plans right now. Especially a bunny-type like Honey. She reminded him too much of his former breasts-before-brains attitude toward women. Honey just wouldn't do.

"I can't," he said.

Honey the voluptuous woman became Honey the ironing board. She simply went rigid.

"I'm sorry," he said, attempting to get the soft, curvy Honey back. "It's the timing. With my show coming up, I can't get my head messed up with a relationship right now. No matter how short."

Honey turned into concrete then and stepped back. She looked as if someone had stretched her face like a rubber band and snapped it back into the meanest scowl on earth.

"Messed up. Short. Wow. I guess you're right. I wouldn't want to *mess up* your head with a silly fling. What was I thinking?"

"Honey, you're taking this the wrong way."

She put a hand on her round hip, worked the kissable neck of hers. "Am I?"

Houston thought for a moment and knew only the truth would come out of his mouth. "No. Not really."

"All righty, then." Honey clapped her hands together then folded them backwards and cracked her knuckles. "Let's get to work."

Houston's stomach felt like he'd eaten something rotten for breakfast. He needed two things—Alka-Seltzer, and to know that he'd done the right thing. Houston had a good habit of doing bad things with women like Honey. He tended to lose his ever-lovin' mind. If he so much as slid a finger inside Honey, he knew it would all be over. The next thing he knew, he'd be all about her instead of all about business.

Nah. He couldn't go out like that. At least, not before he got his show started.

Sorting. That would take his mind off of his lust and her breasts. Sorting would do just the trick. Sorting would keep Houston's hands on boxes and off of Honey's thighs. For the sake of his show, he'd stay focused.

Chapter 10

The work was going too slowly. Houston and Honey had been sorting and dividing for hours. They spent most of the time on their knees, sifting through the contents of all the boxes they'd emptied onto the floor.

Houston couldn't stay focused. Everything he touched, from the lotions to the flavored, removable tattoos, reminded him that he was working in a room with a woman whose eyes blinked to him in sweet Morse code: *I want you naked. I want you naked now.* They'd managed to get through one entire stack of boxes without ripping each other's clothes off. Houston needed a distraction to keep it that way.

"So, tell me something," he said, tired of hearing his own voice go on and on about what to put where.

"What?" she asked, still doing more unpacking than determining what she could get rid of.

"Anything. Tell me about you. Are you anything like your brother?"

"I don't think so. He seems levelheaded. Mindful."

"And you're not?"

"Not even close. My emotions are my fuel. They're why I do what I do. Brax thinks…a lot. My thing is, by the time he's done with all that thinking, he's missed out on something important."

"So, you're a go-for-what-you-know woman, huh?"

"Go for what you know, when you know it."

So far, so good. He'd separated the devices from the latex and the creams, and not one improper thought about Honey *or* her thighs.

"What about you?" she asked. "Do you think or do you feel?"

"Depends on the situation. For the TV show, I didn't think about it at all. The whole thing just felt right. And then there are other things—" he stared into her warm brown eyes—"that I can't shake. That I keep turning over and over in my head because they won't let go…or maybe I can't let go."

"And then what happens?" she asked, looking a lot like a schoolgirl on her first date. Eager for that first kiss, but afraid of it, too.

"And then," he said, feeling himself leaning forward. *Get a grip!* his mind shouted. "And then you tell me the truth about this stuff. That's what's been going on in my mind lately."

Honey clamped her jaw tight, barely speaking. "What truth?"

"I can't believe that people really think they need this stuff. All this batteries-not-included stuff is no substitute for the real thing."

"It's not supposed to be a substitute. Almost all of my regular customers are in committed, healthy, heterosexual relationships. They're couples willing to get each other off in every safe, healthy way possible."

"Puh-leeze! If their relationship was all that, they wouldn't need something else in the bed with them."

Suddenly Honey's eyes sparkled, got large and twinkled mischievously. "That's the virgin talking," she said.

"I haven't been a virgin since I was six," Houston exaggerated. He really lost his virginity when he was sixteen, but the story he told all his buddies was that he had been six. They didn't have to know that's when he had his first kiss. And neither did Honey.

"Aside from that being a bald-faced lie, which I'll forgive you for, you really should try a toy."

"No need. I am all man, baby. One hundred percent Grade A beef. I don't need anything but a woman who knows what she's doing. And she don't need anything else, 'cause I sure as hell know what *I'm* doin'."

"Uh-huh." Honey mumbled something under her breath and rummaged through a small stack of unopened packages and large envelopes. She'd obviously stopped paying attention to him.

"Where in the heck?" she said, rummaging. She tossed aside rubber things. Plastic things. Latex things.

Even glass, uh, appliances. "Damn you, Cliff. You better not have taken... Oh, I remember!" she said.

Houston could all but see the lightbulb go on over her head. "What I need is in my bedroom. Hold on," she said and switched that fine ass of hers up the staircase.

Houston got off his knees where he'd been on the plush Berber carpet stacking more boxes of condoms than he could count in six lifetimes. Ribbed. Lubricated. Triple-tipped. Everybody except him must be having—

The loud, tumbling crash startled Houston before he had a chance to finish chronicling all of the extra-large Day-Glo green Jimmys. He dropped the ones in his hand and took the stairs two and three at a time.

"Honey!" he shouted. A montage of her crushed beneath a mountain of vibrating boxes flashed through his mind. He ran faster.

"Honey!" he called at the upper landing and darted into the spare bedroom. His heart kicked like a bass drum in his chest. A wrecking ball, breaking down walls. "Honey!" he called when he didn't find her in the spare bedroom or the bathroom.

The master bedroom was dark. He jogged inside and fumbled for the light switch. When the plastic snapped around his wrist and he heard the click, his first reaction was to swing out with a big hard fist. His hopeful libido blocked the punch.

"Houston Pace," came the sultry voice in front of him in the dimly lit room, "you don't have the right to do a damn thing except what I tell you. Got it?"

The bass drum turned into a jazz snare. He smiled

and chuckled devilishly, all the while thinking Honey was about to make his sexual dreams come true. And he was about to let her. *Surrender,* his mind shouted. Somewhere in his head, Paul's crazy voice said, "Go on get chu some."

"Got it," he said.

Houston's eyes adjusted to the dimness. He could not have predicted the short, white lab coat, silky brown legs, or the red pumps that matched her red lipstick. The fiendish smirk her mouth held. The allure burning in her eyes.

He hardened instantly. "All right, mama. It's on."

Honey pulled his right arm quickly behind him and clamped the other side of the handcuffs around his left arm. "It sure is," she said.

He barely recognized Honey's voice. It sounded dark, husky, turned on. The way he'd imagined her voice sounding just before or right after she came. He gritted his teeth. His penis was throbbing. If he could just undo his pants.

"Honey—"

"No talking," she said and led him to the side of the bedroom and pushed him against a metal pole. His back smacked solidly against the cold steel.

"Where did this come from?" he asked.

"It's been there for years. You just couldn't see it because of the boxes of toys you don't believe in. Now seriously." She ran her hand from his knee, up to his blood-gorged penis, coaxed a groan, then up until finally her fingers came to rest against his lips. "No…more…talking."

Honey reached behind him, fumbling with the handcuffs, attaching them to the pole.

Honey stood in front of him, pressed against his chest. He groaned as her breasts flattened against him. Damn, if he could just touch…

"What are you going to do?" he asked, surprised by his own lust-filled voice.

"Take you there."

She must have been planning this. All morning. The closed blinds. The pulled drapes. She sauntered over to a line of white candles standing like soldiers on her dresser and lit each one. He stared. Hard. Hoping to get a glimpse of her round, round rear. *Thank God I've got big hands,* he thought.

She blew out a long, wooden, fireplace match and traded the match for a remote control. With one press of a button, smooth, sultry jazz eased out of small speakers in all four corners of the room. On the nightstand, Honey used a smaller match to light a stick of incense. She turned toward him wearing a sexy "I'm ready, are you?" look on her face.

Houston wouldn't have believed he could get any harder, but he did. Just the sheer anticipation tightened him like a lover's firm hand. "Umm," he moaned. Honey's nipples responded in kind, pushing against the cotton fabric of the white coat. Houston bit his lower lip and throbbed.

Honey had mercy on him. Within seconds, she undid his belt and pants and set him free. The air was cool against his skin, but Honey's gaze and mischievous smile were hotter than three ovens.

Touch me, his mind commanded since he was forbidden to speak. They'd been mentally undressing each other, touching, fondling each other since the moment they met. *Linked somehow,* his mind continued. *Touch me. Suck me. Lick me.* "Ah," he groaned, impatient for what Honey would do next. He found he couldn't stand still. With his pants in a puddle at his ankles, he shifted his weight and kept his butt away from the cool metal behind him.

Honey, on the other hand, didn't seem to be able to tear her eyes away from his penis. She'd settled her gaze on it almost from the moment she tugged his pants down. And now, she was licking her lips, as though she were getting her mouth ready. Houston breathed hard and heavy, and hoped.

Honey untied what he assumed was an ascot from around her neck and realized that the black sheer fabric was something else entirely.

She walked behind him in heels so high they almost put her at eye level with him. Her fragrance wafted past him like a hand in the air. Touching him in all the right places. His nose followed the trail her scent left in the air.

"What are you—" he started, holding the vision of velvety thighs disappearing behind him.

Honey slapped him lightly on the shoulder. "You are so hardheaded."

You have no idea, he thought, glancing down at himself, all but dancing at the nearness of her. *Yet,* he added in his mind.

Suddenly her teeth clamped against his ear firmly, and held for a moment, sending a surge of desire coursing from his head to his heels. He sucked in a gulp of air.

"Houston, since you won't close your mouth, close your eyes."

The blindfold came down before he could respond and suddenly, he felt a twinge of vulnerability. For a second, Houston wondered if it would ruin the mood, until Honey's soft, warm hands caressed his thighs. They flowed against his skin as if they'd been hot oiled and trained in Reiki. He closed his eyes.

She tied the blindfold carefully around his head. He couldn't resist a peek. He saw shadows, but nothing clearly. Only her scent and body heat guided his senses, telling him how close she was, feeding his hot urge to reach out, grab her close, strip her down, ride her hard.

Anticipation set his nerves on fire. He imagined lips, a tongue, her hot mouth, a warm thigh against his. He wanted her bad.

Honey's hands caressed and kneaded his thighs, his butt. Rolling erotic heat into his groin. "That feel good, sugar?"

"Yes," he said.

The soft press of her lips on his stomach flared inside him like gas on a fire. He curled his toes and forgot he was cuffed. He strained against the pole needing to touch her soft body, plunge his fingers inside her. Feel her wet for him. "Uh."

"You like it, baby. Is it good?" she asked, washing his stomach with her lips and kisses.

"You know it is."

The woman was into pleasure. Houston approached

the sexual point of no return, hoping that she could receive as well as she gave.

"Come on with it," he said, straining against the pole, wondering if she danced against it. Imagining a slide, spin and undulation.

"You got it, daddy," she said.

The warm tight that engulfed him stole his breath and Houston Pace struggled to remember his name and where he was. More tender and sweet than returning to the womb, Houston felt transported by strong, soft, cocoonlike suction on his hard length. He gasped, struggled for breath and clarity, and surrendered.

The cool, sturdy pole came in handy. He leaned back for balance and fought to make out the sensation. He panted with it. Tongue, mouth, vagina? What the hell was—

"Ah-ah!" he gasped again as Honey's deft hands clamped something against the base of his shaft. Sending sensations of ecstasy hurtling to every inch of his body.

"Ah, aah, *what?*" He started. His eyes snapped open, but all he saw was the blur of her body kneeling in front of him.

"A blow job?" he wondered, but knew no mouth had ever given him a trip to ecstasy as quickly as this ride.

"Honey," he panted. Sweat popped out against his body. The strain, the desire, the need built inside him. Riding hard from a long distance. Coming strong.

The warm suction got hot, pulled him harder, siphoning all his strength. He couldn't breathe or focus. He pumped his hips back and forth. Trying to get closer to the feeling. Out of all control. "Ah! Honey! Damn, damn!"

He called out to her as his semen shot out of his body like a rocket. Houston came hard. Real hard. The force of it snatched away all his energy. His legs failed and before his seed finished pumping out of a penis as stiff as the pole that held him, his ass smacked the carpet with a thud sending yet another sensual jolt from his balls to the edge of his body.

His head slumped as he sucked air and recovered.

"Good, huh?" Honey said.

It was only then that Houston heard the soft, nearly imperceptible hum of something electric. With a soft click, Honey shut it off and chuckled.

Houston couldn't believe his eyes or his penis for responding. He felt as though a giant hand of disbelief had just smacked him upside the head. Duped by a gadget.

Damn, he thought. *I can't believe...* "If you tell anyone," Houston said. "If you even bring this up again—"

"Don't worry."

She moved behind him and removed the blindfold, and there in all his post-climax glory was a red, latex suction glove, clamped down on his penis like a mean DustBuster.

Honey removed the toy. Houston quivered; he was still ultrasensitive and oozing. "Shit," he said.

"Like I said, don't worry. Your secret affair with the Handyman 4000 is safe with me, as long as you give me what I want."

Despite being only seconds from one of the most

intense orgasms Houston ever had, the sultriness in Honey's voice struck a deep sensual chord in him.

"What do you want?" he asked, praying that he already knew.

Honey unbuttoned the lab coat to reveal a white lace bra and lace briefs. She spread her legs just a little and played with a tassel at the center of the lace panties. Her eyes gazed hungrily at his quaking manhood.

Houston smiled with a hunger of his own. "Unlock me."

Chapter 11

Honey had lived her adult life without knowing what it was like to have a man inside her. Whenever the topic of sex came up with her girlfriends, she'd relied on the hundreds of books she'd read on the subject. The how-to's, the romance novels and erotic fantasy magazines.

Just when it seemed that she could put away the dark images of her childhood—images of fists smacking skin and slaps, a pink ripped blouse, her mother being raped by the man Honey'd known as Uncle Turner. Whenever a man got close enough, naked enough, to share intimacy with Honey, her mind draped those dark, screaming, bloody images over her and suddenly she wasn't herself, but her mother with a man violently stealing her most precious gift.

Honey would always panic, lash out and struggle or

sometimes hyperventilate at the critical moment when a man was a breath away from sliding inside her. So far, Cliff was the only man in years with whom Honey had made a determined effort to push aside the torment in her mind, push through the panic and make love to. Each time they tried had ended the same, with Honey breathing into a paper bag and Cliff taking care of his own needs.

He'd been impossibly patient with her for so long, especially when they'd considered counseling. But now the entire world was different. The universe had sent Honey a man whom her soul told her would be the one to get close enough to get inside. She'd been without real sexual intimacy for so long, her body craved the touch of a man, and not just any man.

Houston.

If Houston was that man, she couldn't bear to wait one more second to discover what her body had hungered after for years and her mind had kept from her.

"I can't believe you're making me wait." Honey was pouting and she knew it. The last thing she wanted to do was come off as needy or desperate. But that's exactly how she sounded. Add severe disappointment and frustration to her demeanor. Her shoulders fell. The wall caught her. She tried to look cool and sexy like she planned to post up that way beneath her painting of New Orleans at night. But she didn't think she pulled that off, either.

"Not forever," his voice said, caressing her. They stood in her foyer, staring at each other with new eyes. Honey felt it. She was pretty sure Houston felt it, too.

Something had changed between them, and that something made Honey want to strip naked and sing "Ain't
Too Proud to Beg"—both versions.

"You don't know what forever feels like," she said,
lowering her lids.

"You look unbelievable," he said.

Just then, the sun caught the side of his face and
kissed it. Houston looked like a magnificent prince
standing in her doorway, with all the command and authority of royalty. His eyes brightened. He smiled and
bent to kiss her forehead.

Honey closed her eyes, drank in the feeling of his
lips against her skin. Breathed out. He was leaving
just when she'd opened a door in her life that had been
closed so long it was dusty and cobwebby.

She'd given him her best I-want-you eyes. Wore a
white coat that showed every inch of leg she had,
smelled good, made him come so hard it knocked him
on his ass. In the past, with other men, all she'd had to
do was bat her eyes, tilt her head, or strut, and they
were all begging her for a whiff. But with Houston, she
didn't know whether to be insulted or determined.
Right now, her mind was on overload, and her body
was disappointed that it wouldn't get what it wanted
right now.

"I know me. If we start this now, I'll forget all about
your house and focus on you. Then next thing I know,
three weeks will have passed, I'll be in L.A., and your
brother will think I'm an asshole. That's no way to treat
my friendship, no way to start my new show and…it's
no way to treat you."

"So, this rejection you're giving me, you're saying this is a good thing."

"A very good thing. For now. Let's handle our business so we can *handle our business*."

"Why didn't you say that before you let me—"

"I'm not perfect, Honey. Far from it. Sometimes bad judgment gets the best of me. But I can correct that, if you let me."

"In other words, you can get yours, but I can't get mine."

"Shit," he said, and stepped back inside.

Honey backed up, wondering what would happen if she kept going. Would he follow her all the way back to her bedroom?

He grabbed her by her waist before she could get too far. "Come here," he said.

He pulled her into him fast. Her soft body slammed against his hard muscled one, and he kissed her with such force and intensity she thought she would pass out. When her knees faltered, he caught her, held her up, pulled her closer while his tongue made love to her mouth so completely that her clit responded with slick tremors and soft ecstasy.

When she moaned a long syllable, he pulled away. A proud smile crawled across his lips. His eyes were smoky.

"I need a cigarette," Honey whispered.

"You smoke?" he asked, the smile quickly interrupted by a frown.

"No."

He chuckled. "That was nothing," he said, sounding cocky and boastful. "I take what I do, everything

I do, seriously. And if I can't to something well, I don't
do it at all. Okay?"

"Okay," she said. But was she really talking? She
couldn't tell what was happening since Houston nearly
kissed her into an orgasm. *No more toys,* she thought.
All I need is Houston's lips.

"Look, you planned a little somethin' somethin' for
me. Let me do the same for you. I'm a wine-and-dine
kinda brother…no matter how slam-bam I might look."

That made her smile, but seeing him in her front
doorway so shortly after making him come made her sad.

His eyes swept her living room. "We did good
today, in more ways than one. Now, I haven't always
been chivalrous, but I'm trying to change. Let me—"
he kissed the side of her neck and sent a hot chill
rippling through her "—do you right.

"I'll be back tomorrow. Early. We'll work all day,
into the evening. Two days tops. We'll be done.
Then…we'll celebrate this weekend. How about a
cabin in the mountains?"

Honey nodded. She didn't trust herself to speak. She
couldn't be sure that the words, *Make me come again,
daddy,* wouldn't tumble pitifully out of her mouth.

Finally he left. It felt wrong to watch him go. Her
mind really didn't want to see that. So she closed the
door quickly and stood against it, reliving the kiss over
and over. Even the thought brought up her heat again.
She sank against the wall, slid a hand inside her pants,
stroked the place that so vividly held on to the memory
of Houston's lips and called out his name.

The weekend couldn't get here fast enough.

* * *

The land in that area looked roundup-ready. Thanks to Brax, no doubt. Houston looked on, grateful that his friend hadn't asked him to help. Houston didn't know the first thing about loading small square alfalfa bales onto a flatbed truck. And that's exactly what Brax was busy doing. It would be Houston's luck to break the wire-bound bricks, or get the distribution uneven. That's what he told himself, anyway. The truth was, he just wanted to hang back and see his homey in his new element. The man had a look of happiness and contentment that Houston had rarely seen on anyone he knew. Brax even moved differently—like he'd been born on the prairie and tending a ranch since his first breath. The transformation was dramatic. Houston was happy for his friend and just a little jealous of him, too.

The rolling green land stretched out in every direction as far as Houston's eyes could see. Brax Ambrose pulled soft leather gloves over callused hands and headed for the bales of alfalfa that stood on the east quarter in orderly rows. The hot air held their grassy scent tight and still. Houston gazed into the sea-blue sky of the morning, inhaled the pungent ranch air and gritted his teeth.

Brax tossed him a sideways glance. "Twice in one week. What's up? Is Honey driving you crazy, too?"

"Nah. I just needed to talk to you about something."

"Well, toss it out, man. We don't beat around the bush in the country. We don't have time. Too many chores."

His friend sure looked different. And it wasn't just

his clothes. Even his face had changed. Cooled out. Mellowed. The hard angles and lines and chiseled features women always talked about had been buffed smooth by sun and a good woman. His friend looked...peaceful.

A hard twinge of envy caught Houston off guard. He'd never been a covetous person. But he found himself longing for a life he truly loved one hundred percent.

"So? What's got you bent?"

"Bent?" Houston repeated.

"Yeah. You're standing over there like somebody tied your feet together and pushed you down."

"Sorry. Just thinking about the move to L.A. and hoping it's the right thing."

Brax didn't so much set the alfalfa down as drop it. "Tell me you are not thinkin' twice."

"No. I'm not. I know a good thing when it comes to me."

"Cool. Now help me with this and tell me what's eatin' you."

Houston grabbed one end of the bale and together he and Brax loaded the square block onto the back of Brax's truck.

"Remember what you said about Honey?"

"Man, I've said a lot of things about Honey. What in particular?"

"The part about me staying away from her."

Brax raised the tailgate of the truck and slammed it in place. His body went stiff and the hard lines Houston remembered came back sharp and pronounced. "What are you tellin' me?"

"Something I didn't have to tell you at all. But we're friends, and I want to keep it that way."

"By messin' over my sister? Does Honey know about your track record? Does she know you're not serious?"

"She doesn't care about that."

"How do you know? Did you talk to her?"

"No, but—"

"Tell her who you are, Houston. Tell her *what* you are."

"Look, Brax, Honey is a grown woman."

"Who has the worst luck with men. And you're adding to the scorecard."

"It's not like that. We haven't even—"

"Then keep it that way. Do what you came to do. Be an honorable man for once and then take your touch-and-go ass to L.A. That seems like a good place for you."

"Honey and I are two consenting adults. Whatever happens, happens."

Brax looked like the vein throbbing at the side of his head was about to burst. "You'd better get off my land now. Before I forget my manners and lose a so-called friend."

Houston blew out a breath. He'd thought he was doing the right thing. In the past, he would have just had his way with whomever without a thought. Well, he had changed, a little. Brax had him all wrong. Although Houston had no intention of stepping anywhere close to the vicinity of a relationship, he had no intention of hurting Honey in any way.

"I'm not going to hurt her!" he called back to his

friend as he walked toward his car. Brax didn't answer, but stood like a sheriff making sure that the outlaw got the hell out of Dodge.

Houston kicked back in his hotel room. He'd just ordered room service and was considering a pay-per-view movie, when his concern got the best of him. He took his cell phone from the nightstand and dialed a familiar number.

"I knew I shoulda put your number on call block! The Poonanay Store is closed, Houston!"

"Sylvia—"

"What! Did the women on your speed dial numbers one, two, three, through eighty-something turn you down?"

He didn't have the conceited heart to tell her that ladies rarely turned down Houston Pace. "You're the first person I called. You're the only one I can turn to right now."

Silence. And then, "Where are you?"

"Wyoming."

"Wyoming! What the hell? I don't do phone sex, Negro."

"I'm not calling for sex," he said casually.

More silence. This time, a cold and frozen hush.

"Well, stop the freakin' world. Fine ass Houston Pace is on my line and he's not calling about sex. Is this some trick to get back in?"

"No."

"No? Well, what do you want, 'cause good sex is the only thing I remember us having in common."

"How's your practice?"

"Good. How's your organizing business?"

"Too good to be true. Look, I have a friend, and she has issues with sex."

"I knew it. It's always about sex with you."

"Listen! Sylvia, I'm at a loss here, and I need some advice."

He heard the familiar sounds of her pulling on a Newport and exhaling the smoke. "Okay. What kind of issues does she have?"

Houston sat on the bed and tried to get comfortable. "Sexual ones, maybe. She dresses just two steps away from being a video vixen, and she sells sex toys. The woman just radiates sex in a way that's almost disturbing."

"She's a tease, and I'm insulted that you are ringin' my phone about some other woman."

"I don't have anywhere else to turn."

"Damn, H. You sound serious and kinda sprung."

"Hmm." He would admit nothing. "She's not a tease, although she flaunts her stuff well. But a couple of times when we've flirted, her sexy eyes grew so fearful it was scary."

"Sounds like sexual trauma. Of course, I can't be certain unless I see her for consultation. Any chance of that?" she asked.

Houston shook his head as if she could see him. "I doubt it."

"Okay. Here's my phone doctor diagnosis. She's probably had an incident. Incest, maybe, or rape would be my guess."

"Damn."

"Tell me about it. Some women never get over it."

A ripple of unease snaked through Houston. "Jesus."

"Well, you're on the right track. Praying helps. In the meantime, see if you can get her to talk about it."

"And if she won't?"

"Then you might be calling me back for phone sex after all, or at least to make an appointment for her to come in."

"I just…damn, Sylvia…I want to be with her."

"Just keep in mind that I could be way off base. I'm only going by the few things you've said. Heck, for all I know, she could just be a confident sista not afraid of herself or her sexuality."

Houston checked the time, flipped the TV channels impatiently. "I don't think so."

"Is this a guy thing? A challenge to your manhood or some mess? 'Cause if it is, I'll hang up right—"

"Not even close. I care about her."

Silence.

"I'm telling the truth. I really do care about her."

"Then you've got to reassure her every second that you care, that you're not going to hurt her, that you would never hurt her and that she can trust you. You got to say it and show it until you can't say it or show it anymore. And when you get to that point, keep saying it and showing it. You can't ever stop."

"Oh, is that all?"

"If her aversion is as strong as you say, then yeah, that's all."

This time Houston was silent. Was he up for all that? Was it worth it? Did he have time? "Thanks, Sylvia."

"Sure. Call in any time."

Chapter 12

It took two days for them to get through everything—Wednesday morning to get a rhythm and a routine going, Wednesday afternoon for Honey to get past her separation anxiety and all day Thursday for Houston to kick into high gear and turn most of her first floor right side up.

She had to hand it to him. He had more than a knack for organization; he was a master of it. By the time he finished with the living room alone, Honey would have sworn he'd doubled her living space. But it was just that she'd finally let go and thrown away so much stuff. And what was left, Houston had arranged in containers, baskets and shelves.

Houston brought order to chaos. When they finished sorting and purging, he'd told her to take a day off. Go shopping, see a movie. Hang out with a girlfriend. Just get out of his hair for ten hours while he worked with what was left of Honey's cramped and cluttered downstairs.

He had no idea what a difficult thing he was asking her. Besides having few friends, Honey didn't have much of a life outside of her business, her brothers and her music collection. She spent almost all of her time at home. When she needed something, she usually ordered it from the Internet. Everything else, one of her many guy friends brought to her. She liked her homebody nature. She enjoyed her own company and loved her home. She'd gotten so used to being the only one around that she'd had to adjust somewhat to feel comfortable with Houston at her house every day.

But his visits were more than worth it. She'd see a home she barely recognized. It was a place she hadn't seen almost since she'd moved in. Her belongings placed uniformly in containers, drawers, shelves and bookcases. Her house felt open. And she felt calm. Tranquil. Honey walked in and the sound of her footfalls, her breathing, her relief traveled throughout the downstairs. The smell of new wooden cabinets and wide open space played at the edge of her nose.

"Make every space count," Houston had said. Well, he'd certainly accomplished that. Honey saw nooks and crannies that had been covered up for years. In every direction, symmetry replaced disarray. Stylish solutions replaced piles of unruly boxes. His professional touch replaced her haphazard one. Houston had done it. He'd transformed her living room, dining room and work area. He'd slaughtered the clutter monster and revealed the true beauty that was beneath it all.

"Well?" he said, looking way too smug, leaning against the wall with his arms folded and a broad smile of satisfaction brightening his face.

"I hate it!" she said. "It's terrible. I mean...how could you!"

He stared at her in disbelief. His self-assuredness dented just a peg.

"You are so easy." She laughed. "It's fabulous! I absolutely love it. Really, Houston, I can't...there are no words."

She walked around in astonishment, sparking like fireflies searching for mates. "I barely recognize the place. I mean, is this my house?"

"Yes," he said, stepping away from the wall. "It is now. Before, it was kind of your dumping ground. So, let me show you around your new space."

That tour happened yesterday. Now Honey stood in her bedroom thinking the fates had been kind to her, blessed her, really. One day of organization had shifted smoothly into two and before Honey knew it, Wednesday morning had turned into Friday evening.

Honey felt like a turtle. Not the kind that hid in their shells—although that wasn't too far off, either— the kind that were chocolate-covered and stretched when they were pulled. The kind that were made to be eaten and devoured and brought moans of pleasure from the taste. Houston had done that. Every time she thought of him, she felt sweet and just a little bit nutty.

Honey leaned closer to the mirror on her dresser and

applied a generous coating of cinnabar lipstick to her mouth. She'd finished her makeup before anything else. After taking a shower and putting on lotion but before dressing, she'd painted her face. Put on all the warm colors she felt inside. Golden shimmer. Warm plum. Smoky brown. She couldn't hold them in anymore.

Anticipation fired inside her like rockets carrying her off the Earth. No way she could stay grounded for this. The thought of being with Houston launched her into the sky. Made her float and fly on bliss and the possibility of doing it right this time. Of staying until the end. Of burying the nightmare that had been her life for so long she wasn't sure if she would recognize herself afterward.

But she was damn sure ready to try.

Seven outfits lay against her California king-size bed like a quilt. She couldn't decide among them. Checking her reflection in the mirror, she liked what she saw. She took care of herself. Her body looked good. Nut-brown and lotioned smooth. Too bad she couldn't just slide into a pair of heels and be done with it. But obscenity laws shot that down. It was October, but too balmy for a trench coat. But she did have a mini trench. It was ultralight, and she could cinch the belt at the waist. The idea struck a chord of daring inside her. She picked up her weekend bag that was packed and ready to go beside her bed, slid her pedicured feet into five-inch red pumps and headed downstairs to the hall closet.

Her feet hit the bottom of the stairs with muffled steps of anticipation. She licked her lips, coating her tongue with the flat taste of Fashion Fair cosmetics and prayed that their stay-all-day color was just that. The doorbell ringing didn't allow her the time she'd need to reapply.

For a hot, very hot, second she thought of answering the door raw. Putting all her vulnerability and need on display, not to mention the six-pack she'd been working on since the moment Houston did his strip-tease last week. But that would spoil the surprise. Instead, she flung open the closet door, snatched on her jacket and wrapped it around her with superquickness FloJo would have been proud of.

She tossed the wild curls of her hair one more time, combing through them with her ruby-red manicure, held her breath and opened her front door.

The young woman standing there smashed into Honey's good feelings like a freight train, derailing and grounding every cloud she'd been floating on all morning.

"Yes?" Honey said, hoping the girl was a Jehovah's Witness or a Kirby Vacuum salesperson she could shoo away. But the woman's all-too-familiar features sobered Honey, pulled her down from her emotional high and forced her to look closer.

The woman leaned in as well and struggled several times to speak, only to leave her mouth working, her feet shuffling and her hands fidgeting.

Realization dawned on Honey.

Finally, the woman stood still and tall, looking Honey eye to eye. "Are you Honey Ambrose?" she asked, her voice the only thing shaking now.

Instead of answering, Honey's mouth worked. Dread prevented the words from coming out. Even when Houston pulled up in his SUV, got out and came up on the porch, Honey was still stammering and wrestling with the answer to that question.

"Hey, baby. You ready?"

Houston looked so good in his designer casual clothes. They didn't need to go away. They could have done it right there, in broad daylight on the flat wooden landing of her porch.

But right then, she had a more pressing concern.

"Houston," Honey said, forcing her tongue out of its hiding place. She tore her eyes away from the most handsome man in the world and cast them on a woman she'd never known or seen before in her life. A sickening wave of dread welled up from her stomach.

"What's up?" he asked, obviously sensing her turmoil.

"Houston," she repeated, then swallowed roughly. The back of her throat felt like an emery board. "This is my sister."

Chapter 13

The nut-brown girl was five feet seven inches. Her hair was an untamed mass of ruddy brown waves lightly brushing the tops of her shoulders. The young woman stared at Honey with raven-black, dewdrop eyes. A bob nose, apple cheeks and Cupid's bow mouth completed her sweetly expressive face.

A plum tank top and black skirt hugged her figure-eight shape.

In a corner somewhere upstairs, in a box, in a stack of boxes, Honey was sure there was a picture of her looking very much the same. Wearing similar clothes, her face holding the same frightened, hopeful expression.

The rich color of her eyes could not disguise the pain living there. The girl's too-tight, too-revealing clothing seemed peeled straight out of an uncut hip-hop video.

She shifted her weight from one side to the other, the large black bag in her hand swinging like a leather pendulum.

"I can't believe it! I found you! It's you! It's really you!"

The young woman grabbed Honey in an embrace so quickly and tightly that she didn't have time to react. She wouldn't have known how to, anyway. The young girl put her weight and a good rock into the hug, nearly knocking them both down in the process.

"Wow," Houston said. "Brax never mentioned it. I didn't know you had a sister."

"Neither did I," Honey managed between the girl's sobs. "Until now."

"What?"

"Well, well, well," Honey said, pushing away and smoothing her jacket. "Why don't we all come inside?"

Houston hung back while Honey's Mini-Me wiped tears from her face and slipped past her into the living room.

"A long-lost sibling, huh? Incredible. I'll leave you two alone to—"

"No! Please." Panic cut off Honey's breathing. She didn't know why she felt so uneasy. Not long ago, it was her calling, e-mailing, knocking on the doors of Brax and Collen. And now, someone was doing it to her. But it felt uncomfortable being on the receiving end of the news. She believed that turnabout was fair play, but she couldn't imagine facing this turnabout alone. "Don't go," she said softly, looking down at her hands. They were shaking like the turbo bullets she sold. The young woman looked on as Honey tried to convince Houston to stick around.

"I need—"

"No problem," Houston said, and swung a thick arm around her shoulders. "We were supposed to be together today anyway, right? I'll hang out for a few, then when you're ready for me to bounce, just say so."

With this change in plans, Honey didn't think she would ever be ready for Houston to *bounce.*

"All right. I'm going in," she said, trying to make light of a situation that was almost way too heavy to deal with at the moment.

She hadn't slept longer than fifteen minutes last night. Wet dreams woke her up with dangerous ferocity. She'd washed up and taken a shower long before it was time for her to get up. Knowing that the night and her lust were not going to give her any peace, she'd finally given in at 3:30 and filled some orders that had gotten backed up because of her reorg project. Trying to get her mind on a sudden family emergency was like reeling in a big fish. But since she'd been the little sister dangling from that hook once, she'd give it all her attention and energy.

"Please…sit down…"

"Lela," she said, heading over to Honey's dining room table like she'd been doing it all her life.

Carnetta Rowlins must have some strong genes, Honey thought. There were large chunks of her in Collen's and Brax's faces. But it was in Honey's and Lela's faces where the likeness was goose bump material. There was no doubt they were kin.

Honey thought about skipping the obvious question: *How'd you find me?* Hell, she'd been a bloodhound for five years. If she didn't have a flourishing sex-toy business, she could be a damn good private eye.

While Houston took a seat next to her, Honey slid aside boxes, padded envelopes and papers so that she and Lela would have a clear view of each other. "So, how'd you find me?"

"I knew that when I turned eighteen, I didn't want to stay with my foster family. They were cool for the most part, but I had this itch to get out into the world. See what's out here."

Lela clutched her bag and her purse as if they were the only things anchoring her to the Earth. "So, two weeks ago, I contacted social services, jails, correctional facilities looking for Mama."

A wave of nausea washed over Honey. For her stability, she grabbed onto Houston's leg. He gave her a questioning look, then covered her hand with his.

Lela didn't seem to notice Honey's sudden discomfort. She talked on as if more for herself than anyone else in the room.

"Heck, I even made a list of rehab facilities just in case...but I haven't had a chance to follow up on those."

"So you haven't found her?" Honey asked. Hope and anxiety tightening her hand on Houston's thigh.

"Not yet. But looking for our mother is how I found you. I kept talking to people who said someone else was asking about Carnetta Rowlins a couple of years ago. They ended up giving me the information they gave you."

"So, basically, you just followed a trail," Houston added. He was patting Honey's hand now. She loosened her grip, but not much.

"Yeah. That's what I did. The last guy I talked to…" Lela dug into her purse and pulled out a small notebook from a zippered pocket. The notebook had colored index tabs that Lela used to flip directly to the name. "Scott Weidman, with the Transitions Program, he said he couldn't find her personnel file. He thought it was with some files that had been stored but hadn't been scanned for archiving or something like that. Anyway, he said he remembered talking to you and that he gave you all the information he had at the time. When he gave me your number, and I saw your last name, I couldn't believe it. I couldn't…I couldn't…"

Lela broke down into tears again. Honey's soul broke with Lela's, and Honey got up and went to her sister's side. They hugged and cried for several moments.

"So, you found her, right?"

"Who?" Honey asked, wishing that even as she was consoling Lela, Houston would come to her side and console her.

"Mama. Is she here? Does she live nearby?"

Honey's body stiffened like it had turned to concrete. "No. I never did. Scott couldn't find the file when I called him about it five years ago."

Lela released the viselike grip she had on her purse and bag. Both fell to the floor and Lela slumped into Honey's arms. Her tears were silent this time. The only way Honey knew that Lela was alive was by her shallow breathing.

God, they were alike inside and out. Honey had once been consumed with finding her mother. She'd spent years looking. Fortunately, she'd had help coming to her senses and letting the fantasy of a wonderfully misunderstood mother, who loved, missed and wanted her, out of her head.

Honey stroked Lela's waves of earth-red hair and vowed to help her sister do the same.

"Come on, Lela. Why don't you stretch out on the couch? I'll make us some tea and tell you all about Brax and Collen."

"Who are they?"

"Our brothers."

Chapter 14

Houston stood with Honey and together they helped an exhausted Lela to the couch. Lela lay down in slow motion, closed her eyes and folded up into a half circle.

Honey pulled the throw from the arm of the couch and draped it over Lela. After smoothing her hair again, she joined Houston, looking on from beside an adjacent armchair.

His deep browns grew tender and supportive. "You're a good sister."

"What do you mean? I haven't done anything."

They soft-footed it into the kitchen. Honey took out a teakettle and two bags of green tea. Houston hit the jackpot first time out and opened the cabinet with all of her cups. He selected two large, clear glass mugs. Honey heated the water.

"You okay?" Houston asked.

"No," Honey answered honestly. "Ten minutes ago, I was a completely different person. And now, I'm not sure who I am."

"That's an exaggeration, isn't it?"

Honey fished a spoon out of a drawer and waited for her kettle to boil.

"No. Ten minutes ago, I had two siblings. Ten minutes ago, I had two brothers. Ten minutes ago, I was the baby of the family. Those things are the biggest parts of my identity. And each one of those parts has changed."

"Hey," Houston said.

Before she could speak, he gathered her in his arms. His hands moved in soothing circles on her back. "You really aren't all right."

"I will be," Honey said. "This is some heavy news coming down on me. Especially when my mind—" she slid her arms around his waist and pulled "—was elsewhere."

Houston rested his chin on top of her head for a moment. His chest rose and fell against hers in deep sustained breaths. He was disappointed, too. They both were doing excellent jobs of hiding their frustration.

"I'm sorry, Houston."

"It's cool," he said. But she noticed that he hung on pretty tightly. Probably so she couldn't see the truth in his eyes.

"Besides, you were the one keen for some of this."

"I sure was," she said. Her voice sounded torn and broken.

As the teakettle began to whistle, they both shared a laugh.

"I know we made a huge dent in your house this week. Heck, the only thing left is all the things you won't part with on your dining room table. But I can hang around for another week."

Honey groaned.

"We're not saying never. Just...not now."

Honey tore herself away from Houston's understanding arms and poured the hot water into two cups.

Houston didn't miss the message. "I take it that's my cue to cut out."

"I guess. I'm more steady now. The news that I have a younger sister kinda knocked me for a second."

The expression in Houston's eyes said her disorientation had lasted longer than a second.

She touched his arm. The arm she'd planned on having around her all weekend. "Thanks for staying. I'll call you later. We may still be able to hit the road tomorrow morning."

Even Honey didn't believe what she was saying. Her sudden-sister status nixed every amorous and gettin' busy feelings that she had.

Honey found a tray at the back of a wooden cabinet. She wiped it off, placed a lace napkin in the center. Then Houston helped her put the cups, honey, sugar and lemon on. They walked out together and Houston cleared a space on the coffee table for her to place the tray.

Lela looked troubled. Even though she was resting on the couch, there was so much tension coursing through the young woman's body that it was almost visible in the air.

"I'll walk you to the door," Honey said, setting the tray down.

Houston hesitated before leaving. He stopped with the door cocked open, the morning sun shining against his frame. His skin glowed radiantly.

"Like I said, I'll hang around for another week."

"Houston, you don't have to."

"I know I don't. In the meantime, let 4H give you something to remember him by."

He approached her slowly. Surely. His mouth settled onto hers and pressed warmly against her lips. She felt the blood beating between them. His tongue wandered deep into her mouth. His arms drew her closer. The bliss was dizzying and rose up from her toes to the top of her head. Honey moaned and knew the truth.

The man sure could kiss.

She may not have been able to rattle off her social security number or her address right then, but she did remember one thing. "What does 4H mean?"

Houston smiled and the sun caressed his wondrous mouth. "It's kinda my guarantee. If you spend time with me, you got four thrills coming."

"Only four?" she said, amused and intrigued at the same time.

"That's the baseline, baby. You can have as many as you can stand."

One more smack on her cheek and he was gone. Honey suspected that her heart was going with him.

She'd gotten used to that fine face up in her house these past few days. A silly second went by when she wondered if she could be falling for Houston in some kinda small, weird, inappropriate way. She forced herself to turn away and stop watching his ass in those wonderfully snug jeans and his shoulders testing the strength of the fabric in his Perry Ellis shirt.

"Boyfriend?"

Honey snapped back to reality. The fact that a brand-spankin'-new sister was taking a siesta on her couch was pushed to the edge of her mind.

Lela was sitting up and busy stirring honey and lemon into her tea.

Dang, but Honey would swear there was a younger version of herself in the room. Not a separate and different human being. But Honey from a parallel universe or a bend in the space-time continuum. She was staring at herself through a mirror of the ages. Only this mirror was cracked and broken and too sad for her years. Honey had made it out of her emotional funk. She hoped Lela would, as well.

"He's my birthday present, from Brax."

Lela picked up her cup and blew across the top of the tea. "I'd say brother Brax has good taste. He can give me a gift anytime he wants."

Wow. The reality was setting in. She'd just now gotten used to adding brothers to her gift list. And now, a birthday, Christmas, gifts, cards. Picnics. Cookouts. Thanksgiving would be here in no time.

"I'm so glad I found you," Lela said, looking revived at that moment. That was a good thing. Hopefully she would hold on to that vibrancy long enough to talk to her brothers on the phone.

Oh joy, she thought, heading over to the couch. Remembering how *happy* Brax and Collen had been when they found out about her, Honey wondered how they would react to the news.

She sat down and smiled at the beautiful girl sitting next to her. "Pass me the sugar, will you?"

Chapter 15

"What?"

"Don't play deaf. Her name is Lela, uh, Lela what, sweetie?"

"Ambrose."

"Dang. She's even got the last name. You wanna talk to her?"

"And say what?" Collen grumbled.

"Anything. How about, 'Hi. Nice to meet you. Welcome to the family'?"

"Sounds good to me. Put her on."

"Here's something I'll bet no one has ever said to you. Lela, your brother's on the phone for you."

Lela brightened as if the sun were shining inside her.

She took the cordless phone. "Hello, Collen?"

Honey would not have believed it if she hadn't been

sitting next to her sister when it happened. The solemn-eyed teenager, who had broken down at the sight of a new sibling, blossomed and grinned like a giggly girl with a big present to unwrap.

Honey kept a cool eye on her sister, taking in the happier side of her simply by watching what she did. Smile, nod, sit back, laugh, but most of all talk…a lot. When Honey heard the words *find Mom,* that cold wind that had chilled her before returned, and Honey froze.

"Lela, sweetie, why don't we save the serious talk for later? I want to get 'the family' together for dinner. Maybe we can talk about it then."

Lela looked confused, as if the words Honey used were from an obscure Japanese dialect turned inside out and backwards. "What do you mean?"

"Here," Honey said, reaching for the phone. "Let me talk to Collen."

Lela frowned for a moment and then spoke into the receiver. "Hold on. Honey wants to talk to you."

"Hey," Honey said, breathing a sigh of relief. "I know this is short notice, but how soon can you come up? I'd like to get us all together."

"It's gonna be a while. I just got a government contract to haul electronics from Atlanta to D.C. I'll be ironing the kinks out of that for weeks. At least two."

"That puts us into November. You still planning on coming up for Thanksgiving?"

"Yeah."

"Well, it doesn't make sense for you to make two trips in the same month. I think Lela will have to make do with Brax until Thanksgiving."

An idea straight from her viral show came to mind. "How about Web cam? You free this evening?"

"I'll cancel my plans. By the way, what's she look like?"

"Me," Honey said.

Collen let go a long whistle. "And you say she's only eighteen?"

"Yes."

"Tell Brax he better keep the guys off of her until I get there. Then we'll do it together."

Honey laughed at that. "I'll tell him."

"Okay, Sista Sex. I gotta go, but before I do, hook your brother up with my standard order."

"One box of condoms, three chocolate thongs and three bottles of coconut massage oil. Anything else?"

"Nope."

"Just one question...do they know about each other?"

"Of course, and all at once, little sister."

"Funny. I'll talk to you later. Tonight. Seven your time. Don't forget."

"I won't."

Honey clicked the Off button on the receiver and placed it back on the charger.

"That was the strangest half a conversation I've ever heard. Sounded like you managed to get Web cam, condoms and Thanksgiving all in the same sentence."

Honey chuckled. Lela joined her.

"You hungry?" Honey asked.

"Yes," Lela responded.

"Well, I hope you like Mexican food. My cook Tony, who works full-time for Brax, hooks me up every month. I'll have an elegant Mexican meal micro-waved in no time."

Honey busied herself in the kitchen, while Lela hung around in the dining room.

"So, tell me all about Lela," Honey called from the kitchen.

"I was just about to say the same thing."

"You first," they both said.

Lela poked her head in the kitchen while Honey unpacked tamales, enchiladas and sanchos. She wasn't much for rice and beans. She'd just as soon have two sanchos as have one with two sides.

Everything was packed for individual servings so it was easy for her to put together two of everything in microwave-safe containers and put them in her General Electric for four minutes on low.

She wiped her hands on an amber dishtowel. "Anything I can tell you about me, you probably already know. I'm twenty-eight, I put myself through business college by working for the city in the vital statistics department. I applied for a job as a clerk in that department for the same reason you knocked on my door. Ms. Carnetta Rowlins. And just like you, my search turned up a sibling. And then another. While Carnetta was nowhere to be found."

"I have extensive files. It's just a matter of time."

"Well, that's just great," Honey said, forcing a smile. "Anyway, after more dead ends than I could stand, I stopped looking for Mother and started my own business. When I had more clients than I really knew what to do with, I quit that job. I've been working out of my home ever since."

"Really?" Lela asked, finally stepping all the way inside the kitchen. "What do you do?"

Honey only hesitated for a moment, then decided that in this day and age, an eighteen-year-old could take the news. "I sell toys...sex toys."

At first, Lela didn't say a word. And then, "Why?"

The microwave beeped as the Defrost mode went off and the timer automatically kicked into full heat.

"Because people deserve to have fun when they have sex. And if they need a little kick, a little zest, a little something extra to get them off, well, then they come to me. And I provide them with safe, healthy, respectful ways to give and receive pleasure."

"What about S&M?"

Honey whipped around and fixed her eyes on her sister. "Not from Fulfillment. I do have a line, and hurting someone crosses it."

"So, no bondage?"

"My stuff's lightweight in that area. Cuffs. Scarves. Feather whips. Soft crops. I've been thinking of discontinuing even that. It's just too severe for me. Why are you asking? Are you into that stuff?"

"No. Some girls I know are. I'm a man-on-top kinda girl myself. Pretty unimaginative when it comes to those things. No back door, no sixty-nine, no—"

"Okay, sweetie. I know we're blood, but that's a little more than your big sister is prepared to hear. You are using protection, right?"

"The whole time. Every time."

"Good girl."

According to the timer on the microwave, their meals would be finished in four and a half minutes. But Honey's appetite had dissolved into the air as soon as she discovered her teenage sister had more experience in the bedroom than she did. She had to turn her mind from that irritating fact.

"So, what about you? What's your story?"

"Short story," Lela corrected. "Foster care, school, here."

Both women took a seat at the dining room table.

"There's got to be more than that. Interests? Hobbies? Did you like school? How did your foster parents treat you? What about plans for college?"

"To answer all of your questions. None. None. No. Okay, I guess. Definitely not."

"You cut to the chase, don't you?"

"The whole time. Every time."

"Hmph. You and Brax will get along *real* well. What about a boyfriend?"

"There's no shortage of guys that want to go out. That's for sure. I just take my pick when I get bored or tired. But I'm too young to get serious about anybody."

"Well, keep in mind Collen is the overprotective type. He almost got into a fight with Cliff—who was my other half at the time—just because Cliff made a smart-aleck remark to me. Do yourself a favor. If you ever get serious about a man, don't introduce him to Collen until you're married and even then, be careful."

Lela laughed and smiled sweetly. Honey recognized that reaction. The idea of having a blood relative in your life who approved of you and had your back was intoxicating. Honey didn't think she'd ever fully sobered up from that wonderful glow inside that told her she was connected to someone, a people, a family. People to whom she mattered and who mattered to her. She wanted Lela to have that feeling and know that among Honey, Brax and Collen, they were all the family she needed. Otherwise, she'd feel lost and disconnected forever.

"What's the matter?" Lela asked.

"Nothing," Honey said. Moist eyes belied her words, but not a single tear fell. Honey had moved on from all of that mess too long ago to rotor it up now. Besides, her role in the family as the one looking up had changed. Lela was the baby of the family now and looking up to her. Honey was determined to make a real good example. Honey accepted her new role with relish. Loved the taste of it. Smacked her lips with it.

The microwave signaled that dinner was ready. Honey served it up on china and in no time they were quiet into their meal.

It had been a long time since Honey felt a purpose beyond paying her mortgage. Her business had started out that way at first. Creating ways to have honorable rather than hurtful sex. But she'd allowed so much of her original drive to fade, it was hard to stay in that emotional place for long periods of time. But Lela had set a new fire in her soul. Given her something new to wake up for. God had blessed her with a sister. She would not make Him regret it.

Chapter 16

"**C**ompliments of the lady in red." The bartender placed the cognac snifter next to the one that was nearly gone. Houston let his ego rise with the drink and sent a nod and a smile over to the woman who was indeed in red—lips, pantsuit and heels. She sat opposite him at the bar like a corporate seductress, fresh out of the boardroom coming to the local watering hole and looking for a fresh conquest. He knew a briefcase came with that smile she returned, along with athletic, no-strings-attached sex. As horny as he was, he wondered why he wasn't feelin' this woman or the other three women who given him just-say-the-word eyes since he'd sat down.

He drained the rest of the liquor from his glass, pushed it off and pulled his fresh drink into place. The cognac didn't dull his senses like he'd hoped. Instead, it made them more acute. Colors brighter, sounds sharper, thoughts clearer. He couldn't concentrate on or consider the other women in the bar because Honey kept pushing them out of his head.

He knew that as a professional organizer, he was privy to people's private lives. He had access to things and information that others rarely had. People revealed themselves to him in the things they collected and allowed to accumulate. He saw inside his clients by touching what built up outside them. He liked to think of himself as a social anthropologist. Learning about people by coming into contact with how they lived.

Normally, he found his discoveries about people fascinating But what he found out about Honey had tied him to her. It was as if she'd put all these aspects of herself on display so that he could lose himself in the playground of her life. And that's exactly what her world felt like to him—a playground. A fun and energetic place where life was lived seriously but not taken seriously. Life was meant to be explored in all its intoxicating allures and every boundary respectfully pushed until the only thing left was a good life on your own terms.

Buried beneath all her adult toys, he found the real Honey in self-help books on healthy relationships, couples and family magazines, newsletters on treating people with respect.

Honey's unabashed approach to life captivated him more than a cognac ever could.

The music in the background was so shallow and distorted, it sounded like it was coming out of a tin can a hundred miles away. Houston had spotted the bar on the way back to his hotel. He had to have passed it at least three times since he'd started working on Honey's place. But today, the sign Brother's Tavern caught his attention like a finger beckoning him inside. The air was thick with the smell of draft beer, hot wings and raging pheromones. Houston adjusted himself on the bar stool, realizing that instead of cooling his disappointment with the missed rendezvous with Honey, he'd stoked it. Made it so powerful, he couldn't shake it out of his head.

He'd dated enough bimbos to know that some of them only pretended to be dumb because far too many men were intimidated by intelligent women. Some actually were as stupid as their actions and words conveyed, and others such as Honey came with great brains and great beauty but worked their sex appeal like a casino dealer workin' a deck of cards.

What really pulled Houston in from the get-go was the hidden part. A mystery lived inside Honey. Houston could smell it. He'd been invited into enough people's lives to where he could diagnose their personalities like a shrink. From the moment he'd discovered what she did for a living, Houston had felt compelled to uncover what would drive a woman into the line of work that Honey had chosen. And the fact that she was highly successful committed him even more to finding out just who this woman with erotic toys alongside figurines of happy couples and angels was.

"Looks like you came to drown your sorrows," the woman said. Houston blinked and gritted his teeth.

The room had changed or maybe he had, but the woman who was seated across from him had miraculously appeared in the seat next to him. He hadn't even noticed her approach. He gave her a quick appraisal. Formfitting suit. Still wrinkle-free after a hard day's work. The body in the Prada suit was long and slender. L'Oréal makeup. And those soft leather pumps… were…

Damn. He was slippin'.

"Nah. Just washin' down a few regrets is all."

She gave him an up nod and pursed her lips. "I'm Cynthia."

"Houston," he said. "Thanks for the drink." He picked up the cognac and took a cool-suave sip from the rim that Billy Dee would be proud of. Old habits, he thought and decided to dial back the charm.

"You looked like you could use one."

Houston smiled. He never was one for hiding his emotions. He raised his glass in salute. Cynthia matched his move and they drank together.

"Well, today, I had my mouth all fixed for something and then something else came up."

"Do you need to beat somebody like they stole something?"

Her eyes danced with the question, and her mouth turned up real pretty with a smile. Last week, Houston might have been swayed by that. Probably given in.

But a lot had changed in a week, like the fact that Houston was looking forward to spending more time with Honey, not just a weekend. He was hoping the weekend would be the beginning of how he would spend the rest of his time before he left for L.A. But those plans were probably dashed. Vanished with the sudden appearance of a long-lost—or in this case never-known—sister. Houston downed the remaining liquor, gritting his teeth while it burned the back of his throat and warmed up his stomach.

"Look," Cynthia said. "I don't ever do this, but I'd like to give you my number." She reached inside a tiny red leather purse and pulled out a business card. She wrote her number on the back of it with a pen that probably cost more than Houston's entire wardrobe. Not only did she have good taste, she had some ducats, too. Nice.

Houston took the card, but decided to be honest. "I can't make any promises—"

"That's okay." Cynthia finished her drink and pulled her purse strap up onto her shoulder.

"You don't have to go," he said.

"Yes I do. Before I embarrass myself by saying something like, 'I'd love to help you fix your mouth.'"

She blew out a breath, shook her head and pushed a full head of bone-straight hair back from the front of her face. "Sorry."

"Don't be," Houston said, placing the card in his back pocket, hoping the gesture would help the woman save face.

"Next round on you?" she asked, then slipped off the bar stool and headed toward the door.

"Deal," Houston said, but the woman was already gone.

Chapter 17

The evening couldn't be going any better if Honey had been planning it for weeks. One brother and his wife in the living room, the other on a big-screen TV, by way of wireless Web cam, and all of them getting along with Lela. Honey had spent the better part of the afternoon trying to whip up something brilliant in the kitchen. The result was a Mexican fiesta. Ariana, her sister-in-law, even brought dessert. A sweet potato soufflé which tasted like sweet potato pie only with glazed pecans on top.

For the first time in months, Honey's home was filled with laughter and lots of it. It reminded Honey of the childhood she'd always wanted and never had. To have it now meant the world to her and brought a sting of fresh tears to her eyes. Her heart swelled in her chest. Honey was so overjoyed, she excused herself and went into the kitchen where she could dab at her eyes in private.

A few moments later, Lela came cautiously into the kitchen.

"What's wrong, Honey?" she asked. A dark shadow of sadness fell over Lela's eyes so quickly, it hurt Honey's heart to see it.

"Nothing," she said in a strong voice. She stepped away from the sink and walked toward her sister. "As a matter of fact, it's been quite a while since I've been this content. I was just too embarrassed to let you all see my happy tears."

Gratitude swelled again inside Honey, cutting off her words, so she opened her arms instead. Lela stepped right into them.

"I'm so glad I found you," she said.

Honey held her tight. "Me, too," she managed. "Me, too."

"God dang. Do you two need a mop?" Brax said, coming into the kitchen, glass in hand.

"No," they said in unison.

"I'll come back in a minute."

Lela looked after him, then turned to her sister. "Not the touchy-feely kind, huh?"

"He's a lot better since he married Ariana."

"That's better?" Lela asked.

"Yeah."

They both laughed at that.

"Hey, can you give me a minute? I need to make a phone call."

Lela's eyes softened. There it was again. That sadness. It took over her sister's eyes at the strangest moments. In time, Honey knew she would ask her sister about it. Right now, while she had so many good feelings bouncing round inside her, she wanted to share her joy.

Lela went to the refrigerator, took out a cold beer and headed back to the living room. "I'm sure this is what Brax came in here for."

"Thanks, sweetie. See you in a minute."

Lela went back to the family and Honey dialed the phone number that had burned a place holder in her memory since the moment she got it.

Listening to the number ring, she pressed the phone closer to her ear, held the receiver tighter and shifted from left to right. Two rings. Three. An eternity. She needed to hear his voice.

"Hey, lady," came the smooth velvety voice on the other end. Honey breathed a sigh of relief. Gave her heart permission to beat again.

"Hey," she said, suddenly questioning the reason for her call. Houston might not be missing her the way she was missing him. What if the moment has passed and he was no longer interested in getting together with her? What if he'd already gone out and…and… She swallowed dryly, her mind unable to finish that thought.

"How's Lela?"

"She's good. We're good. She's meeting the family. Brax and Ariana came up. We've got Collen on Web cam. It's…it's real good."

"I can tell. Your voice sounds like it's dancing. You must really be happy."

"I am."

"I'm glad."

"So, what are you doing?"

"Actually, I'm doing the family thing, too. I just finished dinner with my aunt and a couple of cousins. We're outside trying to make good use of the weather."

It had been unseasonably warm for the beginning of November. Sixties and seventies. Early fall weather, although Cliff had blamed the temps on global warming.

"Well," she said, "I don't want to keep you from your family."

"Don't worry about it. It's cool. I'll take a call from my favorite client anytime."

Honey twirled a strand of her hair around her finger. "So, now I'm your favorite client?"

"Absolutely. You're the only client I've ever had where organizing came with enchiladas, deep kissing and a Handyman 4000."

They shared a laugh. Then Honey got serious, suddenly questioning her rash act.

"I'm sorry about that," she said.

"You shouldn't be. If me," he lowered his voice, "falling on my ass didn't tell you how much I enjoyed it, then I don't know what words I can use to convince you."

A bold streak of audacity bolstered her confidence. "You can say that you'll come get me on Friday so we can have our weekend."

"Wild horses couldn't keep me from it."

Honey felt like Houston had just turned a light on

inside of her. The power of her reaction surprised her. She was humming like one of her top-selling products.

"Umm," she said, purring her response. "I can't wait."

"That makes two of us."

"So," she continued, getting bolder by the minute. "What should we do until then?"

"Call me back later on tonight."

Honey got a little wet just from the insinuation of phone sex with Houston. "Wild horses couldn't keep me from it."

"Okay. That's what I'm talking about."

Honey felt tingly all over. As if she'd swallowed a giant Fourth of July sparkler. The weekend couldn't come soon enough.

Funny, people always made comments about toys spoiling for a man. Honey suspected that after a weekend with Houston, the opposite might be true.

"So, Friday?" she asked.

"Friday."

The silence between them then was so awkward, Honey didn't know if she should hang up right then or figure out a way to keep him on the phone a little longer. Their weekend plans had pulled them into a world where they were the only inhabitants. Her heart sounded as if there were a microphone next to it and a subwoofer on the floor next to her feet.

They say absence makes the heart grow fonder. Well, it sure was doing a number on Honey. Already. By the time Friday arrived, she hoped she'd still be able to behave like a polite woman.

"Ah, Houston, just one more thing."

"Yes…"

Honey stood by the kitchen door and glanced at her living room—the clean, neat and tidy living room where her family was sitting and enjoying themselves. "I couldn't have had my family over if it weren't for you. Thanks for everything."

"You're welcome, Honey."

Honey smiled, wishing she could stay on the phone with Houston much longer. "Well, I better let you go."

"You sure about that? Your voice sounds tentative, like there's something else."

"That's just me getting the dessert ready," she lied. "I probably sound distracted."

"Okay then," he said. "Have a good time with your family."

"You do the same," she said, but her voice purred with all the sexuality and allure she could muster. What she was really saying was, "We're going to have a good time with each other tonight." She hoped he picked up on it.

She hung up with a jolt of sadness. She did miss him. It was a cold, empty feeling. A sense of being disconnected and floating randomly.

"You keepin' all the dessert for yourself?"

"No," she said, answering her brother. She hadn't even heard him come in.

He grabbed plates, forks and napkins. "So, what's the holdup? You thinkin' about Lela?"

"No. Actually, I was—" she wasn't ready to tell Brax how the nature of her relationship with Houston had changed "—thinking about business. I'm backlogged with orders. Catching up has been a monster."

"Um-hmm," Brax responded. "Well, the real monster is sitting out there having the time of her life."

"Are you talking about Lela?"

"Who else?"

A hot streak of worry straightened Honey's back. "Lela is not a monster."

"Really? What do you really know about her, other than she showed up yesterday claiming to be our sister?"

"I know she's telling the truth."

"How? Have you seen a birth certificate—not that one can't be faked. But have you seen any paperwork that proves she's even related?"

"I don't need the paperwork."

"How do you not need proof?"

"Because the proof is in her eyes. In case you haven't noticed, they look just like mine. Hell, for that matter, she looks just like me—all of her. And we all know who I look like. So, besides that, I got nothing else. But then again, I don't need anything besides that."

"Honey, even if she's related, you don't know anything about her. She could be a meth head, a thief, a pyro, a—"

"Stop! She's not any of those things. I would feel it if she were!"

"I just don't see what sense it makes to take her into your house. You really don't know her from—"

"Take her in? What do you mean take her in? She practically collapsed yesterday, so she slept on the couch last night. As far as moving in with me, no one's talked about that. I hadn't even considered that."

"Well, somebody better tell Lela that. 'Cause she's

under the impression that she's staying with you. Pretty much got the week of sisterhood all planned out. We all just assumed you okayed it. If you didn't, you better get her straight right now. And if you didn't offer your home...why didn't you?"

"Because—" Honey began and then cut herself off. She was going to say, she didn't know Lela well enough to invite her to stay, but that would have played right in to Brax's line of thinking. Big brother know-it-all.

Brax waited for her to finish. A look of expectancy hardening his handsome features.

"Because I hadn't gotten around to it yet."

"Right," he said, obviously not buying it. "Look, if you're gonna do this, do it with your eyes open, your guard up and your valuables locked away. At least until you can feel her out. See what she's about."

Honey knew that the last thing Brax wanted to hear was that she already knew what Lela was about. It was the same thing Honey had been about when she first met her brothers. Their mother. Finding her. Bonding with her. Picking up with her as if nothing had happened. Honey knew from her own disastrous experience that was a road best not traveled.

At least by taking her in, keeping her close, Honey could make sure that the same pain she experienced would not come to Lela.

Honey picked up the soufflé and stood beside Brax. "Thanks, big brother. Good lookin' out and all that. But I got this covered."

Her brothers either didn't feel the same pain of rejection that she'd felt or they were damn good at hiding it. Either way, as men, they probably couldn't understand the mother-daughter connection and how acutely powerful it can be. Honey understood every aspect of that power. With her help, she was certain that Lela would come to understand it, too.

Brax headed out into the living room and Honey pressed Redial on her phone receiver. Houston picked up on the first ring.

"You change your mind about waiting until Friday?" his voice asked with equal parts of eagerness and sensuality. The tones of his voice sounded like they'd been dipped into hot caramel before they came out.

"Yes," she said. "Can you come over tomorrow?"

Chapter 18

"**C**ome *on!* It ain't that much pretty in the world!"

"Not pretty. Handsome," Houston responded. His cousin had been pounding on his aunt's bathroom door for the past ten minutes. "Besides, you don't have to shower or nothin', you just want to see how I look."

"You damn skippy!" *Bam! Bam! Bam!* "Now come out, come out, whatever you're wearing!"

Houston swung the door open, feeling real good about his appearance. Hugo Boss from neck to ankle. Steel-gray body sweater and matching slacks. He put his big studs in his ears tonight. One carat. He topped that off with his favorite gold watch and Stacy Adams shoes the color of smoke.

"You crazy, Paul."

"Sweet Pea! Sweet Pea! How many times do I

have to tell you? What do I have to do, spell it for you?"

"You can if you want. Just so we have an understanding, I'm never gonna call you by that ridiculous name. Ever. Your momma named you Paul. I'm gonna call you Paul."

"Not in front of people, though, right?"

"Shut up. But before you do, tell me how I look."

"You look like you're ready to get your ride on. If you weren't my cousin—"

"My right hook and uppercut would be all over you."

"Okay. Right. No need for graphics. Anyway, you look like you're going to need a whole box of Trojans."

"And I know just where I can get them."

"Get outta here, Negro. And make sure you call me when it's over. I want all the details."

Houston gave his cousin a look that he knew conveyed how inappropriate he felt that remark was. And the fact that he had no intention of sharing one second of the details with him.

Paul crossed his arms and had the nerve to rock his head. "Well, *dang.*"

"Tell Auntie I'm not sure when I'll be back."

At that, Houston grabbed his Andrew Marc badass jacket from a coatrack in the hallway with only one thing on his mind...flippin' the script on Honey. When he got finished with her, she'd be like, "Toys? Are there toys?"

He made it to her home quickly. The fastest time on record. Twenty minutes. He gave himself one more appraisal in the rearview mirror and stepped out of the car. Early fall at its best surrounded him—sapphire sky, with nary a cloud to cover the vibrant and shining sun. A warm breeze blew around him. It held just a hint of the cooler weather behind it. The air smelled vibrant and full of change.

His body was on full tilt. He could barely stand being without the heat of Honey's touch one second longer. After her call yesterday, he guessed she was feeling the same way. He knocked on the door, then rang the doorbell, then called out, "Honey!"

When the door whooshed open, all sense of common decency evaporated. He grabbed her, pulled her into him as tightly as he could and kissed her like nobody's business.

Their lips and tongues rolled together in a frenzy of need, each seeking the other in the most urgent way. Honey's body softened, turned to butter, tasted like vanilla espresso. Hot. Invigorating.

Houston didn't want to breathe.

He just wanted to keep kissing, keep filling himself with her essence. His whole body broke down and went erect at the same time. They wouldn't make it to any cabin, bed or couch. Their clothes wouldn't last another—

"Excuse me!"

Houston and Honey stiffened, peeled away from each other slowly, then looked toward the sound of the intrusion.

Lela.

She stood with her arms crossed and her hip

cocked and her mouth bent in frustration. "Are we going or not?" she asked, obviously upset about... something.

"Hey, Lela," Houston said, in a lust-drugged voice.

"Hey," Lela returned. Her voice sounded the same way she looked. Annoyed.

Honey adjusted her hair and her blouse that had gotten mussed in their energetic exchange. "Yeah, sweetie. We're going. It'll just be a second, okay?"

"Okay," she said, and plunked down on the edge of the couch. Her left foot swung back and forth impatiently.

Honey turned and pressed herself into Houston's erection. He guessed she was trying to hide it from her sister.

"Lela, give us a minute."

The young woman glanced at her watch and screwed up her mouth. "You want me to time you?"

"What the—?" Houston's anger flared at the girl's impertinence.

Honey gave him a gentle stroke on the arm. "You know what I mean."

Lela blew out a long hot breath any dragon would take pride in. "All right. A minute."

Houston watched the girl walk with heavy feet up the stairs. If she moved any slower, she'd be standing in one spot.

"Can a brother come inside?" he asked finally.

"Sorry," Honey said, planting a quick smack on his cheek. "Come on in."

She stepped aside and let him enter. It was the first

moment since he arrived that his mind was clear enough for her attire to register.

She was wearing a long-sleeved plaid shirt. Powder blue and baby pink. Hideous. The damn thing had the nerve to have two front pockets. Her shirt was tucked into a pair of jeans so tight, Honey shouldn't be able to breathe, let alone talk or kiss. Those he approved of. He could have done without the belt, though. Three inches of rawhide leather with a buckle the size of a cell phone.

The crowning glory was actually at the opposite end of her body—a pair of tan cowboy boots, with thick black heels.

"You got a hat to go with this getup?" he asked.

"Of course!" she said, scurrying over to her work-table and picking up the Stetson. She plopped it down on her head like she'd been born in a saddle.

"Yee haw!" she proclaimed.

Houston moved to her side. Pulled her against him again. He couldn't help himself. Even dressed as a cowgirl, he found her irresistible. "I smell Brax."

Honey's eyes sparkled. "Yep. I'm taking Lela to his ranch. I thought it would do her good to see it."

He kissed her forehead to mask his disappointment. He assumed she'd called him to come over for something entirely different. "So, how do I fit into all of this?"

Honey slid her arms around his waist. The gesture was so familiar, as if they'd been lovers for years. "I want to hire you."

"Huh?"

"I want to organize everything. My whole house... even my garage."

Houston stiffened and not in a good way. "You what?"

She had to repeat that. She couldn't have said—

"Since Lela's gonna be living with me, I need to get my act together, or rather, my house. So, I figured—"

Houston pulled away, amazed that Honey would do such a thing. "She's *living* here?"

"Yes."

"You just met her."

"Why does everyone keep *saying* that?"

"Um." Houston scratched his goatee, ran a hand over his bald head. "Because, now let's see…oh yeah, it's true!"

Honey popped him on the arm. "Smart-ass!"

She tried to walk away. Houston pulled her back, not quite ready to let her go. "You trust her?"

"Yes. It's like…I *am* her. Or at least I was. I know everything she's going through, and believe me, I went through a lot. If I can keep her from some of the pain that's in front of her, well…"

Her voice trailed off. A lonely tear tracked down the side of her face. Damn. Tears. Superman had kryptonite. Achilles had that tiny spot on his heel. Houston had a woman's tears. They brought him to his knees every time.

He wiped the tear away and replaced it with a kiss. "You can't afford me."

At that, a sweet smile broke through the sadness on her face. "I bet I make more money than you."

They shared a laugh and a tight hug. For a moment, Houston wondered where all the lovey-dovey stuff was coming from. It seemed like they'd gotten awfully close awfully fast. He guessed that after you've seen someone naked or come in front of you, anything is possible.

Houston pulled back, gave his new employer a good once-over. "So, while you two ride the range in Nebraska, I stay here and get your house in order?"

"You catch on fast."

He smiled. "You have no idea. Okay, to make this work, I'm going to need some supplies and an extra hand. I'm sure my cousin Paul can bring me what I need and help out, too."

"Sounds good to me. So how long?"

"Is this a rush job?"

"Are you ready yet!" Lela called down as if on cue.

Honey bit her bottom lip. "Yeah."

"Just so you know, I get time and a half for rushes," he said, chuckling.

"Deal."

Houston released his remaining disappointment in a long breath. "Give me two days."

"You got it," Honey said, smiling as sweetly as her name.

Honey and Houston finally let go of each other, and Honey walked to the foot of the staircase. "Get your stuff, Lela. I'm ready!"

Houston couldn't get enough of Honey's curves. The vision of her standing there reminded him of the place on his body that responded to all those curves by going straight. "One more thing," he said.

She turned, just the slightest hint of worry clouding her features. "What's that?"

"This is the last rush job you get. From now on," he

said, imagining her beneath him, pumping, moaning, "I take my time."

Honey didn't have to say a word. Her face told it all.

Chapter 19

"Oh hell no! You got me up in here on some false pretenses. Some humbug mess. Some U-Haul craziness!"

"Calm down, Paul."

"Calm down? *You* can be calm with your big burly self. Me, I'm a delicate flower. A *fragile* thing."

Houston ignored Paul. Then Paul got his five-ten, two-hundred-pound fragile self up in Houston's face. "Look here, homeboy, I don't pick up anything heavier than a fat wallet. You dig? So, if you think I'm gonna bust my back movin' boxes with you, not only have you lost your mind, you must not have had a mind to begin with."

"The only reason you're so upset is because you know you're going to help me."

"Oh no you didn't just try to use that vice-versa, psychoanalyst crap with me."

Houston didn't respond to his cousin's tirade. He simply grabbed a stack of boxes, moved them to the hallway and went back for another.

Out of the corner of his eye, Houston caught a glimpse of Paul's face contorting from willfulness to acquiescence. Finally, Paul huffed a short string of expletives and picked up an even shorter stack of boxes. "Okay, Mr. Clean, where do you want these?"

The two worked in that manner, Houston doing most of the work and Paul helping a little and complaining a lot the entire first day. Surprisingly, they were able to get everything out of the upstairs and sorted. Most of what they were organizing was product, so it was quick work once they got a system and a rhythm.

Since Honey wasn't there to tell Houston which of these products were big sellers and which weren't, he'd relied on Paul's…suggestions.

"Oh, now this right here is a monster, mister. Go from zero to the Big O in six seconds…so my *sources* tell me."

Along with an education and an explanation of what Honey's toys did, Houston gained an appreciation for Honey and all the work it must take to keep her one-person business running so successfully that she could afford the lifestyle she led.

"Yes, yes. Your girl is makin' money fist over fist. These thangs are not cheap," Paul assured him, waving something around that looked like a model of the space needle.

"She's not my girl," Houston insisted. Then curiosity got the best of him. "How much money?"

"For the top of the line, which this is, her customers have got to be droppin' at least three hundred."

"What?" Houston said, standing up from the bin he was filling with shipping supplies.

"Um-hmm. And I'll bet this is one of, if not the, bestseller. This big puppy alone will take care of her mortgage every month."

Houston shook his head. *Maybe she does make more than me.*

"Hey," he asked, making room for the next in an assembly line of bins, "how come you're such an expert on women's toys?"

"Women's? You're kidding, right?"

Houston remained silent.

"Don't you know that with just a slight adjustment, you can—"

"Never mind! That's one family secret you can take to the grave with you."

"Fine," Paul said, pouting. *My cousin,* Houston thought. *The world's greatest pouter.*

They went through a first sort, placing items into categories of either Unload or Make Room. They plowed through the overrun and clutter, repurposing rooms, and zeroing in on anything that had obviously outlived its life span.

Bringing his cousin in to help was the best idea he'd had. It was cutting the hours it would take to finish the job big-time. Two men working like four. He and Paul worked well together. Both focused and goal-oriented.

"This chick sure does hold on to a lot of junk. Has she thrown anything out, ever?"

The two sat in Honey's kitchen eating a pizza they had had delivered. Honey'd said they could help themselves to anything they wanted to eat; Houston preferred to order lunch in.

"She must have gone through a time in her life when she was without. So now," Houston said, taking a big slice of sausage and onion pizza, "she surrounds herself with abundance."

Paul swallowed a mouthful, wiped away the string of mozzarella hanging from his chin and gulped down his orange soda. "You and your psychology. I hate to jump on your couch, Sigmund Pace, but this heifer is just lazy."

"Don't call her a heifer."

"Why? What you gonna do?"

Houston didn't say anything. He just eyed his second piece—the one with all the cheese—and wondered why what Paul said bothered him.

"Ooh, you are *feelin'* Little Miss Clutter Bug. Only there's nothing little about her. Except maybe her waist. Which makes her just your type, too. Alphanumeric. Look at her from the front, she's a number eight. From the side, she's a capital *S*. Go on, get you some!"

"She's cool. That's all. She deserves respect. She's just got…issues." Houston scooped up that other piece. Paul was busy scarfing down the side of wings. "Maybe she's hiding behind her things. Or she's trying to keep something out."

"Or maybe…she needs to move that big ass of hers and get rid of this mess!"

Houston ignored Paul and thought he'd hit upon something.

* * *

Houston and Paul cleaned up the table and after a quick check of the sports channel—Houston to see how well his Atlanta Falcons were doing and Paul for reasons Houston didn't want to know about—they headed back upstairs to start putting things in order.

Houston had moved everything out of Honey's closet except an old metal lockbox with a broken lock. That piqued Houston's interest. If there were personal items inside, Honey would probably be tickled to come back to find them preserved inside a fashionable, yet secure storage container. Houston had purchased several yesterday just in case.

Houston reflected on what his cousin had said. If Honey was trying to keep something out, she'd let him in a lot easier than he would have expected. He had no doubt that she asked Brax to vouch for his character. But Houston felt it was the way something between them just…clicked.

A feeling.

The way they liked to look at each other, with the same things on their minds. *Intimate connection, baby,* his mind sang.

And it was intimate. This was not the way Houston typically worked. He was the coach. The cheerleader. The voice of reason and solution with his clients. He pitched in, yes. But the work was done by the clients. To make the organization meaningful. To help them understand what it took to make places for things, to recognize unnecessary items and to practice the habits of decision-making and purging.

clients went through their things, then
Houston rode in on his white—better living space—
and completed the transformation.

But this with Honey, going through her things, was
like opening up her psyche and immersing himself in
it. Houston discovered that the woman had a penchant
for all things seductive. From the usual shoes, lingerie
and perfume, to art, color schemes. Even her shampoo.
When she did put things in containers, the containers
were in exotic shapes. There were very few straight
lines in her home, especially upstairs. Everything con-
toured and curved. Bent and sloped. Mirrors. Paintings.
Statues. Jewelry boxes. Perfume bottles. Her stereo
and bedroom furniture. Houston felt seduced just by
being upstairs. Honey didn't even have to be in the
room with him.

He always had special feelings for his clients.
Usually fond memories and good thoughts of success.
But after organizing the most intimate parts of Honey's
life, Houston felt a special bond. A strong one. As if
he knew her on a crazy deep level now and they could
speak without saying a word.

"You want this last slice?" Paul asked.

"No," Houston said. But what he did want was
Honey. Now more than ever.

Houston opened the box and found it swollen with
important papers. The title to Honey's home and car. In-
surance papers. Honey's diplomas—high school and
business college. A handful of photographs of Honey as
a girl—hair in untamed pigtails, short dresses with

ruffles, patent leather shoes. The same weak smile in all
of them. Honey was a cute girl, skinny, all legs. If
Houston didn't know any better, he would have mistaken
her for being happy. But he and Honey had talked over
dinner those first few days helping her with the downstairs. Honey's childhood was far from cheerful.

These things deserved a great home, Houston
decided, and picked out the best-made of the three
cases he had with him. Not just simple containers, they
were elaborate storage units that would accent any
elegant living space.

He reached down deep into the box and pulled
everything out.

A folder, worn and splitting, slipped out of the pile.
The contents spilled on the carpet. Houston dropped
the papers in his hand into the new curvy, more decorative container he'd selected and gathered the papers
that had fallen.

Houston recognized the research from his discussions
with Honey. This was all information about her mother.

The folder looked old, likely due to constant
handling. Dark worn edges. Ratty tab. The manila had
long since turned a pale gray. The stiff card stock
softened by wear. It nearly ripped apart as he knelt to
put all the papers back inside.

Then it dawned on him. It was Honey's birth certificate. A birth certificate belonging to Carnetta
Rowlins. Divorce decree. Death certificate for James
Ambrose. A page torn from the white pages with a
listing of Ambroses. A newspaper clipping of an
assault-and-battery sentencing. Business cards from
several people in the social services industry.

The document that caught his eye was the handwritten one. There were six addresses written on it, all of them lined through except one. The last address had a circle around it. Houston wondered if this was Honey's final lead. The last known whereabouts of her long-lost but not forgotten mother.

"Ooh!" Paul's voice startled Houston as he stared down at the writing. "You're going through her personal papers."

Houston felt like he'd been caught with his hand in the cookie jar. "I'm just picking up some papers that I dropped."

"Um-hmm. Anything good?" Paul's eyes widened with bright curiosity.

"No," Houston said. He gathered up the papers, placed them in the box and stood. "I was not snooping."

"Ain't nobody said nothin' 'bout you snoopin'. But since you brought it up—"

The sound of the front door creaking open ground Paul's accusation to a halt.

Frustration set Houston's jaw. "They're supposed to be gone another day."

"Maybe there was some drama at the ranch and they told that little adolescent trick to go back where she came from."

"Back off, Paul," Houston said, heading for the stairs.

Paul followed. "I don't know why you're defending her, the way you said she acted up!"

"Whatever."

Houston took a deep breath and tried to ignore his disappointment. When Honey returned, he wanted everything to be perfect. Everything in place for the big unveiling.

"Hey! What are you doing in here?" a man yelled.

He was tall, a bohemian-looking type, with Birkenstocks, loose khakis, wrinkled Jimi Hendrix T-shirt and a scraggly goatee. His glasses made him look intelligent despite his hey-dude, sleepy-eyed appearance. Ol' boy's skin was the color of blanched flour.

"Look, man, you can leave nicely, or I can call the cops. Your choice," he said.

"Okay, now that's a bold paleface right there!" Paul said, slamming his hands down on his hips.

Houston stepped closer, not wanting to strike the beatnik-looking man, but ready with his right fist. "Who the hell are you?"

"Cliff," he said, defiance riding his stern features. "Who the hell are you?"

"Houston," he answered.

The man's features brightened in recognition. "Oh, hey, man. Wassup?" he asked and extended a hand. "Honey has told me way too much about you."

By day two, no one would have recognized the upstairs of Honey's home. Not even Honey. Houston barely recognized it himself. So much potential, especially with all the clutter and junk and inventory out of the way. And that's where Paul really came in. Houston had an eye for redesign. A damn good one. Paul's eye was Houston's eye...on blast. He had a wilder, more eclectic taste than mainstream America, but he had just the kind of "out there" vision that Houston had a gut feeling Honey would appreciate.

So on the second day, Houston followed Paul's lead this time for containers, arrangements, storage bins, placement and the overall look of the upstairs rooms. From Honey's boudoir to a second, high-tech office, to a bedroom and living space for Lela. The transformation was enormous. And by the time they were finished, they were both sweating with pride.

"Good work, Paul."

"Not bad, Houston. I think we make a good team. We could be the dynamic duo of Bravo TV."

Houston laughed. His cousin had been trying to scheme his way on to his show since the family found out he'd signed the contract.

"Well, I tell you something, Paul. You really came through for a brother. I mean, this is better than anything I've ever seen you do."

"That's 'cause I got skills."

"It's also because you're trying to prove you deserve a spot on my show."

"Damn that sibling ESP!"

"You're not my brother."

"You know what I mean. We family, and you just know me so well."

And there came the pout. Right on cue.

"Tell you what. I'll compensate you by flying you out with me when I go. I'll get you on set somehow. They may put you to work, you know, behind the sc—"

The bear hug Paul attacked him with cut off

Houston's breath. His cousin squeezed tight. "Thank you. Thank you."

"No problem," Houston said as Paul released him from a near headlock. Houston's ears throbbed from the grip. "Fragile my ass."

Houston couldn't tear his eyes away from the transformation. It was momentous. He made a mental note to take his After pictures before Honey got home—which, according to her phone call, would be in the next hour. He fidgeted. Pushed back a cup holder. Slid over a basket just a hair. Thumbed a painting on the wall up a notch. Adjusted the books on the headboard shelf.

"Chill out, Mr. Clean. It's done. You can't improve on perfection."

He stood back again, feeling like a director trying to get just the right angle and panoramic view of his scene. It had to be good.

"She'll like it," Paul said, frowning.

"She better," Houston said on the outside. On the inside he thought, *I hope so.*

Chapter 20

The end of the Nebraska prairie—with its savannah-like grasses and expansive green of trees, ever-bright sunflowers, so late into the season—transitioned into the lifting landscape of Wyoming. The Nebraska landscape, which had been experiencing such unseasonably warm temperatures, didn't realize that it was autumn and held on to its early fall colors with a glad hand.

Wyoming's countryside hadn't been so lucky—it had turned a dull brown. The temperate spectrum brought on the quiet calm of a season in slow transition.

Honey drove fifty-five miles per hour on the two-lane highway, basking in the calm. It was the first moment of peace she'd had since she and Lela left for Sugar Trail Ranch.

Honey was reluctant to glance over at Lela for fear of stirring up the hive's nest of questions Lela seemed to have been stirring almost all her life. The girl was SOM—Stuck On Mother. Honey hadn't wanted to use the word like Brax and Tony had moments after she and Lela arrived, but after two days, her sister's heightened fixation was undeniable. Honey didn't realize there were so many variations of the topic, so many ways to get to the topic and so many triggers to the topic of their absentee mother. Lela didn't need six degrees of separation. One or two, and she was right there, back on Carnetta Rowlins and questions about her possible whereabouts, her likes, dislikes, memories, things she left behind, jobs she had, last known addresses, numbers of times she'd been in jail, her drugs of choice.

At one point, when they were all out riding, Honey's head started swimming so badly, Brax had to gallop to her side and steady her on her horse. She said she was just a little light-headed from being up on such a large stallion, but Brax's frown told her to stop lying.

Honey fought that dire sense of nausea the entire time. The threat of something spoiled and putrid coming up kept her mind spinning and her mouth clamped tight. Lela was determined to find out what they all knew about their pasts and create a picture that would lead them to the only missing piece that seemed to matter to her. Honey merged off of Interstate 80 onto Highway 87 North, wishing Brax was in the car to fend off Lela's pursuit of the past.

No matter what Honey did, her mind ticked back

to the way Lela had grilled them like steaks at a cookout. Honey didn't hold up too well when her emotions were pressed to the wall. Right now, Honey felt flattened but the wall was missing. Brax. He'd answered every one of Lela's questions, like a tennis pro returning a serve. Giving her *an* answer, but not quite answering the question all the way, either. After a while, when Lela's insistence put them all on edge, Honey had had enough.

Right in the middle of dinner—a smothered burrito and queso soup, and Honey knew she didn't like to be disturbed while enjoying one of Tony's good meals— she quietly and calmly placed her knife and fork on her plate and folded her hands in front of her.

"Lela, no disrespect, sweetie, but you are walking on old wounds with spiked shoes. And for some, this wound is still painful, still raw and open, still bleeding. Not only is what you're doing rude, but it's starting to get obnoxious, and quite frankly…you just got here. So, please *chill out!*"

After that, Honey proceeded to unlace her fingers, pick up her knife and fork, and go back to her burrito.

The shift in conversation, mood and emotion in the room couldn't have been stronger if an earthquake had split it in half. For nearly five minutes after that, a mouse walking on cotton would have been a loud noise. Honey was hard-pressed to hear chewing, swallowing, or silverware clinking a plate. It was a hard silence. As well it should have been. Three of the five people in that room had had harsh, push-pull childhoods. The kind not everyone can recover from. They were healing. Coping. Dealing. There was only so much prying into something ugly that they could take. If Lela wanted to be welcomed into the family, it was better that she learned that from the get-go.

Everyone stared at Honey with a mixture of shock and surprise. All except Brax, who reflected appreciation and approval in his wise eyes.

Lela's mouth worked, but no words came out.

"I'm sorry," Honey said quickly before the situation had a chance to deteriorate any further. "I shouldn't have said that that way, but please understand you have really asked enough questions about our mother for one day. For three, actually. Let it rest awhile, okay? We'll pick back up on Monday. Start fresh. Just, right now…it's just too much."

Honey didn't know then if her words had made things better or worse. But Lela abandoned her barrage of questions, and the family had a reasonably comfortable two days together. The underlying tension didn't ruin the mood too badly; it just kept Lela a lot quieter. All Honey could think was *good*.

Sometimes it's good to just listen, especially if you're the newbie.

Honey headed into Cheyenne proper. They'd made it in just under an hour. It was early evening, but Lela was asleep in the passenger seat—or maybe resting but not moving. The only thing she'd said after they loaded up the car and got inside was, "I'm tired. Is it okay if I just sleep?"

"Sure," Honey said. Her mind screamed, *Thank God!* She wasn't sure what the drive back was going to be like, but she assumed it would be awkward. Even with Lela's head lolling back and forth according to the roll and twist of the road, Honey felt closed in and uncomfortable. It was like being in the car with their mother. Lela looked so much like her. Wavy, ruddy brown hair. Large forehead. Eyes so intense, you know she'd already seen too much. Strong cheekbones and apple lips.

She even slept like their mother. When their mother went to sleep, she was out. But not in the wild-horses-couldn't-wake-her-up kind of way. In a limp doll way. Their bodies went completely soft. It was as though they both used every spec of strength they had when they were awake and conscious. So when sleep took them, their bodies collapsed, needing every minute to recover and build energy for the next time they came to. Honey wouldn't have been surprised if Lela slipped right through the seat belt and pooled in a soft brown heap of flesh and soul on the passenger-side floor.

West Lincolnway, Pershing Boulevard, Lyons Park. Five minutes. Just five more minutes. Honey wasn't claustrophobic, at least not overly so. But riding back in the car with Lela couldn't be over fast enough. The weekend had started out on an uncomfortable note and was ending on an awkward one. The sooner they got home, the sooner they could start over—get off on a better foot this time.

For thinking about the positive side of the situation and not panicking like she usually did, Honey allowed herself to have half a thought about Houston. And then a full thought and then two, three. She opened the floodgates that had been threatening to burst free the entire time she'd been gone.

Honey thought about the upcoming weekend with Houston. About his hands and how she wanted them on her. About his hips, the movement of them that she memorized, and how she prayed he would move that way when he was naked and inside her.

Honey had brought her Body Buddy with her. A little device that she never left home without. It looked just like a tube of lipstick, but instead of rolling up ruby-red when you turned the base, it vibrated. Nice and quiet. Quick and fast. Honey kept it with her for…emergencies. She'd known that fantasizing about Houston would put her body in a state of emergency. And she was right. But the tension between her family members put out her heat like a fire hose.

"O-kay," Honey said out loud, pulling into her driveway. She'd hit the garage remote almost two blocks back. The door was nearly open by the time she turned into the driveway.

Lela stirred.

Just what I thought. Light sleeper or damn good actress.

"We're here," Honey said. She cut the car's engine and gave Lela's thigh a gentle shake. "Lela?"

Her sister unfolded from her curled and tucked position on the passenger side. She stretched like a cat and yawned like a man.

"Car rides always make me sleepy," Lela said with a foggy voice. "What time is it?"

Honey glanced at the clock on the dashboard of her sports car. Just after six.

"Wow. You made good time, and I'm going to bed."

As they entered the house, the garage door closed behind them, shutting off the sunlight. The car motor hummed like a loud bee.

"You'll wake up in the middle of the night. Why don't you hang with me for a little while? We can play backgammon or chess." *Or talk about the future for a change,* Honey thought.

Now that Honey had the company, she wanted to experience what it was like to sit up with a sister and talk. She'd had a taste of that the past few days before they left for the ranch. She liked it and wanted more. Especially if Houston made any kind of dent in the madness upstairs. Honey and Lela could hang out in Lela's room, in their pajamas, and just talk. Create new memories. And besides, Honey wanted to extend her sister a peace offering.

The anticipation of seeing Houston's work got the best of Honey. She stopped herself from running up the stairs, but she couldn't stop herself from mentioning it.

"I wonder how far he's gotten."

"Who?" Lela asked, frowning. She really did look asleep on her feet. Wobbling. Moving in slow motion. Eyelids heavy and hooded. Honey guessed their talk wouldn't be as long as she'd hoped.

Honey flipped on the kitchen light and without anything in there being different, Honey sensed a change. A lightness.

"Houston. Remember? He was going to tackle the upstairs. No more sleeping on the couch for you."

"Oh," Lela said and rolled her sleepy eyes.

Honey hoped Lela was rolling her eyes because she was sleepy and not as a reaction to Houston.

No sooner did Honey think the words *reaction to Houston,* than she had one. He was coming down the stairs. Finer than she remembered. There was the thinnest layer of sweat and exertion on his skin, and he looked delicious. Honey's whole body ached with an inner longing. He'd been working. Moving something. She liked the idea of a man, especially that particular one, doing things for her. Getting sweaty for her. Because of her.

Suddenly, the thought of her sister going to bed sooner than later didn't seem so bad. If Houston could stick around, Honey and Lela could have a quick conversation, recap the visit to the ranch, then off to sleep, at least for Lela.

Honey had things, and a man, to do.

Chapter 21

Houston had always been told that absence makes the heart grow fonder, but no one, not even his boys back home, told him anything about absence putting your libido on tilt.

It was as if he were seeing a woman for the first time. Adam's first look at Eve. Honey came toward him on the staircase with a sexy smile and hips that rolled like a mighty ocean.

Relief and appreciation washed over him in great breath-snatching waves. What did he think? That she wasn't coming back? That he'd never see her again? He winced. That thought cut him and made his insides thrash with pain. He clamped his mouth shut, afraid of what might come rushing out. Uncool things like, "I'm so glad you're back," and "You sure look good," and "I missed you."

Her smile brightened. His heart hammered. "Hey, Houston!"

Houston grinned. "I'm glad your back. You sure look good. I missed you."

Damn!

She giggled a bit. Smiled even broader. "I missed you, too."

A well-aimed feather could have toppled him. But it didn't have to. Seeing Honey again had done it. That great big pretty smile. Drinkable mouth. He could stare at those lips for a lifetime. Kiss them even longer. She trotted up the remaining stairs to the landing and hugged him like a chum. Sweet, quick so that essential body parts didn't get too close. He had to change that. As soon as...

"Are we gonna see it or what?"

"Oh *no!*" came Paul's pained reply.

Paul sauntered down the stairs to the landing, his back as straight as the number one. Eyebrows knit together in disapproval. "You are way too snappy, Little Miss Pretty Thing. That attitude is not allowed near my masterpiece."

Paul planted one hand on his thin hip while the other arm flailed demonstratively in the air.

Lela rolled her eyes. "Who *is* this?"

"My cousin," Houston said. "Paul, make nice with Honey and Lela."

Paul bowed slightly at Honey, then did a visual spot check of Lela. "Pleased, I'm sure."

Lela sucked her teeth and crossed her arms over her chest. "Are you gay?"

"Are you?" Paul asked, as smug as Warren Buffett on a good Wall Street day.

Houston clamped a hand around Paul's flying arm before it hit someone. Mini Honey was shutting down all Houston's "my woman's back" feelings. And Houston couldn't have that.

Not wanting to wait another moment for Honey to see her improved and reorged upstairs, he took her hand. "Since I'm here, why don't I give you a tour?"

"Because we're tired. I'm going to bed," came Lela's dry reply.

Honey's smile lost its seduction. "Lela's tired. She fell asleep in the car. It was a long couple of days."

"Little Miss Thing, why don't you let me show you your new digs."

"I know where my room is," Lela huffed and pushed past all of them up the rest of the stairs.

"Ungrateful heif—"

"Paul," Houston interrupted. "Can you wait for me downstairs?"

"Sure. Just how extensive is your cable, Ms. Honey?"

"Satellite. Three hundred channels."

Paul's hand flew to his throat. "Ooooh! I may never leave."

Houston and Honey watched Paul jounce down the stairs happy as butter on a biscuit.

Houston took a settling breath, grateful to be alone with Honey, even if it was on the landing of a staircase.

He took her hand. "Come on. At least let me show you the hallway."

Man, quit lying. You know all you want to do is take her to her bedroom and hope that she likes it enough to invite you to stay.

They climbed the stairs together and Honey shook her hand free as soon as they got to the top. She covered her mouth, but Houston heard her reaction loud and clear.

"Oh, my God!" Her eyes grew wide and bright. Houston couldn't tell if it was shock, horror or surprise. Damn. Did she like it? She had to like it, right? He had her taste down. He'd been through her things intimately. Knew her. Inside and out now. She had to like it. Had to love it. He was confident. But for some reason, it was hard to breathe just then.

"I have a hallway!" she shouted. "And it's gorgeous!"

"Shut up!" came the call from both upstairs and downstairs. Paul and Lela didn't blend well in each other's presence, but once out of sight, the two had the same mind.

Houston and Honey laughed quietly. "What do you think?" Houston whispered.

"I think you're a genius," Honey whispered. "I felt so light coming in here. I felt like I could float or something, you know?"

"Like you could breathe?"

Her eyes sparkled and her smile came back. "Yes!" This time, she took his hand. "What else?"

"Well," he said, leading her down the hallway. "Your bathroom is pretty sweet."

"You did the bathroom?"

"Yeah." They rounded the corner and stepped inside. "Check it out."

Honey folded her lips together and pressed them tightly, but her expression said everything. Cupboards above and below the basin. The windowsill and alcove space displayed decorative bottles, brushes and small baskets. Short shelves served as holders and accents on the wall. Tucked into every corner were hide-away spots for laundry bags, sponges and extra toilet paper. Everything color-coordinated in muted gold, ginger and deep red.

"It's fantastic!" she said, her voice rising above a whisper. "It's so me. Utterly. Completely."

Just then, her eyes moistened and his heart stopped beating.

"Houston, it's so…I mean, guys do stuff for me all the time. Because they want…" She touched the hamper, twirled in the free air. "You *get* me. You really got inside to wear I live. Downstairs and now up here. No man's ever…"

She stopped and took a deep breath, then planted an exquisite kiss against his cheek.

Houston's ego expanded. Wave after wave of relief hit him. He straightened his back, leaned against the wall and crossed one Cole Haan–clad foot over the other. Honey examined, touched and delighted in every area of her newly arranged space. Houston liked to think of bathrooms as rejuvenation areas. That's exactly what he'd created for Honey. Something special. She deserved a peaceful, tranquil, spa-like space in her home. He imagined that running an online business was demanding and tiring.

"I thought you should have a power-down space. You know, somewhere to relax."

"I love it," she said. Then she lowered her head. "I just get so busy, you know? I don't ever take time to..."

"Hey," he said, peeling himself off the wall. "I do this for a living, remember? I know how it is. People have busy lives."

"Yeah, but you do more than just de-clutter and straighten out rooms. The people who come to you have...issues. And you help them. I just don't want you to think—"

"What?" he asked, stepping closer. In the confined area of the bathroom, the scent of her perfume surrounded him, drifted into his senses, excited him, drew him even closer. "Think you have issues. Everybody has issues."

"Really? What are your issues?"

She looked up then, delight simmering in her eyes. Her excitement was still present, just subdued. Hesitant.

"I like to help other people deal with their problems so that I don't have to think about my own."

"Which are?"

Houston took a deep breath, wondering if he was going to go in all the way and realizing that, yes, he was. "I tend to date the same kind of woman. Over and over."

Honey furrowed her brow. "What kind of woman?"

"Airheads."

"Why?"

"So when I end the relationship, they won't have sense enough to be mad."

"That's cruel, Houston."

"It's the truth."

Honey took half a step backward. "Hold up. Don't tell me. Let me say it. 'You're different now.'"

"I'm trying to be. Yes."

"Um-hmm."

Suddenly the shoe was on the other foot. Talk about feeling light. Houston felt as though he'd just been given wings but didn't need them to fly. He could simply look up and take off. What a release to unburden himself of that awful part of his past that he was working so hard to bury and pat smooth.

He thought about the upcoming weekend, all the things he wanted to do to Honey before he left for L.A.

"But, one thing I know for sure. There's not an airhead bone in your body. Besides, we aren't talkin' about a relationship. Just an early fall slap and tickle, right?"

He heard himself ask the question and wondered about the feeling of apprehension knotting inside him as he waited for the answer.

A fling! his mind shouted. *And then I'm out!* But the connection he felt with Honey seemed to demand more than a fling. Too bad the timing was so bad on this one.

"Yeah," she said finally, a little of that delight coming back into her eyes. "As long as I get to do the slapping."

Houston laughed at that. And liked it, too.

He moved closer. Closing the gap she'd created just a moment ago. "You ready for it?"

Houston held out his hand and smiled devilishly. His heart slammed against his chest in anticipation.

She placed her hand gently in his. "Yes, I think I am."

Houston licked his lips and led her to her bedroom.

Chapter 22

The current of electricity that moved from her hand into his spread throughout his entire body. "Um," he said under his breath. His mind was playing tricks on him. Was that two hands between them or just one? *Shake it off, man. L.A., remember? L.A.*

His idea had been to create a sanctuary within a sanctuary. A place where the sexiest woman on Earth lived and called home.

The moment she entered her bedroom, she stopped and her hand went slack and her mouth made a luscious *O*.

Natural materials all in her favorite color scheme—red, butterscotch and sage. Everything that was out—clothes, books, CDs, toiletries—had been put away into baskets, wicker storage containers, barrel-front

side tables and elegant cargo bins. Houston had transformed her overfull bedroom into an oasis of classic
lines and open areas. Accent fabrics on the windows
and behind the bed created a warm, relaxing welcome.

The man truly knew how to make an impression in
every room.

Nearly a minute had passed and she hadn't said
anything. Just stood and stared.

"Don't make me wait," Houston said, eager for
her reaction.

Her left hand glided slowly across her chest, down
her side and against her thigh. "It makes me feel…"
She turned her lust-filled brown eyes toward him and
bit her bottom lip.

"Come here," Houston said, tugging her gently and
spinning her into him. He bent in and set his lips free
against hers. He drank her mouth like a love-starved
fool. Got serious with it, and real hungry as his tongue
told her just how much he'd missed her those two days
she was gone. How much he'd wanted her. And how cold
and empty a hotel bed could get. How hard it had been
for him to sleep at night when he dreamed so vividly of
plunging inside her, keeping her wet. That he woke up
every day since he'd met her hard as steel and sweaty.

When the kiss ended, they both exhaled and moaned
against each other, holding strong.

Houston buried his fingers inside Honey's curls,
gently pulled a fistful of strands to his nose. Filled his
lungs with her scent. Rose and something deeper. San-
dalwood, maybe. Or jasmine. The aroma increased
his need.

"I can't wait until Friday," he said, hoping. He kissed her cheek. Followed the line of her jaw with his lips and tongue to the crook of her neck. Slid his tongue over the soft, yielding flesh. Then to her shoulder.

With his hands, he kneaded her back slowly, pulled her closer. Stepped into the swell of her breasts and pressed inside the softness.

"Um," Honey moaned. Her arms traveled the length of his back, settled against his butt and squeezed. Houston closed his eyes and nudged her closer to the bed.

"Wait," she said, her voice whispery. "Lela. I can't… Close the door, Houston."

"Nothin' but a word, baby," he said.

The speed at which he closed Honey's bedroom door and got back to that luscious body amazed even him. He scooped her up, quickly before she had the chance to think twice and placed her on the bed.

Her eyes looked apprehensive. He placed a kiss on the eyelid of each one and felt her relax beneath him.

Her skirted, four-poster bed was draped with natural textures and colors. Stone and beige blocks contrasted with a bleached wood duvet. She settled comfortably into thick, soft heaven.

Honey's arms came up, slid around his neck, caressed his face. "What about your cousin?"

"Probably watching reruns of *America's Next Top Model*."

Honey smiled and nodded.

Houston slid his hands into her skirt, and slid off both her skirt and thong with practiced hands. Her skin, a smooth warm stroke of chocolate flesh, molded to him with his every touch.

Houston soon discovered that it wasn't just the scent of her hair that drove him to distraction. The sweet aroma of her body wafted into him. The jasmine was ambrosial and clingy, like the woman arching toward him.

"Houston, please," she said. "I can't wait, either." Her words sounded stretched out. Needy. Infused.

She was going to have to wait. Just a second. They both were. He couldn't stop looking at her body. Even as he removed her blouse and freed her breasts, he stared, took in every inch of her body with measured glances and soulful appreciation. Curves and mo' curves. Soft, brown, sloping, winding curves. The only place in the world he wanted to go right then wasn't L.A. or back home to Savannah, but everywhere those curves went. Every direction. He would follow forever, get lost and never come up for air. He held her gently, like those dreams he kept having, so as not to break the spell.

He took her right breast in his hand, moaned at the feeling of her full round flesh, and fingered the nipple before he slid it into his mouth and sucked rhythmically.

His mouth pulsed. His tongue swirled deftly around the tip until it got as hard as he was. He worked his fingers down the center of her body, slid them inside her wet opening and rocked his first and second fingers against her clit. Bringing it to a hard slick pebble.

Honey gasped and tensed at the same time. Houston sensed a change in their sexual rhythm. Her legs went stiff. Her thighs closed around his hand.

"Relax, baby," Houston crooned.

Houston straightened and unbuttoned his shirt. Honey's hands reached up to help him. He shrugged off the garment while her hands roamed freely over his pecs and abs he worked so hard to keep. Her eyes roamed with her hands, as if she'd never touched a man that way before. Houston moaned at each hot sensation her playful examination stoked inside him. She loosened up a little.

Houston finished undressing and Honey smiled like a sexy, delicious diva. Her lips said, "Come on, let's do this."

He lowered himself on her curves. "Like I said, nothin' but a word."

She was so wet and ready for him. And his organized, thoughtful and horny ass made sure she had a cache of condoms within reach of every area of her bed. He grabbed one and put the packet between his teeth. But the next sound he heard set his teeth on edge instead of allowing them to rip open the extra-large Trojan.

"Somebody better come get this little hooker before I slap her into a brand-new day!"

Houston didn't move except to make sure that Honey's vital areas were shielded from Paul's rude eyes. "Get out, Paul." The words fell like bricks between them.

Paul didn't move. Instead he said, "Dang, cuz. You been workin' out?"

"Out," Houston ordered though his teeth.

Paul's eyes got as big as CDs. "I'll just wait for you downstairs."

Before the door closed, Paul stuck his slender head

back in the room. "Honey…sweetheart…if those are
real… You *go,* girl!"

"Paul!" Houston's torso stiffened, but his arousal
was doing just the opposite. *Family!* he thought. *That's
why I keep my distance.*

The door slammed and the opportunity for Honey
and Houston to quench their thirst for each other closed
with it. It just wasn't the right time. Houston should
have been more respectful of Honey's sister and his
cousin. Besides, Honey deserved a special celebra-
tion. Rose petals on the bed, scented candles, music
playing. She'd seduced him in all the right ways. He
needed to return the gesture.

He sat up.

"No," Honey said, her eyes frantic and hands
grabbing for him. "Let's just… I really want…please,
Houston. I need—"

He shushed her with his mouth, calmed her with his
lips, tasting, licking her sweetness. He hoped she
understood. Her urgency built beneath him. He felt the
heat rise from her body and seep into his. A few more
seconds and there would be no stopping either of them.
He pulled back, smoothed her swirling hair with his
hand.

"The man I used to be wouldn't care, Honey. You
understand? But I care…about you. And this isn't right."

When Honey's hot hands wrapped around his
arousal and massaged, Houston gulped at the quick
rising sensations and he almost lost himself right then.
"Um," he moaned, feeling himself sway to her persua-
sions. "Ah-ah," he moaned louder.

"Ho-ney!" The shrill voice pierced the lust-choked sounds coming from Honey's bedroom. Lela's frustrated voice was unmistakable.

Honey's hands fell away and her eyes closed. A barrage of expletives went off in Houston's head. Disappointment rolled inside him like a sharp boulder.

He took in Honey's amazing beauty one more time. Admired it. Memorized it. "You don't know what kind of self-control I'm calling on right now to not ride you till you scream."

He got up before that control faltered and the respectful man disappeared and the lustful animal inside him took over.

Honey laid back completely open, arms at her sides, legs parted, lips spaced apart. Everything about her inviting except her eyes, which she squeezed shut. *Damn, she feels it more than I do,* Houston thought.

He picked up his clothes that had mingled with Honey's in a heap on the floor. She looked so sad and wrung out, like they'd never have another moment. Her dissolved expression compelled him to reassure her.

He bent down, took her left nipple between his teeth, flicked his tongue against the still-tight orb, then let go. "Friday," he said.

She nodded silently.

"And until then," he said, handing her her blouse, "no goody drawer."

Her eyes snapped open. "What do you know about my goody drawer?"

"Nothing, except for the fact that I'm sure you have

one. Probably packed with more high-tech gadgets than a James Bond car."

That remark brought back the smile he liked. "You got that right," she said buoyantly.

"Promise me," he said. "No toys. No erotica. Not even…" He took her hands and kissed the fingers of each one. She sighed and the mere breath of it made him throb. "These."

Honey frowned as if he were speaking a foreign language in reverse. "I don't know, Houston. I have needs."

"And I'm going to take care of every one."

"But by Friday, I'll be—"

"Just the way I want you," he said.

Honey sat up, picked up the rest of her clothes from the floor. Houston watched every move. The tilt of her head. The pitch of her hair. The fall of her breasts. The turn of her waist. It was going to be a long week.

"What about you? That means no pulling the pole for you, mister."

"I'm cool with that," he said. His hand could use the rest. His regular fantasies of Honey had gotten the best of him and he'd…tried to alleviate the tension they'd caused. To his surprise, he'd only created more tension.

"And another thing," she said, standing, allowing him another exquisite view of all those curves.

"What's that?" he asked fighting the painful urge to reach out and touch.

"We've got to keep off of each other until then. No kissing. No stroking. No petting. No panting."

He hadn't thought about that. Somehow that didn't

seem fair. Before he could open his mouth to protest, Honey took a step toward him, placing featherlight touches against his thighs, his groin, on his stomach. He placed a hand over hers.

"You want to do this right, don't you? Build it up?"

"Yes," he said, his voice barely above a whisper, anticipation deepening the bass.

They dressed quickly and watched each other intently, each careful not to touch or brush up against the other. They kept contact with their eyes, which never faltered or looked away.

Fully clothed, Honey headed for the door.

"Hold up," Houston said. The need in his gut had gotten the best of him. "One last kiss until Friday."

Honey stopped, turned and looked at him with eyes so sexy he had to blink to make sure they were real. She took a slow, easy, seductive step closer to him and tilted her head slightly, exposing the delicious smooth skin of her neck. She licked her lips, and Houston leaned in.

"No," she said, then smiled sweetly. "You just have to wait."

Honey headed out the door, leaving Houston stuck in the kissing position.

He'd make her pay for that tease. She'd pay with deep moans and long groans of pleasure. She'd pay with quivering thighs and back-to-back orgasms.

Houston smiled smugly as he left Honey's bedroom, the bedroom that he'd re-created just for her pleasure. She'd pay with rapturous tears and screams of ecstasy.

Oh, hell yeah. He'd make her pay big.

Chapter 23

"Lela! Put that lamp down!" Honey shouted.

"This little skinny heifer came down here startin' trouble!"

"You lie!" Lela bent forward, eyes hard, body stiff and poised to pounce.

The two stood in the middle of Honey's clutter-free living room like WWE wrestlers about to grapple.

"I was sitting in the big chair, changing channels when she takes her bony fingers, with that bad acrylic job, and snatches the remote," Paul accused.

"I asked you to hand it over, and you acted like you couldn't hear me."

"That's because I always ignore rude children."

Lela bristled. "What'd you say?"

Houston set his jaw to keep from cursing. Honey

clamped a hand over her mouth. They both slid glances toward each other in disbelief.

"So, that's when I snatched the remote from her triflin' behind!"

Lela's finger went to work then. Making nah-uh motions in the air. "Not for long ya didn't. I snatched that sucker back and took the batteries out!"

"Then *I* grabbed it and popped Miss Thing upside the head with it. *Ka-boing!*"

"Which is why I picked up this lamp and started swinging!"

In one quick motion, Houston grabbed the lamp from Lela and held it away. Honey batted the remote out of Paul's hand and shook her head. "You're both acting like children!"

Lela folded her arms across what was going to be an ample bosom one day. "All I wanted to do was watch Lifetime." She stuck out her lip, frowned and looked ten years younger.

Paul opened his mouth to protest, then placed a hand to his chest. "Well...dang... Me, too, girl."

Houston placed the lamp beside a brown leather chair. Well out of Lela's reach. He kept his frustrated eye on Paul. "Out!" he shouted.

"Well, now wait a minute. She said Lifetime. In case you don't understand, my movie's on!"

Houston gave Paul a stiff nudge toward the door. "I'll call you, Honey."

"If I don't call you first," Honey said without thinking. Damn, she wished she could take those words back. They made her sound...sprung. The last thing she wanted to come across as was whooped. Men tried to walk all over you and take all kinds of advantage if they thought you were gone over them. She wasn't about to give up that hand, not even to the man who remade her house into a home. A man who was so deliciously sexy, Honey knew she would never recover from seeing him naked. Judging from the way she still tingled from head to heel, her body would never stop thrumming from the sight.

Houston's sexy-as-hell eyes twinkled and turned her legs to jelly. "You do that," he said, perfect teeth sparkling.

Without another word from either of them, Houston and Paul were out the door, leaving Honey and Lela staring at each other in an all too uncomfortable silence.

"What's gotten into you?" Honey asked.

"Besides eighteen years of neglect?" Lela asked. Her body jerked straight and her eyes went liquid. "Not much."

Honey's hard edge dissolved and her heart ached for her sister. So much turmoil. So much pain. Would she ever get past it? For the first time, Honey considered the thought that Lela might not be able to, then quickly chased that thought out of her mind.

"Come on," Honey said, picking up the scattered batteries.

Lela picked up the remote. "I think Lifetime is Channel 28." Her mouth said the words. Methodical and caring despite the fact that she felt like half her soul had just walked out her front door.

Honey headed for the couch where Lela was already leaning into some drama playing on the flat TV screen.

"Slide over," Honey said, hoping there was a good-woman-leaves-abusive-husband movie on to take her mind off of things. Off of Houston.

Houston shoved a barely folded silk shirt into his Louis Vuitton luggage and pressed down. The darn thing was swollen with shirts, slacks, T-shirts. He hated packing. And hated moving even more. For himself, that is. Houston was grateful that the only thing he'd done for the L.A. move was pack clothes, and then he hadn't needed to do that. The studio had sent movers, the good kind that packed everything in rows with good folds and bubble wrap. Everything he owned, except the three suitcases in front of him, was in an L.A. storage facility. Waiting.

Houston was waiting, too.

He was in desperate need of a sign that his work with Honey was complete, and he was free to leave for California. Every time he spent more than three seconds with Honey, a feeling of unfinished business consumed him. Houston pushed against the front compartments and grunted as the side zipper resisted the bulge and force of clothing that refused to be confined. For a while, the clothes won. Then, with a grunt of determination, Houston pulled the zipper across. It sounded bright, loud, like tiny teeth chattering.

The hotel was getting way too expensive, even if the studio had given him a substantial allowance. He didn't have to spend the money as soon as it came in. Instead, he decided to take his aunt up on her generous offer and stay with her. Houston yanked the heavy suitcase from the bed, told himself that he was still black, that he grew up in the projects and headed to the 'hood.

Houston guided his SUV through traffic while images of Honey dominated his thoughts. Each in vivid color. Damn if the woman's juicy butt and hot-fudge skin didn't appear again and again as if she were right there beside him. Houston switched lanes, imagining Honey riding one of Brax's big horses. Slow at first, then turning him loose to run as he pleased. Galloping. Turning the dry grass and hard earth into dust clouds. The hooves beating the earth, rumbling against the surface. Sounding like his heart.

Because he'd spent so much time stacking, sorting and rearranging the contents of Honey's home, the details stuck into Houston's mind like hooks. Fixed permanently and dug in tight.

Her favorite color—brown. Her preferred toys—ben wahs and bullets. Her favorite fragrance—Ylang Ylang. Her style and taste—urban, contemporary, exotic. Her touch—velvet and hot.

In addition, African violets, mother-in-law's tongue, red ferns and bamboo filled her house, making it tropical and alive. Underneath her brown thumb was a green one.

And all her plants were thriving. Bright green leaves and dark green vines. One philodendron had leaves the size of his head. She placed decorative sucker hooks on a corner wall and let the plant climb and thrive. Not a dead, dry leaf on any of them. Honey took care of business when it came to her plants.

Houston smiled as he managed to marry the image of healthy plants and hearty sex. "Talk to me," he imagined himself saying. "Talk to me like you talk to your plants. Make me grow."

He forced the image of Honey naked and whispering against his hard length from his lustful mind. His time was coming. He just had to be patient.

On the ride over to his aunt's house, Houston stared ahead at traffic on that bright morning. The sun was wide-awake and shining full force, belying the fifty-degree temperature and the pure blue sky.

Houston knew he was going to a place that was roughly the same size as the suite he just checked out of. But instead of a wet bar there would be a portable one that hadn't been moved since the day his uncle bought it thirty-five years ago.

There would be the vacant lot across the street—one that doubled as the broken-down furniture burial ground. Only none of it was ever buried; it just rotted there but not before becoming a nest for snakes, mice and fearless rabbits and squirrels.

Rather than a balcony, Houston's aunt had a stoop she liked to sit on to watch the cars. No chairs. No outdoor furniture. Just slap your butt down on the cold, hard concrete and cop a squat.

Houston smiled. That was real living.

May he never lose touch with his roots. Being a professional organizer allowed him to see that the folks who could afford his services had lives cluttered with indulgences. His aunt's home was cluttered, too. But mostly because her home was so small she didn't have the room for all of the things that mattered.

And unlike clients who had walk-in closets filled with clothing they never wore, everything in his aunt's home had a story. A significance. Her home told the tale of his whole family. He'd found that out when he'd tried to help his aunt "purge" her clutter. She promptly gave him a lesson in being the family historian. Although she would never refer to herself that way, that's exactly what she was.

Nah, no way Houston wanted to lose this. His authentic self. The last time he'd been to L.A., he'd seen more plastic surgery, more spray tans, more fake hair, fake nails, boob jobs and hair plugs than he could fathom. He appreciated the fact that Bravo wanted him because he was a little rough around the edges. A straight-up brother, complete with Tims, slang and earrings. Bravo wanted it all. Just as he was. He couldn't have lucked into a better deal. Life was good—real good.

"You just help yourself to that room upstairs now, y'hear? You ain't got to worry 'bout no stuffy hotel. No tellin' what kinda soap they usin' ta clean thangs. Shoot, they might not be usin' no soap at all down there."

"Yes, ma'am," Houston called, halfway up the stairs with his luggage. He couldn't help noticing that his cousin was conspicuously absent just when he could have used an extra hand with his suitcases.

It was just as well. Houston planned on getting settled quickly. He'd been thinking about Honey all morning. It was time he reached out.

Back in the day—which was actually only about six months ago—Houston would have taken every gift the company was generous enough to give. A rented car. A suite. He would have taken advantage of every luxury, and treated a lady or two to his boon.

Maybe he really was growing. In a healthy way, like Honey's plants. Being responsible felt good. He hoped that staying at his aunt's was another good step in his journey to anchor himself to what was valuable and real.

Chapter 24

Honey spent the beginning of the next day catching up on work. She'd posted a notice on her site that she was taking time off and that she would resume filling orders in a week. Well, it hadn't been quite a week, but she still wanted to get back to it. The last thing she wanted to do was alienate her regular customers. Her bread and bouillabaisse. So, while Lela was still getting her beauty sleep, Honey went downstairs, checked her backlog. To her surprise and anguish, it was long. Those folks didn't listen one bit. They placed their orders after all. A couple of them had typed things in the special-instructions field on the online order form.

Just hit me up when you get back.

I'll wait.

No rush.

It brought a tear to her eye and a warm caress to her heart to know that her customers, who could have gone elsewhere for their orders, were willing to wait and get them from her. Cliff had told her all along that it wasn't the merchandise they were buying, it was her. With her funky Web site, her hard-to-get, high-end, high-quality products and her Webcast, Honey's personal stamp was all over every inch of her business. When customers bought from Fulfillment, they bought a little piece of Honey herself. Honey smiled like a girl and felt bubbly like one, too!

She didn't sit like she usually did. Instead, she turned on the CD player, pushed Play on the remote. The latest release from Allgood—her favorite singer— made her sway in front of her new order center—à la Houston Pace—and began to work.

She figured she had a full day's work ahead of her. She would get as far as she could until Lela woke up and then she'd fix them breakfast.

A strong bass and Allgood's voice penetrated her skin, reached down into her soul, reminded her of her femininity. She touched the work space, imagining all the places where Houston's hands had been. Impulsively, she printed her order sheet, then flipped her computer to the desktop where she'd changed the background to a picture of Houston that she found during her Google search.

It only took her a minute to get used to her new setup.

After that, she was filling orders like crazy. All her most popular items were at her fingertips, along with the correct size boxes. Houston had installed an overhead peanut packer. The material came down a cone-shaped shoot and spilled just the right amount into each box. At the end of the assembly line, she had a new scanner.

While Allgood sang "Can't slow down my love— It's comin' on like a storm—'cause the way you keepin' me warm—takes my heart, takes my heart away" she remembered the way Houston stared at her. All of her. Her eyes. Her face. Her hands. Most men just stared at her breasts and talked to them as if they could speak back. If Houston was checkin' like that for her body, he wasn't letting on…much. He seemed much more interested in her mouth and her mind.

Memories and music took over Honey's waist and hips, and they danced as she worked. Each item she scanned generated a packing slip and return address label. They spit out of the printer just as she was ready with the tape runner. Slick.

In thirty minutes, she'd gone through a quarter of her orders.

Houston Pace was a genius. He'd do well in L.A., she thought. Two weeks, her mind told her. Just two more weeks and then he'd be off to his show.

That thought brought down her mood.

Two weeks was not nearly enough time for all of the things she wanted to do with him. But that was just her luck in life. Finally feeling comfortable enough, trusting a man enough, to let him touch her in the most intimate way and their time together would be brief.

Suddenly, the idea of waiting until the weekend seemed absurd when they'd have so little time together anyway.

The soft, quick beep on her computer brought her out of her thoughts. She stared at the pop-up on her screen. An instant message.

Honey moved closer to her computer while Allgood sang. "I keep drinkin' from your lovin' cup—No matter what I do, I just cain't get enough—You give me just a little and still I want more—Always come when you call, baby—'cause I want it all—I want it all."

No matter how many times she asked her customers not to send her instant messages, some of them never listened. She had a few hardheaded ones. They didn't bother her all the time, just when she was busy and didn't have time to chat. She considered making her online ID invisible, but life without female friends meant that, now and then, an online "Hey, what's up?" was nice company.

She sealed the order she'd just packed and leaned over to glance at the screen.

What are you wearing?

Oh great, just what she needed, some per—
The e-mail address said PICKUPTHEPACE. Houston!

I wanna wet them lips up.

Hmm…I was thinkin' the same thing, she typed.

Damn right.
Honey inserted one of her *special,* graphic smilies.

What's the world coming to when you can download sexually active and boldly explicit round yellows?

Now that's what I'm talkin' 'bout. You live up to your name?

Absolutely! Finger-lickin' good. You better come hungry.

Don't worry 'bout me. You better come ready to come.

Oh, you got skills, huh?

Mad, crazy, stupid skills, baby. My love's bananas. Make you scream in three different languages.

Is that right?

Like you're speakin' in tongues, baby. Can you hang?

The question is, do you?

Do I what?

Hang? LOL!

You tell me.

Honey thought back to the memory of him naked against her. The brother was packin' like U-Haul. She selected another choice smiley to show her approval.

What are you wearing? she asked, letting excitement get the best of her.

Nothing.

Got a Web cam? she asked.

Built in.

Honey didn't realize she'd been circling her nipple until the bud had bloomed between her fingertips. A soft moan escaped her mouth as she anticipated Houston's Webcast. All they needed to was select a chat area, and then—

"What are you doing?"

The question spun Honey around like a top and sent her pulse revving. "Lela, you scared the crap out of me!"

"Sorry," she said. But she didn't sound sorry. She sounded nosey. A few quick keys and Honey closed down the pop-up box with her and Houston's flirtatious exchange.

"You hungry? I was thinking about Belgian waffles."

Lela nodded. "Sounds good. You have strawberries and whipped cream?"

"Sure do!" Honey assured her.

Lela's eyes sparkled like tiny stars. Honey's heart warmed. Having a sister was going to be cool, after all.

"What the—"

Honey turned to where Lela's eyes stared with wide-eyed disgust. Another pop-up window had appeared on Honey's screen. The image of a handsomely naked Houston peeled down by the inch. Honey switched the image to the next order to be filled but couldn't keep herself from giggling.

"I think Houston and I were about to have cybersex."

"Ugh!" Lela said. She rolled her eyes and headed for the kitchen. "I'll make my own breakfast."

"No, no," Honey said, feeling a stretch in the connection between them. "Houston and I have this weekend thing planned. Plus, we're supposed to be chillin' until then anyway. He was just trying to...tempt me."

And doing a darn good job, Honey thought.

Lela came back and stood in the kitchen entrance. "You're going to be gone all weekend?"

"Yes," Honey said, imagining how the weekend would start and feeling tingly.

"When were you going to tell me?"

"Uh, I don't know. I guess I hadn't thought about it."

"I just got here and already you've forgotten me? You're leaving me?"

"It's not like that," Honey said while typing an IM to Houston.

Something's come up. Gotta go. IM you later.

Honey signed off before giving Houston a chance to respond. She had to smooth things over with her sister. The girl was obviously suffering from abandonment issues. Honey had them herself for a while. Heck, maybe she still did. She understood this kind of reaction and wanted to do whatever she could to help her sister through it.

"Well, I don't have to go away this weekend. Houston and I can go next weekend. You *did* just get here. It's rude of me to think of leaving you so soon."

That seemed to cheer Lela.

"Why don't you and I plan something for Saturday? We'll hang out. Just the two of us."

"Cool!"

After the abrupt end of Honey's IM, Houston waited and waited for her to get back, but she never did. No e-mail. No IM. No phone call. Houston wanted to know how the upstairs reorg was working out. He wanted to make sure they were still on for the weekend. And besides all that, he just wanted to hear her sexy-as-sin voice. Just the way she said his name made him want to strip her naked and drape her in diamonds. He imagined the ice against her skin, both flawless. Um-hmm.

"What you mumblin' about?" Paul sashayed into the room, flashy flamboyance dripping like an ice-cream cone in August.

"Honey," Houston said, rubbing himself absent-mindedly. "That right there is the kind of woman that makes a man wanna put in work."

"So, what you doin' here?"

"We made a deal. No...nothin' until Friday night. Come Friday, anything goes."

"So, what are you going to do—or should I say *who* are you going to do—until then?"

"Nobody," Houston said. The word came out of his mouth so definite and easy, it surprised him.

"Nobody? Whaaaat? Is this Houston *Can You Keep Up the Pace* talkin'?"

"Yeah. It is." Houston felt good about being good.

"Well, Honey must have a gold clit for that to come out your mouth."

"Hey, hey!"

"Hey my sweet ass. I've never known you to wait for nooky in my life. You must have mellowed in your old age."

Paul eyed him as if he were examining a dead fish. He felt Houston's forehead. Held his wrist and took his pulse. "Oh my gosh. Are you having…problems? 'Cause I can call my girl Sabrina. She can be here with some bootleg Viagra in fifteen minutes."

"Don't even joke about it. I gots no problems when it comes to that."

"Well, then what's up? I can't see you bein' alone like this."

Houston shook his head. It's funny the way other people peg you. Houston always had a lady on his arm. He wore a beautiful woman like a Rolex. Never left home without one. But now, besides the whole turning-over-a-new-leaf thing, just thinking about Honey made him feel as if she were right there with him. Just imagining her laugh, her smile, those curves that wouldn't quit. Um. He had enough to keep him company until Friday.

"Oh, good God in heaven. Hell is frozen over."

"What?" Houston asked then turned away. He

didn't want to see the look on his cousin's face. And he damn sure didn't want Paul to see his.

"For once, a woman is calling the shots. Hey-hey!" Paul laughed. "How's that other foot feel? You know, the one with that shoe on it?"

Houston rolled his eyes and shook his head. "That sounds like something Auntie would say."

"And that sounds like you tryin' to dodge my question."

"Whatever," Houston said, waving him off. Paul was being ridiculous now. Houston turned his attention to his laptop. Honey's Web site was in his Web browser.

"Admit it, Negro. You sprung."

"Now you sound like me."

"And you sound sprung. Heh, heh. Sprung!"

"Don't make me cuss you in yo' mama's house."

"So, you can cuss, but you cain't answer a simple question."

Paul made a flicking motion with his fingers, then a *boing* sound with his mouth. "Sprung, sprung, sprung."

"What happened to Ms. Sweet Pea? I think I like her much better."

"Uh-uh. Sweet Pea had to go. This is your stomp-down cousin right here. And I want *all* the dirt."

"You can take the colored people out of the South—"

"No, you can't. They never leave. No matter where they are."

Both men laughed at that. Then Paul got serious. "Now you can tell me or I'm going to call Honey and ask her myself. And you know I will."

"There's nothing to tell, man, really. I like her. What's wrong with that?"

"Nothing. But I should have known you didn't have me up in that woman's house givin' her upstairs the best that I got just because of some debt you owe. I should have known there was more to it."

"What more to it? I owe a debt. You helped me pay it off. And now, I'm going to get a little somethin' somethin' on top of that. I like to think of it as the best kind of send-off a brother can have before he heads West."

"And you waitin'?"

"Yeah," Houston said. "Friday is only two days away."

But Houston had to admit to himself it was going to be a long wait. He'd been the one who suggested no playing around until then. They both were supposed to be on a full tank sexually. But they never said anything about not seeing each other. And Houston had been sitting around—moping around—jonesin' for some of Honey's brains and beauty. Like a cup of coffee, he kinda felt as if seeing her every morning would set his day right.

And quite frankly, it was a little bit more than just missing her company. Actually, it was a lot more than that. Although Honey seemed so ready to take it to the next level, there was hesitation there, too. A hesitation Houston was determined to break through.

Heck, he did wonder how everything with the upstairs was going. It probably wouldn't hurt if he stopped over tonight. Just for a minute. And, if for some strange reason, his lips happened to touch hers or his tongue slipped into her mouth, well, shucks, accidents do happen.

Chapter 25

"What are you doing here?"

Houston strode into Honey's living room looking off-the-chart sexy and staring at Honey in a way he never had before, a storm of emotion brewing in his eyes. It filled the room and damn near lifted the sheers with its force.

"3221 Larimore. L-Lover99." He placed his cell phone on the table between them. "4HoneyNow," he said. Never blinking, barely breathing. Immobile.

"What's that?" she asked, not sure why her heart felt like it was about to beat right out of her chest.

"My aunt's address. My e-mail password. My cell phone lock code."

She bit her lip and trembled.

"Check 'em," he insisted. "Check 'em all."

Honey ran a hand through her crazy curls. Felt sexy and powerful. Felt like a woman.

"That's *my* hair you touchin'," Houston said. He still hadn't moved. Hadn't taken his eyes off of her. Hadn't stopped making her feel hot and sticky, like a chocolate bar melting.

"Look, I'm here. I'm yours. Every part of me. Damn, woman!" He ran a hand over his bald head then. "When I told you who I was, I told the truth. And the truth after that is that I'm a new man. And I can only take credit for some of that. I had the intent, but you…whoo…you brought the action. You took it there. You brought the change in me. I can't even look at another woman without comparing her to you. And you know what? Other women come up often and come up short every time. You know how strange that is?"

Honey couldn't hold back her smile. It stretched all the way across her mouth and reached down into her soul.

"I put all my standbys on Call Block. Ain't that crazy? You and me ain't even official, but what we got is more real to me than…than anything."

"Houston—"

"No, don't stop me now. I'm on a roll."

"Houston!" she said and skipped over to him. So happy she felt silly and young and alive and vibrant and…she flung her arms around his waist. "I love you!" she said. She couldn't hold it back anymore. She had to tell him.

He let go a long, strong breath and pulled her close, stroking. His heart sounded like a djembe drum against her ear.

"Thank you," he said. His head dropped down against hers. His favorite position. "Thank you for loving me."

Honey waited. There should be an *I love you* coming back from him. When he didn't say it, she started to worry.

Before she could talk, he went straight for her spot. The place at the crook of her neck that made her toes curl and her nipples hard. Painted a symbol of love with his tongue. Leaving his mark with his mouth. Whispering, "Mine." And right now, if she weren't careful…

"Where's your sister?" he asked, the words coming out like a whiskey-soaked slow drag.

Honey's eyes fluttered closed. "Sleepover… Houston." She pushed away with unsteady arms, weakened by Houston's skillful mouth.

"What you want, baby? You know you got it, right?"

Houston's voice sounded love-drugged and dipped in lust. Honey tingled with excitement and anticipation. "I want you to say it," she whispered into his mouth. "I need to hear it."

Houston pulled her back and took her mouth in one swift, urgent motion. The storm of his emotion covered her like chocolate drowning a cherry. His feelings were torrential over her body. A hard steady rain, drenching and so powerful she could barely breathe.

Then he broke the contact, but just barely. His lips were still against hers. His breath was still flowing inside her. "Can you hear me now?" he asked.

"Houston—" she began.

He grabbed her hand. "Come on," he said and led her upstairs.

A thousand volts of electricity flowed from where he held her hand. They spread to her shoulders, her hips, her thighs. She floated up the stairs and into her room, so ready for him her thighs quivered.

"Me first," he said. He slipped out of his clothes and let them fall on the floor with a soft thud. "Now you." He removed Honey's outfit, even though she already felt naked in front of him.

"You wanna do it?" he asked, reaching for her condom dish.

"Yeah," she said, just barely above a whisper. *Finally,* she thought. *This is it. I'm really going to go through with—*

She took the foil packet from him and sat down on the bed where she was at mouth-level with his arousal. She tore the packet open. Her breath came quickly as she rolled the latex down his hot hardness. Hungry for the sensation of him, she opened her mouth and leaned forward. He caught her head and moaned.

"Maybe later, baby," he said, then laid her back against the bed. His sliding kiss eased her down. His roaming hands opened her up. Her legs. Her soul. Her breath came in puffs and gasps. She drank in the rock-hard muscles and chocolate sinew comin' at her in every direction.

He ground his hips against her. His hard length like iron throbbing hot and passively on her skin. She wrapped her arms around his neck. Glanced up at his face. Houston's brows knit together. His expression intense, focused, almost pained. "Let me know," he said, still grinding and then sliding into her dripping wet center. "When you hear it."

They both moaned as he pushed his long inches inside her and began to move in circles.

He filled her so completely. Her core wrapped around his thickness. Tightened against him as he drove wave after wave of pleasure into her body.

"What's that say?" he asked. His eyes were piercing. They never left her face. But Honey couldn't speak. She could only groan in response. The sound came from deep inside her, animalistic and wild.

He slid a hand beneath her buttocks. Pulled her closer. "What's that word?"

"S-s-s-s," was the only response she could give.

So soon. Too soon. She felt her peak building. In response, Houston slowed down. Slid in and out. Tortured her. She clung tighter. "Houston, Houston!" she flung the words out of her mouth.

"I know I'm whispering right about now, but you hear me, right?"

"Ah." Honey's response came out loud and husky.

"Shhh," Houston said. "Listen. I'm talkin'."

Houston's other hand slid beneath her. Pulled her up from the bed against his thighs. She wrapped her legs around his waist. Matched his stroke.

"There it is, right there. Is that what you need to hear?"

Honey's nipples hardened and ached. Her juices flowed like a river, getting them both soaking wet. Houston brought her love all the way down, and Honey began to thrash wildly. Sensation after sensation rocked her with each thrust. Bringing her closer the deeper he drove.

"Three words," he whispered against her neck. So damned close to her spot. Honey felt her body unravel. Her entire soul coming undone. "One for each time I'm gonna make you come."

"A-ah!" Honey's scream started low.

"I," Houston said, kissing her spot.

The rush of ecstasy came faster than Honey could stand it.

"Love." He was tonguing her now. Right where she loved it. Where she had to have it!

He grabbed her up. Pumping long and strong. Then faster. Deeper. Her core sounded like a faucet running.

"What you checkin' for, baby? That?"

He rode harder. "Is that it? Shit!"

Warm tears slid down Honey's face. She shuddered while Houston's love took her over. How could she have doubted? Doubted this?

"Ooh, b-bay-beeee," she whimpered. He had her so right, she couldn't remember anything before he kissed her. She felt so good. So damn luscious. She pumped back hard and crazy against him, like she was losing her mind and had let go of everything.

"A word, right?" His lips brushed against her neck. "Hell, a word ain't got nothin' on this," he said, and settled into her.

"Or this. Is this the word you want? Huh? How 'bout this one? Am I sayin' it now?"

"Yes."

"What?"

"Yes."

He loved her so right. Lifelong and bone-deep. She came again.

"You sure, now?" he asked, circling his hips, giving her some of his gettin'-greedy-with-it lovin'. Takin' all she had.

Honey held on desperately. Aching to come again. "Bring it!" she yelled. "Tell me some more."

She felt his soul flow into her then. Like he couldn't hold back anymore. All his control gone and pulsing between her legs.

"I love you. Z-z-uh. You want me...to shout it? Ah—I love you, Honey!"

Houston got a rhythm and pumped it into her.

"It's so sweet, right now," he said, his eyes closed, his head buried against her neck. "Sweet like you, baby."

They caught a groove and rode it like it would never end.

"Don't worry," he whispered. "I got this. I ain't comin' no time soon."

He licked around her spot, vibrating her clit like no toy ever could. "But you are."

The moment Houston sucked on her neck, Honey came harder than ever.

"Hmm," Houston said, when her scream subsided.

"What you know 'bout me now?" he said, lifting his head. His eyes bore into hers, liquid with desire.

Honey spoke through her sobs. "I know you love me. Oh, God, Houston, I know, baby. I *know*."

Houston settled back into his stroke, and when he finally came, it was two hours and three trembling orgasms later.

Chapter 26

Honey had suggested a girls' night out. Dinner and a movie or her favorite: shopping, fast-food salad, then more shopping. Lela wasn't interested. She wanted dinner in and time with her sister. Lela wanted to see photos, any Honey had of herself growing up. There wasn't much.

Honey went into her bedroom closet and pulled out a box of photos and other memorabilia. Mementos of her childhood. Special memories. Important moments.

A ticket stub from her first concert: Boyz II Men. A red ribbon from coming in third in the one-hundred-yard dash in high school. A program from a Sunday-school play. Recent photos of Brax, some of Collen, a couple of the three of them together.

Most of the photos she had of herself were Polaroids

taken when she lived with the Vale family. She'd asked for Polaroids because film sometimes never made it to the developers. And then, Honey might have moved on to another family and not have anything to remember herself by. Other than adding the recent photos of her family, Honey hadn't spent time with her treasures in years. With every photo or memento she added, she always promised herself that she would one day put a memory album together. She'd just never gotten around to it. Now, she wished she had.

Her memories were becoming just as faded, dull and frayed around the edges as the items themselves.

Lela had been fingering a plastic gold coin from a Mardi Gras school program as though it were an actual gold piece. The girl looked pensive, sad and lonely.

"You should put these in something...like an album."

"I was just thinking about that. I meant to. I even went to one of those scrapbooking places and bought all the stuff to do it. I just never made the time."

Suddenly Lela brightened. "Let's do it now! You can tell me about everything in this box. We can write stories about each thing and put it on the pages. I did a project like this at school once. It was...kinda fun."

Honey hadn't seen Lela's face that bright and cheerful since the girl had shown up on her doorstep and realized she'd come to the right place. Honey would do anything to keep that warm shine going.

"Okay. Let's do it!"

Thirty minutes later, they turned her dining room into a sprawling craft area. A pang of guilt made Honey wince. She'd just gotten comfortable with order—real comfortable—and here she was creating an artistic mess with her sister. Honey moved around the table arranging the items into a logical order.

"There," she said, pleased by what she'd done. "That gives us an assembly line kinda thing."

Lela smiled. "I was just about to suggest that."

Honey saw that her sister had a knack for putting things together, making arrangements, layouts. It was that putting-things-in-order gene that obviously had skipped Honey. She was impressed and did what she could to help.

"I can get a basic look, you can glue everything down and then I'll write the journaling."

"Deal," Honey said, and they went to work.

Before long, they had finished six pages and two Belgian waffles doused with strawberries and whipped cream.

They traded stories about best friends, favorite toys, worst subjects in school and first kisses. They reminisced on clothes, hair and dances neither of them attended. They compared skinned knees and favorite candy. All telling the story of how to grow up sans parents without ever mentioning it.

The memories came back slowly to Honey, like children themselves, not knowing if it's cool to come out and play. At first every muscle in her body tensed at the idea of looking back and digging up the past. But Lela made it easier. Her eagerness to hear and know gave Honey the confidence to share and tell. By noon, the book was almost complete.

"Ready for a break?" Honey asked.

"I feel like my whole life has been a break. I can keep going. But if you want to stop—"

"No, that's okay," Honey lied. Even a stretch break at this point would probably do them both some good. "Why don't we—"

The doorbell came right on time. Honey didn't care who it was. It could be Cliff for all she cared. She welcomed a brief respite.

"Be right back," she said, rising. She stopped for a moment to stretch and lengthen her body before opening the door. The sensation felt good after sitting so long.

When she opened the door, Honey felt even better.

"Houston," she said. She couldn't stop her eyes from roaming. She took him in, head to toe, then toe to head and then once more. Even though they'd technically forfeited their agreement, the man came dressed to impress for their *date.* Honey tried not to stare, but it was hard. Houston's chestnut-brown skin radiated from the inside out. He looked as though the sun were shining from inside his skin. It made him luminescent and impossible to look away from.

He came impeccably groomed. His bald head was smooth and delectable. His goatee was trimmed to perfection, with every hair in place. Black sweater, black slacks, shining black leather shoes. Looking every bit of Armani and smelling like Polo Double Black.

Lookin' good. Smellin' good. And he had Honey *feelin'* good. Her legs felt like warm grits. "Um. Um. Um. You are lookin' finger-lickin' good."

"Speakin' of lickin'," he said. His tongue lightly

grazed his bottom lip and left that part of his mouth moist, sending a strong invitation.

"Mr. Pace, what are you trying to do to me?" Honey asked, daring to wonder out loud about her own feelings.

"Seduce you. What else?"

"Well, can I tell ya, it's working. Get in here!"

While Houston got his sexy swagger on, Honey admired the view. And she'd been wrong. He came dressed to undress.

"You're a hot drink of water up in here, brother. What are you tryin' to do, bring back the summer?"

"Ah, you know. I gotta be right."

And he was. A clothing designer's dream. And an amorous woman's dream come true.

Houston did everything but turn and pivot. It was obvious, he was checkin' for her checkin' for him and enjoying every minute of her appreciation.

"You wanna give up now or five minutes from now?"

Honey laughed. "Neither," she said a little more solemnly than she'd expected. "Lela and I are working on a scrapbook. You can join us if you like."

Houston's broad magnetic smile faded just a bit. "Hey, Lela!" he called, following Honey into the dining room.

"Hey," she said, not looking up. She kept working on the reunion page with individual pictures of all four brothers and sisters.

Houston stopped short of sitting down at the table. "No, thanks. I'll stick with sorting bins and space planning."

"Fine with me," Lela said. Her eyes still on the photos, arranging them, trying different layouts. This one was taking her a minute to put together. It was like her great sense of creativity had dried up.

"Lela, let's take a break. We've been going at it pretty good all morning. Let's give our brains a chance to power up again. Okay?"

"Whatever," she said. Lela pushed the page she'd been working on away from her and got up.

"I'll fix us some lunch and then we can start again," Honey called after her sister, but Lela had already stormed up the stairs.

Houston sucked in a breath. "Okay, I *know* I'm outta pocket, but your sister...her attitude..."

"I know. It's severe. But she had it rough. For some folks, growing up without your mother—your real mother—is tough. It was hard on me. When she lashes out, or gets angry, or acts out, I know why. I understand her. I guess...I was her."

"Please don't take this the wrong way, but I don't care."

"What do you mean?"

"I mean what I said. There is a way to treat people, and she doesn't know it. Or at least, she doesn't seem like she knows it. Now either she's just rude and lacks social skills, or she needs help. If she's just rude, somebody needs to check her. If she needs help, I suggest you call a therapist. An attitude like that can get you into all kinds of trouble."

Honey bristled. "Thank you for your opinion, although I'm sure I didn't ask you for it."

"Honey, I'm just sayin'... That's the third time she's been rude to me. I know I'm just a step above a 'hood rat, but where I come from, you got one time to mess up like that, then it's your ass. Now, you might be willing to let her disrespect a guest, but I'm not in the habit of being disrespected."

"What's that mean?"

"It means, if she jumps outta pocket again, and you don't say anything, I will."

So this is what it means to let a man inside, Honey wondered, feeling torn between Houston and family. The choice was simple. Honey chose family. "Well then maybe you should leave."

"So, it's like that?" Houston asked. The man had the nerve to look hurt.

"Like that? Like what? I barely know you."

"You knew me well enough to get me off. Now you gonna play anonymous?"

"Lela's my family."

"The way you was callin' me *daddy* the other day, you would've thought I was the only family you had."

Houston's words stung her soul. Honey had heard enough. She walked to the door then and opened it. Houston wasn't the booty call she thought he'd be. He wasn't even the companion she'd hoped he'd be. He was just another man with a one-track mind. And when it seemed something more was developing between them, he flips on her.

"Good thing I found out how you are now. I was starting to really like you."

Houston stopped at the door. The fine asshole. *Get out already,* her mind screamed, so she could start forgetting about him.

"Me, too," he said and headed to his car.

Too bad. Honey's mind formed the words, but her heart had a different feeling. More like shredded and ripped apart. More like the last chance for Honey to feel like a whole woman was driving away. It was then that Honey realized that even without making love, Houston had already made her feel like a whole woman.

She closed the door thinking, family was family. Blood was thicker than water. And cursing under her breath.

She couldn't have a relationship with someone who didn't respect her sister, could she? No. She couldn't ever consider becoming involved with a man who would cause that kind of a grief, right?

She went back to the dining room table, with no in-clination to eat. She moved the photos and embellishments into an order, a pattern. Everything touching, overlapping. The objects ran together like her thoughts and emotions. Tangling. Fighting. She closed her eyes before she allowed herself to get all revved up. This was usually the point where she called one of her brothers, nearly in tears, wondering what to do, asking for their advice.

Well, this time she was going to take her own advice. The advice she'd given Lela so often these past few days.

Let it go. Let it go. Let it go.

Honey applied adhesive to the photos, pressed them into place and let Houston go.

Chapter 27

It had finally happened. Houston had lost his flippin' mind. Brax had warned him that it would happen one day. Years ago, when Brax fell hard for Ariana and all his friends teased him, Brax had assured him then.

They'd been having a drink at a bar in Savannah. Race Jennings and another partner of theirs, Philip Brown, were into a serious dart game when out of the blue Brax said, "She's coming for you, man."

Being the eager bachelor he was, Houston glanced around the bar hungrily, assuming that Brax had noticed a honey coming their way. When he saw that there were no hips en route, Houston's anticipation collapsed, and he took a drink from the neck of the Heineken. "Who are you talkin' 'bout?"

"The woman who will stir up your emotions like soup and then feed them to you."

"Man, please. I belong to the Hugh Hefner players' club. Bachelor for life, baby. Cain't no she tame me."

"What you say now, but I'm telling you, if it happened to me, it's gonna happen to you, and it will damn sure happen to Race."

They laughed at that. They both knew Race was the romantic, leading-man type out of the bunch of them. Houston took another drink then and pointed the neck of his bottle at Philip, who was losing badly. "What about your boy?"

Brax didn't look at him. He just stared straight ahead like the future was in the bar mirror instead of reflections of liquor bottles. "Philip is reckless."

Brax was right. Philip became HIV positive just two years later. He handled it, though. On the best medication and healthy as a track star. Houston didn't put much thought into Brax's pronouncement at the time. He was too busy trying to bat it away.

"Man, not the kid, okay? There are too many women out there for me to get bent over just one."

"Well, you just keep that wish ticket in your pocket. And when she comes for you, you pull it out and remember I wrote my name on that mug."

"Man, drink your drink," Houston had said.

Today, he was pulling that ticket out of his pocket, smoothing out the creases, picking off the lint and reading the letters B-R-A-X clearly.

He headed toward the back door of the only house

in the neighborhood done in a colonial style, knocked on the door and marveled at how right Brax had been.

Houston knocked on the door again and waited. He knocked again and waited longer. Finally, the stomping of feet, probably size fourteen, preceded the door swinging wildly open.

Cliff Watson had obviously been asleep. He frowned and blinked, as if his eyes weren't working properly. Then his body relaxed a bit as realization smoothed out his facial features.

"What happened? Did she push you off after three kisses, too?"

Houston's bravado leaped to the surface and took over his mouth. "Nah, man. Nothin' like that." He shook his head and smiled, implying that he'd made several touchdowns without one call of pass interference.

The insinuation was not lost on Cliff. "Dude, what do you want?"

Houston's insides were tied into crazy knots, but he pressed on. "I need a favor."

Honey paced back and forth in her nice neat living room with her fingers against her wrist. Her pulse had to be way over one hundred beats per minute. Her blood pressure was probably one seventy over one ten. And she was about three short breaths away from hyperventilating.

Sweat sucked her clothes to her skin, and her head pounded. She went to the door again just as she saw the pickup turn into her driveway.

Honey closed her eyes as a mild wave of relief flowed down her body. Thank you, she whispered.

Her brother Brax climbed the stairs and walked in without knocking.

"It took you long enough!" Honey snapped. She regretted the words as soon as they slipped out of her mouth. Her hormones were probably raging like her emotions.

"Sorry," she said.

"I'm here now. Ari's not too happy about it, but I'm here."

"What's got her gauchos in a wad?"

"You're kidding me, right? You can't keep calling me to come to your rescue. I got a wife, we're trying to start a family—"

"What? You and Ari?"

"Yeah," Brax replied, smiling broadly. "We're trying to get pregnant."

Suddenly Honey felt incredibly selfish. She was so wrapped up in her life and her own drama, she forgot that her brothers had lives and goals and challenges and triumphs all their own. She couldn't help believing that if she wasn't so wrapped up in herself, she would have known about Brax and Ariana starting a family. She didn't even know her brother wanted kids.

Honey plopped down on her couch. Most of her energy had been eaten away by worry. Funny, all she'd wanted her entire life was to have a family and now that she had one, she realized how hard it was being a sister.

"Where's the note?" Brax asked.

Honey pointed to her worktable, too choked up to speak.

Brax picked up the note and read it out loud. His first time, her fiftieth.

Dear Honey,
Thank you for everything. For years, I dreamed about having a sister. Sometimes more than one. You made me feel like family, better than any dream I ever had. I know you want me to let go of the past, but our mother is out there somewhere and I can't. So, wish me luck while I keep looking.
I'll be in touch.
L.

Brax looked up with a frown. "Any idea where she went?"

"No," Honey said. Her stomach pitched with the word.

"You tried to find Carnetta for a long time. You share any of that with her?"

"Only that the trail to Mother led me to a dead end."

Brax nodded. Then their eyes met, and Honey knew. For the first time, she realized that both knew the truth about their mother. Honey prayed Lela would never come face-to-face with that truth.

"What about her cell phone?"

"I blew that up when I discovered the note. Her mailbox is full now."

"She's eighteen, Honey."

"She's an open wound, Brax."

"She took care of herself enough to find you, right?"

"Brax—"

"She's not a missing person. She's a grown woman. Who, quite frankly, is showing more maturity than you are right now."

The sincerity in her brother's voice and eyes sliced her like a knife through the gut.

"I hate it when you're right."

He took a seat next to her. Tossed the note on the table. "No, you don't. You just hate when you're wrong."

Honey leaned across the sofa and landed on Brax's broad strong shoulders.

He blew a breath of exasperation through his lips. "Unless she's got a wad of dough, she had to take the bus. I'll call the station and see what I can find out."

"Don't bother. They're the second place I called. They wouldn't give me any information."

Brax wrapped his arm around her. "Then you gotta believe what she said. She'll be in touch. Let her do this. If anyone had tried to stop you, what would have happened?"

Honey couldn't restrain the soft chuckle skipping up to the surface. "I would have run over them like a steamroller."

Honey let her head fall to her chest. She was tired. Lela had dragged up all the turmoil of her past. The stress made her so tired she couldn't think straight anymore.

"Honey, I love you. You know that. But here's the thing. No, here's two things. First, I'm your brother, not your knight in shining armor. Second, you need a man and a life…in that order.

"No," he continued, "I got one more. You need to let your sister learn what she needs to learn—what we all learned."

Honey swallowed the hard lump in her throat. She nodded, thinking none of them had learned the lesson that Honey had learned. As far as Honey knew, Lela didn't have any real leads. Honey could only hope that after running into a few dead ends, Lela would give up and call. Or better yet, just come back.

Honey gave Brax's broad shoulders a quick squeeze. "Thank you for coming to see about me."

"No problem," he said.

"Liar," Honey responded. "Now go home and get on your job. I can't wait to be an aunt."

Brax pushed up from the couch and tugged at the bottom of his black leather jacket.

"Why don't you get some rest? Go for a walk or go get a massage. Relax and throw off that stress."

"Yeah, maybe." Honey didn't know if she could relax. Maybe she'd go through her CDs. Put on some Brule. They usually chilled her out. Heck, she'd even light her incense.

With a kiss on the cheek, Brax was off in his pickup and headed toward the highway. Honey closed the door and took steps to change her mood.

She filled her CD changer with favorites like Brule, Lotus, Michael Franks and Nina Simone. Then she dimmed the lights and put her incense on blast. After that, she did something she hadn't done since Lela showed up—she took off all her clothes, wrapped herself in her favorite blanket and stretched out on her sofa. By the time Marcus Miller started singing "Boomerang," Honey was toasty. She couldn't have been more relaxed if she had finished a glass of merlot before lying down. The only thing that might have made her feel cozier was if Houston's arms were around her instead of her favorite blanket.

Honey closed her eyes, realizing Houston was another source of stress she needed to shake out of her head. The man hadn't called once since he'd insulted her sister. No *I'm sorry.* No *Let's start over.* Nothing. Honey had way too much time to think about the incident since then. She was even starting to wonder if Houston could have been right.

"Ah," she said, interrupting Raphael Saddig's voice harmonizing with her favorite bass player. "Let it go."

But just like the song, memories of Houston and her desire for him always came back like a boomerang.

Honey stretched long and languorously, her determination restored until her doorbell rang. A bolt of adrenaline shot through her body and she found herself wishing for Houston like crazy.

She pulled the blanket around her and shuffled to the door. "Who is it?" she asked, too eager to gaze out the window or get an eyeful out of the peephole. Even though Cliff always used his key to get in, he hadn't come over in such a long time, it would be just like him to be that formal.

"Houston," the voice called, turning Honey into a yearning lump of throbbing flesh. All he had to do was say his name, she chastised herself. It wasn't good for a woman to be this vulnerable to a man. But then, most men weren't Houston Pace.

She opened the door, holding back a smile and all her emotions. He had some apologizing to do, didn't he?

She stared at him stiffly, not willing to move.

"May I come in?" he asked, looking every bit the elegant, sophisticated man with just a splash of thug.

Mr. Pace could hang some clothes. The television cameras in L.A. would love him. Without a word, Honey stepped aside.

Houston brushed lightly against her, a trail of cologne following behind him. She used all of her willpower to keep quiet instead of moaning her approval.

Houston looked from the incense burning, to the subdued lamplight and the stereo, then back to her, concern knitting his brow. "Am I interrupting something?"

"No," she said then waited a beat. When he seemed reluctant to speak, she decided to push the issue. "So, did you forget something?" she asked, closing the door. For a second, she was about to fold her arms across her chest, but she couldn't do that and hold on to the blanket, so she just stood still.

"Yeah. You can say that." Houston looked just as troubled as Honey felt.

She waited. She'd never seen him at a loss for words. It was interesting. She wondered how long it would last.

He rubbed his palms together, then grabbed the back of his neck and let out an exasperated breath. "I forgot something real important. My head."

Honey hadn't expected him to give in so easily. Relief flooded her from head to toe. She stopped fantasizing about his rear and started paying attention to his words.

"The craziest thing in the world happened to me when I met you. It's like I'm this person I never knew I could be. I actually want to spend time with you and *do* things—talk, listen, hang out. I've never just wanted to *be* with someone before. And when Lela showed up, it felt like my time with you—what little I have left before I leave for L.A.—was being cut off. So what you heard the other day was stupid frustration. I really could have handled the situation better."

"Yes, you could," Honey said, finally.

Houston looked even more handsome when he was humble. He had the make-up face on. Those please-take-me-back-I'll-do-better-next-time eyes. Simply luscious. It was the sexiest she'd ever seen him.

Right on time, her mind told her. Just the distraction Honey needed. Her clit beat like her heart. She shifted her weight beneath the blanket and gazed at Houston through lustful eyes.

He stared back with a look equally as intense and hungry. "Why do I get the feeling that you're naked under that blanket?"

"Because I am."

"Um," he said. The intensity of his gaze increased as if he had X-ray vision or wished he did.

"Uh, like I was saying…I came over to, ah, make sure things are…cool between us. Will you accept my—"

Honey dropped the blanket and placed a sassy hand on a round hip.

"—apology." Then without another word, Houston picked her up and carried her upstairs to her bedroom.

Houston laid her on the covers and re-created the downstairs atmosphere by lighting a candle, closing the drapes and putting her slow jams mix into her CD player. Since he'd rearranged her bedroom, he knew where everything was. It didn't take him long to create the perfect atmosphere.

Houston took his clothes off, much too slowly for Honey's taste. He was teasing her. It was working.

Honey pressed her thighs together and squirmed in anticipation.

Houston stood before her only a moment before he climbed on the bed on top of her. He looked harder than she'd ever seen any man before. Tighter.

Honey reached up, pulled Houston's face to hers and kissed him deeply. He responded with his lips and his hips, both circling her skin. Circling. Mesmerizing. Controlling.

She started it, but Houston finished it, taking his mouth away and giving it back. Being stingy and generous. Teasing and tasting. Honey wanted more. Pulled him closer. Matched his circles.

Houston kissed the side of her face, her chin, the crook of her neck where it made her crazy and got her juicy. His tongue caressed the sensitive area. Like a master, or a selfish man who'd discovered gold.

Honey gasped and clung. He'd found her spot. Zeroed in on it. Worked it until she arched against him and spread her juices on his stomach. She shivered with delight as he kissed and sucked and licked her just behind her ear.

He moved down farther. His lips across her shoulder. His fingers twisting a nipple. Honey rubbed the bare skin of his back and shoulders, begging him to enter her with her hips.

Houston grabbed a packet from a dish on her nightstand, tore it with his teeth and quickly rolled the latex to the base of his hard length.

Too long, Honey thought. He's taking too long. She stiffened when his weight returned and his arousal probed her opening.

"Don't make me stop," he panted, but paused anyway. "You want this…right?"

"Yes, yes, Houston, I—" A whisper of uncertainty passed between them.

He plunged inside her so deeply, Honey gasped in shock and pleasure. She grabbed on to him, not sure what to do next. It had been so long.

Houston pumped in and out of her and Honey closed her eyes as slowly her inclination to pull away faded, replaced by her desire for more. More of Houston. More of this feeling inside her.

Honey felt like she was drowning. The sensations came too fast for her to sort them out. She clutched at his skin and gasped. "Houston, Houston!"

"Shhh," he said, taking it slow. Pumping easy. "Let me sit back in it," he said. "Get comfortable. Yeah. You feel that?"

"Yes," Honey said. "I feel it."

"Don't think about anything else." Houston stopped for a moment. Kissed her collarbone, then her neck and then…

"Just this," he said, as his tongue slid across her sweet spot and Honey screamed in ecstasy. Her body went into a wild buck dance beneath him as wave after wave of pleasure hit her from the inside out.

Her body felt stretched out. Strung out. Jonesin' and coming. She felt all the sensations of her sensual journey. Instead of chasing away her butterflies, his lips played with them. His hips stroked them, saturated her body with pleasure. Her body softened and pitched to his featherlight touches across her thighs. Her blood ran hot and tender at the same moment. Where Houston's wondrous mouth thrilled her to the marrow, she shuddered at the flicker of unease.

Suddenly, Honey felt awkward and self-conscious about her inexperience.

"Houston…"

He kissed her jaw. Held her tighter. "Yes," he answered, his voice a hot whisper against her ear.

"I…I don't know how to…am I… Is this right?"

Was she keeping up? Was she moving her hips right? Did it feel as good to Houston? She'd been consumed with pleasure their first time, but now, she wanted to get it right.

"This…is new to me," she admitted.

"It's right, baby," Houston said. "It's so right. And so good."

Houston's voice trailed off, his hand scooped up her right leg and he leaned into her core.

"Ah!" she moaned, feeling him more fully. Thrusting inside her.

A feeling taking her over, pushing her to the edge again. She could get used to this. The weight of his body. The smell of his sweat mingling with hers. Another moan in the room besides her own. Even the bed creaked differently. And she loved it. Loved the out-of-control sensations. Sharing control of her pleasure with someone else—with Houston. She could—

"Oh, Houston—"

"Come with me, baby."

"Yes," she moaned. "I'm, I'm…"

Honey's whole body came alive. Every nerve ending ignited with fire and passion. She closed her eyes and squeezed herself tight.

"Ah!" Houston moaned, thrusting powerfully.

She matched his rhythm and heard her mind say, *I love you, Houston,* as her heart exploded.

Chapter 28

Houston's eyes peeled open slowly. He rolled over and glanced at the clock on the nightstand: 4:00 a.m.

He smiled at the woman hugged up against him. Her breath a hot rhythm against his chest.

He played with the tendrils of her hair so he wouldn't wake her. He wanted to reflect on their evening before he roused her for a repeat performance. They'd been good together. Better than he'd imagined. All he'd wanted to do was stay inside. Keep her coming. Honey's body and Houston's stamina had seen to that several times over and long into the night.

They couldn't stop touching each other. Couldn't stand for their skin to be separated. Every time Houston came, the urge to come again was so strong, he kept rubbing and sliding against her thigh until he was hard again. Then, it was off with that condom and on with another.

His fingers stroked deeper into her curls and waves. He stroked more deliberately now, feeling his desire rise one more time.

Honey stirred, moaned softly and clung closer.

Houston flicked his index finger against a nipple and after a moment, lowered his head to it. His lips and tongue pulled on the soft tight flesh while his fingers found her feminine opening and massaged gently.

Honey snuggled closer, moaned louder.

"Wake up, baby," his lips coaxed. He made a come-here motion with his finger inside her. She moistened with the movement.

Honey's eyes fluttered open. She stroked Houston's neck. "You want some more?" she asked, her voice sleepy and sexy.

He abandoned her nipple, but only for a moment. "What do *you* think?"

"Um," she said, arching, aching "Me, too."

Houston spent time getting to know Honey's body. Tasting each sweet place with his lips, his tongue. Realizing that the taste of her body lived up to her name— Honey.

He loved making her moan. Making her happy. The night couldn't have gone any better if he'd planned it. But of course, he had planned it.

"One more time," Houston coaxed after Honey's first shuddering release. "Come for me again."

"Ah, Houston, Houston," she said. She was so giving and so wet and so—

"What was that?" she said, tensing.

Her body froze immediately, like it had been turned to stone.

"That's just me," Houston said, pumping slow and deep like she liked it. "Doin' you right."

"No," she said, moving to sit up. "I heard something."

Houston would not be dissuaded. Not when it was this good. "You heard me, swimming in this."

"No," she said, pushing him. "Get up. Lela's back."

Houston gritted his teeth. She was killing the moment. He rolled off, but tried to reassure her. "It's not Lela."

Honey was already up and grabbing a robe from her closet. "Honey!" he called after her.

Houston rushed down the stairs after her, pulling off the barely used condom. *What a waste,* he thought. *She only got one orgasm out of that bad boy.*

Honey reached the bottom of the stairs and flicked on the light. Soft halogens filled the room, and Houston's eyes started to adjust.

"It's not Lela," he said.

Honey looked around for a futile moment then sunk down on the couch. She dropped her head into her hands, and her shoulders shook.

"Hey, hey," Houston said, taking a seat beside her and putting his arm around her shoulders. "It's cool."

"No, it's not." Honey lifted her head, her red eyes tired and sad.

"I didn't tell you this earlier, because I was trying to take my mind off of things, but Lela is gone. She left me a note, but she didn't say where she was going. I've been worried sick ever since I found it.

"I thought being with you would chill me out, you know, but I guess worry is getting the best of me and now I'm hearing things."

"Well, don't worry. I have a feeling Lela is fine."

Houston swallowed a lump of what was steadily turning from pride to a twinge of conscience. He had more than a feeling about Lela.

"Look, Honey. I wasn't going to say anything, unless Lela said something when she got back. I sent her to Laramie. She's—"

"You did *what?*"

"When I was putting the finishing touches on the spare bedroom, I found a box with papers from when you were probably looking for your mother."

"You went through my personal things!"

"Of course I did. That's what organizers do."

"But you, you—"

"Hold on. Before you blow this all out of proportion, Cliff let me borrow his key yesterday—"

"Cliff! My Cliff? What's Cliff got to do with anything?"

"If you'll just calm down for a second, I'll tell you. I used his key to get that last known residence document you had. Then I called in a favor from a friend of mine who checked it out and said that your mother might still live there. So, I figured, Lela could be the one out of all of you to make contact since it seemed to mean so much to her. I thought by helping her, I'd be helping you."

"When did I ever ask you for that kind of help? You idiot! You stuck your nose someplace where it didn't belong, and now, as if her heart wasn't hurt enough, you're going to break it all the way!"

"What? I don't understand."

"You sure as hell don't." Honey went over to the phone and quickly dialed a number.

Houston had never seen Honey so pained. She looked as though she'd been told her mother was dead instead of possibly found. "I need to speak to Binky." She waited a beat and then... "It's Honey. Yeah," she said, turning her back to Houston. "I just thought I'd call and tell you that Lela is on the way to see you. She's—"

"Damn. What did you tell her? What did you—"

Honey held the phone away from her ear and stared at it. The phone began to tremble in her grasp. Houston caught it, before it fell to the floor.

A look of shock and confusion pulled his features tight. "Was that your mother?" he asked.

Honey felt like half a woman. The other half had been siphoned away by that brief conversation. "Yes."

She plopped down on the couch and Houston grabbed the blanket in a heap near the door and tied it around his waist.

"You *know* your mother...know where she is...all this time?"

"Yes."

A steady stream of tears fell from her eyes. She'd mentioned Lela's heart being broken, but Houston would swear right now it was Honey's.

"Why didn't you ever say anything?"

"Because she doesn't want me. She doesn't want any of us. She never did. Least of all Lela."

"Honey—"

She turned, her face pale and her eyes dead. "You need to go now."

"You're joking right? I'm not leaving you like this. I want to help."

"Get out. Please. You've done too much already. Don't do any more. Please. My heart can't take it."

She was so flat and lifeless, it was as if all of her curves and buoyancy vanished into the night air. And *lifeless* was the operative word. The vibrant, luscious, juicy woman he'd come to know and shared his body with all night was as dry as dust and just as vulnerable to the wind.

Her words deflated Houston. He felt crumpled and useless. It was a terrible, lonely feeling. One he didn't want to last any longer than it took for him to put his clothes on and leave Honey's home.

Honey might have been sitting in the same spot on her couch for days if it hadn't been for her brother.

No more rescues.

Even with a family, she really only had herself to rely on. She also realized that if it hadn't been for Houston clearing out breathing space in her home, Honey could have quite easily curled into a ball and tried to sleep away the anguish coming to her in fresh waves.

Would it ever be over?

Just when Honey thought she'd moved on—healed, dealt with her past—something would trigger an emotional relapse and she'd sink into every regret she ever had about having a junkie for a mother. Having a mother who didn't give a damn about her. Knowing that her mother was less than sixty miles away living her life without her children.

Being rejected.

That's what it was. All her life, she'd been so afraid of being rejected by others that she pushed them away before they had the chance to reject her. Men. Women. It didn't matter. She'd told herself for years that people just didn't *get* her, but the truth was, she never let them.

All except Houston. She'd thought he was different. So different that she'd let him into her body and in doing so, he'd gotten into her soul.

How could he go behind her back like that? Break into her house, go through her private papers and then send a teenager on a trip that would surely end in disaster.

In the shower, Honey stopped soaping up, stood still and let the water hit her face in soft blasts. She had to find Lela. She'd put her business on hold. Put her life on hold. Do whatever it took to find her. No telling what Carnetta, aka Binky, had said to her. If it was anything like Honey's *reunion* with her, it was anticlimactic and painful.

Honey finished showering and dressed in a dark silence. She didn't have a plan and beyond Laramie, she had no idea where she was going or how on God's Earth she would find her sister. But she had to find her.

Honey grabbed her purse and keys and headed for the door just as the doorbell rang.

Lela, her mind whispered. *Please, please,* she

begged to any god who would listen. *Let it be.* Her heart pounded right through her chest. Her breath stuck and adrenaline rushed in her veins as she snatched open the door.

"Thank you, Lord," she said, gazing at her sister who looked as if she'd aged five years and had been crying for at least that long.

"Lela!" she said and rushed out to hold her sister, who collapsed in a puddle of tears and anguish.

"It's okay," Honey said, holding her tight. "I got you. You hear me. I got you. It's all right now. I'll make it all right."

And with no meddling man in the way to create unnecessary drama, Honey vowed to do just that.

Honey kept her mind occupied by finishing her backlog. She had to admit her fulfillment station worked the way her mind worked. She couldn't believe how quickly she could get orders out the door.

She'd considered branching into other online novelties or even creating a few of her own. With this setup, she could do it easily.

Lela was upstairs taking a shower. She'd been up there a long time. Honey remembered her first meeting with her mother and how she felt the need to wash every emotion, bad memory, all the tears off of her body. Lela must have had the same idea.

By the time she came downstairs, Honey was finished with her backlog and only had the day's orders to fill.

"You hungry?"

Lela's expression said, *You've got to be kidding.*

"Good," Honey responded. "'Cause I didn't feel like cooking."

They both sat down in the living room. Honey popped in an old Sounds of Blackness CD and wished Lela would say something. Her heart ached for her sister. She wanted so much to take the pain away.

"You want to talk?" she asked but couldn't imagine Lela saying anything Honey didn't already know about. Roach-infested halfway house where most of the boarders were halfway high. Fresh tracks on their mother's arm. Ashen brown skin and bone. A drawn and sunken face that used to be beautiful. Their mother cycled in and out of a special rehab program where as long as you stayed out of trouble and pretended to look for a job, the state gave her a free place to stay and a food stamp card, which she traded for drugs.

"There's nothing to say. I mean, you tried to tell me, right?"

Lela looked down at her hands, so dejected and crushed. Honey wanted her to know that she wasn't alone.

"It's hard. It's the kind of thing that can break you down or make you bitter. I was bitter for a *while.*

"I wasted *so* much of my life trying to find her. Trying to find Brax, Collen and you, too.

"Then, after all these years, you know what her first words to me were?"

Lela looked up, eyes curious and vulnerable. "What?"

"'You smoke? Your mama needs a cigarette.'"

Lela's eyes rounded like saucers for a moment. Then she covered her mouth and choked back what sounded like a chuckle.

Honey felt perplexed.

"She said the same thing to me."

Honey's heart sank until Lela started laughing. In seconds tears came with her laughter, but her eyes sparkled.

Honey got caught up in Lela's giggles and had a laugh herself.

"You create this image in your mind. Funny how your brain tries to protect you. Make you think it's not that bad. But in reality she's...she's..."

"Absolutely nothing like the image in your mind?" Honey finished.

"Yeah," Lela said. "Why couldn't she be—"

"Because nothing in life is that perfect," Honey said. "And the sooner you learn that, the better. What's even more important is that we don't let it stop us. You hear me?"

Honey wrapped her arms around her sister. "Now that you know, no matter how much I wanted to save you from this, you gotta believe this is the beginning. Not the end."

Lela stared at Honey, a tiny spark of her determination shining in her eyes. "I came from that, but I'm better than that."

"You got that right!" Honey said.

While Sounds of Blackness harmonized the words "I believe," Honey and Lela held each other tight. In that embrace, each silently promised the other to be there. To be the family the other needed and deserved. And to rise above their pasts together.

Chapter 29

"I feel like I'm corrupting you," Honey said. She couldn't believe that she was allowing her eighteen-year-old sister to help set up her Webcast.

Since Houston made her order area look like something out of California Closets, Honey hadn't had a chance to reconnect her broadcast equipment. With Lela's help, it was going smoothly.

"Just one more USB and we're good to go," Lela said.

"How do you know so much about electronics?" Honey asked, remembering how she usually called on Joshua Crane down the street whenever she had AV issues—much to the chagrin of Mrs. Crane.

"My teacher-mom was crazy about gadgets. I picked up a few things."

Honey realized Lela had picked up a lot. Mostly her

attitude. Since the incident with their mother a week ago, she'd gradually returned to what seemed close to normal. From what Honey could tell, she was almost there.

"So, you all set?" Honey asked. She hoped the question came out calm and clear. Inside, Honey was worried to distraction. Lela had made friends with the Johnston sisters who lived two houses down. They always seemed like nice teenagers. They had invited Lela out for a movie and a visit to Arcade Palace.

"Yeah. What about you?"

"Oh, I've done this hundreds of times. I could do this upside down and backwards."

"I wasn't talking about your show."

Honey caught Lela's meaning and blew out a breath of exasperation. "No. Never be ready for that."

"But I don't want you to call for you. I want you to call for me."

"So you said."

"I *do*. I might owe him an apology. I was kind of—"

"A brat?"

"Yeah. But it was all that mom stuff. It just made me crazy. Ya know?"

"Do I ever."

"Well, at least think about it."

"Why are you so into Houston all of a sudden?"

"Because, despite what happened, he helped me when he didn't have to. So, really think about it. I know you want to."

"You act like you know me."

"I'm your sister, remember?"

"I'll never forget it," Honey said, grabbing Lela and

hugging her. She had no idea she could hold so much love for someone. She didn't feel this close to her brothers, and she'd known them longer. The only other time she could remember feeling like her heart was about to break open from love was...Houston. And he had to go and act like a fool, like a common thief, robber, burglar—

"Too tight," Lela said.

"Sorry," Honey said, letting go.

"I guess I got a mom now, huh?"

"I didn't mean to—"

"No, it's cool. I like that you're worried about me."

Fresh tears stung Honey's eyes. "Okay. You go on to the movie so I can do my show."

"Break a leg," Lela said, heading for the door.

"Have a good time."

Lela grabbed a jacket from the closet and shoved her arms into it. "Call Houston!" she shouted and then dashed out.

Honey shook her head yet stared at the phone. She left her computer/camera setup and walked over to it. She even picked it up. But waves of mistrust mixed with feelings of betrayal overcame her.

He went through my private things and sent my eighteen-year-old sister away. It was not just audacious, it was arrogant.

And it was wrong.

Honey put the phone back on its base and went over to her computer. It was time for FulfillmentTV.

"Now you're talking! Way to get creative. If you can't get your girlfriend off with clit-stim gel, a bullet, a G-spot vibrator and a butt plug, you might want to take her pulse. Make sure she's still among the living. Okay?"

Honey placed each product in a line on her desk, so viewers could get a good look. She changed the camera views to shoot close-ups of each one and then pull back to a full shot of her at her desk.

"Thanks, Honey."

"You're welcome, Hank from Arizona."

Honey disconnected the call, and the next one in the queue came in behind it.

"You're all the way live in the Beehive. Welcome to the show."

"Thanks, Honey. My name is Felicia. I'm from Pittsburgh. I've called in every week since your show began. This is the first time I've ever gotten through."

"Thanks for hangin' in here with me. I appreciate your persistence. What's on your mind?"

"Well, with the last caller, you mentioned the clit-stim gel. I've had some for a long time and I've wanted to try it, but I'm reluctant to put it on because, well...is it really safe?"

"If you've had it for a long time, check the fresh-ness date. It might be time to treat yourself to a new tube. But this product—"

Honey focused the camera on the tube on her desk. "It's safe if used according to the instructions."

"Okay...but...like...how does it work? How does it make you feel?"

"Actually, it's like taking menthol and putting it on your clit. It has the icy/hot action goin' on, and it makes you ultra, ultra sensitive. So anything that feels good without it, feels awesome with it. And as far as the big O goes…super size me, okay?"

"Well…okay."

"How about this? All things in moderation. Buy a new tube. Try a tiny amount. If you like that, try a little more and a little more. Just don't exceed the maximum. Then call me back and let me know how much you loved it."

"I will, thanks, Honey. Love your show!"

"You're welcome, Felicia!"

Honey pressed the button for the next caller. "We have time for one more question," she said just as her front door swung open.

"Look who I found," Lela's voice called.

"Collen!" Honey shouted.

"No. My name's Curtis," the voice coming through Honey's computer speakers responded.

Honey got up from her desk, trotted over to her brother and flung her arms around his neck.

"Hey, sister. What ya know good?"

"I'm looking at him."

He planted a kiss on her cheek. "Nah. I'm as bad as they come."

"Honey? Are you there? Did the system crash?"

Honey let go of her brother and dashed back to her desk. She adjusted her cordless headset. "I'm sorry, Curtis. Something, or I should say someone unexpected has come up. Please feel free to send your question to me via the Web site.

"I want to thank everyone for a wonderful show. I'll

be back next week. Until then, respect yourself and each other. Honey Bee out."

She turned to her brother. "Collen, what are you doing here?"

"I heard what happened with Lela. I knew you'd be upset, too. I wanted to check on you both."

"Thanks, big brother."

"Don't worry about it. Besides, why should Brax have all the fun?"

Collen was a tall man, easily six-seven. He had a runner's build and a warrior's eyes. His skin was the color of strong ginger and when he walked into a room, you had the feeling that a great mountain had just risen in your presence. At first blush, he came off as demanding and, well, full of himself, Honey thought. But underneath, and protected by all that, was a heart like a barn door. Big. Wide. Open. Sometimes it just had to be excavated.

"So," he said. "Were you doing your show?"

"Yeah."

"She made me leave," Lela said.

"She should have. How old are you again?"

"Eighteen."

"Too young," Collen declared, not missing a beat.

"It's not like I've never had sex."

"Ah. We don't need to have this conversation." Collen slammed his palm against the side of his head as if his ear was plugged up—or he wished it were.

Honey crossed her arms over her bosom, a knowing sensation gnawing at her patience. "Okay. I know you care about us. I'm sure that's part of the reason why you're here. What's the other part?"

"What kind of brother do you think I am?"

"The kind who will get away with whatever he can get away with for as long as he can get away with it."

Collen was about to respond when Lela came back from the kitchen with the drinks.

"So, what's up with you? You look like a man who's just been kicked to the curb."

"Kicked to the curb is such a…strong description."

"I knew something was up."

"Nothing is really up, trust me. I just need a vacation. I haven't had one since Brax and I started Big Rig Trucking. Since he's no longer a partner, the business has been workin' me like a sled dog.

"So if it's all right with you, I'll just kick it here until Thanksgiving."

"Yes!" Lela said, pumping her fist.

Honey's happiness went into overdrive. She'd spent much more time with Brax than she had with Collen. This would allow her to get to know her family better. She couldn't have asked for a better blessing or more to be thankful for.

Or could she?

No matter how she tried to evict Houston from her thoughts, like an obstinate tenant he stayed up in there. He was hooked in good. Darn-near permanent. Why did Mr. Organization have such a tight hold on her?

Because, her mind told her, *he's seen you, everything about you, every crack and crevice, every place and space. He knows all your faults and dirty secrets.*

He's been through them. Touched them with his hands.
And he still looks at you with adoring, appreciating
eyes. Even when you made him leave.

She'd let him into her life, into her body, all the way,
and because of that, she felt a deeper-than-intimate
connection that was unshakable.

How could she have been wrong when everything
about Houston Pace felt so right? His intelligence, his
attentiveness, his interests, his goals, his looks. Honey
even liked the way he walked—like a man who owned
the ground his soles touched. His determination was
unshakable—even if it was misguided. His loyalty to
her brother. His ambition. His relationship with his
cousin gave her an insight into how he treats his family.
His pull-no-punches attitude.

As far as Honey was concerned, the man had
everything in the right place. And just the right size
and grind, Honey's mind reminded her, flashing back
to their lovemaking.

There was more chatter in Honey's house than a tree
full of randy squirrels during mating season. Catching
up, getting to know kinds of words and sounds for
days. Honey was uncharacteristically quiet as Collen
and Lela went on about their lives, their experiences.
Now and then, the conversation would dip into childhood memories, where the ink of stories there was
still fresh, painful and bloodred. Honey was concerned
that touching that past might keep Lela feeling blue
and far away. Collen took care of that. He stepped in
like the healing balm Lela needed. His strength, hard-

truth honesty and straightforward way of dealing with things helped her see a different side. A side Lela needed to know about. A side Honey needed to be reminded of.

"So, cooking. Can you cook? 'Cause we all seem to have a different relationship to food preparation. Honey can cook, but she doesn't. I can make a kitchen smile like it's got big teeth. Now, Brax on the other hand…he'd rather not have to even go into a kitchen if he can help it."

"Yes. I can cook. And I actually enjoy it."

"My girl!" Collen said. "I guess we know who will take care of Thanksgiving in a few days. Now, I have two rules: the turkey and the mac and cheese are my domain. You can have anything else you want."

"Cool. I'll take dressing, yams…"

Honey's thoughts trailed off with her family's holiday plans. Her mind had been occupied the last three days with them, but it has also been busy with other concerns. The main one—if she would ever see Houston again.

She'd kicked him out, sure. She'd yelled. Been rude. And thrown the force of her anger in his face. Yep. She'd done all those things. And now, seeing Lela, safe, sound, and having turned a major corner of her life because of him, she wondered if she'd been way too rash.

And in all this time, she also wondered why he hadn't tried to call, e-mail, text or anything. He'd disappeared from her life. It was as if he'd never existed.

Except that he had. And he'd created something new in Honey she never believed she would have.

Peace.

He'd started with the simple gesture of putting her house in order. By the time he'd finished, he'd put her soul in order. Not only that, he'd stepped up to the plate and helped her sister, when all Honey could think about was her own pain and how much she never wanted to peel back the scab of that old wound.

Honey had been afraid that she'd never get healed again. It had taken so long the first time. She'd never quite healed from her childhood. Maybe she never would. But one thing was certain. The one person she believed could ease her through any hurt was on his way to California.

"There she goes again," Collen said.

"I know," Lela responded. "She's been that way since Houston left."

Honey ignored her brother and sister. It was probably best not to give them any more ammunition. Anything poised to come out of her mouth at that moment would have done just that.

"Okay, look. You know Thanksgiving is my thing. You can't be down in the mouth, sis."

"I'll be fine," Honey said.

Lela blew out a breath. "I don't think so."

"You've got two choices. Let go, or go get. Now which one's it going to be?"

Lela and Collen waited expectantly, their eyes wide with curiosity. Anticipation sat heavy in the air. Honey felt it push down on her shoulders, nearly sticking her to her chair. Her insides felt like warm soup.

She didn't want to ruin Thanksgiving for her family. The first time they were all together, it was important that it be special and not drama-filled. Honey decided to do what her mind had been pushing her to do all day.

"I'm letting go," she said.

"I'm putting them away as fast as I can! Most folks pay me a thousand bucks a day to do half what I'm doing here. So cut me some slack. I only have two hands."

"And half a brain."

"Oh no, you didn't just talk to my mother like that!"

Paul scurried into the foyer and stopped inches from where Houston was on his hands and knees, shoulder-deep in boxes and stored items that his aunt hadn't opened, dusted, touched or probably even wondered about in the forty years she'd lived in that house. Since she was kind enough to let him stay, and he did have skills, he offered to do something for her. Who knew it would be to unpack boxes from when the eighty-year-old woman had first moved in.

"All right. I'm sorry. I'm just—"

"Suffering from a bad case of blue balls and Honey withdrawals."

"Why must you—"

"Because somebody should, and most folks don't have nerve enough or sense enough. So God created me. And honey, when he did, there was no mold. Just *BAM!* And here I am."

Houston pulled out six unopened boxes, all from a company called Ronco.

"You gonna take your frustration out on my mama and her junk, or are you gonna deal with the real?" Paul asked.

"Look," Houston said, standing. He pulled out the rest of the boxes that hadn't seen the light of day since the seventies. He brushed cobwebs and ancient dust off of his hands and trousers. He buried his face in the crook of his elbow to stifle a sneeze, then turned toward Paul. "She gave me the boot. One of those stiletto-heeled, pointed-toe boots, too. The kind that leave an imprint on your backside that never goes away. Even when you meet someone new, your ass still hurts."

"I wouldn't know anything about that. I've never been in love."

Houston frowned at his cousin's remark. Paul was straight-up crazy. Houston wasn't in love. He decided that ridiculous notion didn't deserve his attention. Otherwise, the truth of it might crush his heart. "Anyway, Honey made it clear. She doesn't want my help. She doesn't want me."

"You sure about that? You call her? 'Cause you lookin' like somebody took your train set. And you snappin' at folks like you want a beat down. Now, I may be…delicate…but I ain't scrurred. Ya heard?"

Houston took one look at the seriousness on the face of his reed-thin, Sisqo-short cousin and laughed for the first time in days. "You're serious?"

"Like Oprah's accountant."

Houston took a seat on the floor next to all the boxes. His aunt would have to go through them, but the least he could do was unpack them. There were only three days before his plane left for California. He wondered what family treasures were tucked away in the cardboard boxes. His mind flipped and he wondered what

kind of family treasures he and Honey could have
created. God, he loved her that much.

Damn. His heart hurt anyway.

"Paul, I'm going to take your advice. I'm going to act
like I've got some sense, finish up here, pack my clothes
and be ready when that plane leaves on Thursday."

"What about—"

Houston didn't look up, but he flashed a stopping
hand in front of Paul's face. *No more,* he thought. *I
knew better than to start up with someone. I knew
better. I should have followed my first mind.*

His second mind, since the moment he met
Honey, was his show. Selfishly, he pulled it to the
forefront, determined to leave Cheyenne with his
soul intact.

Easy come, easy go, his mind said, but his heart
wasn't so sure.

When the phone rang, Honey thought she recognized
the number on her caller ID, but she couldn't place it right
away. She was just finished with the final batch of orders
for the day. For some reason, Fulfillment was having a
run on love games. Holidays were like that. Folks started
getting ready for those special intimate occasions,
planning surprises for significant others as well as themselves. Often, the trends came in waves. Like a signal
from a high tower broadcast to the populace about what
would get them off this time of year.

Houston had built in flexibility into her work area
so that when there was a run on an item, she could set
up her packing and shipping bins to accommodate the

item. All movable parts. All interconnected. She could shift and sort at will.

"Hello?" Honey said.

"You better come get this Negro, before I have to kill him!"

Paul's voice blared through her receiver loud, clear and just as demanding as ever. A jolt of surprise and gladness traveled her body like electricity.

"Paul! What's up?"

"My blood pressure and my fist. Houston is getting on my last mahogany nerve."

"Why? Is something wrong?" The electricity turned into bright concern. Honey took a seat at her order station.

"Hell, yeah. You…him…not together. That's a whole lotta wrong. Now I'm no marriage counselor—"

"Marriage?"

"Okay, couples' therapist, but I ain't stupid, either. You two should be together. So can you tell ol' boy something so he can pick up his bottom lip?"

"He's sad?" Honey asked, perking up. Not that she was pleased Houston was sad. Just intrigued by the idea that he might actually miss her or be as bummed about not seeing her as she was about not seeing him.

"Girrrrl, a Bobby Brown comeback album has a brighter future than Houston Pace right now."

"Has something happened with his show?"

"Not yet, but if he reports for work like this, they'll even cancel the *rehearsal*. Folks be walkin' 'round talkin' 'bout Pick up the what? Who?"

No. Houston was the most talented and visionary man she'd ever met. He deserved his shot.

"Now, I'm buttin' in where I don't belong, only because I do belong."

"Huh?"

"That's what I'm trying to tell you. Our family, we keep to our own. We live and let live. We stay out of A/B conversations. We don't get up in folks' business unless they ask…or unless they're family.

"Houston must have felt like your business was his business. Right or wrong, he was treating you like family. Like more than somebody to kill time with. You know what I'm sayin'?"

"Yeah."

"I'm not being disrespectful. I'm being real."

"Did he ask you to call me?" Honey hoped that maybe Houston had taken a step toward her.

"Hell, no! If he knew I was even talking to you, he'd stop talking to me. For a minute."

"Paul, thanks for the call. I appreciate it. I'm grateful and all that. But I don't know what to do. I pretty much slammed the door on the relationship."

"Then open it. You know all the ways to get in touch with him. You're the Webcast diva. Do something electronic. But do it quick."

Honey thought about the timid approach. A text message. An e-mail. Heck, she could send an electronic voice mail to be delivered later, just so she didn't have to eat crow right away. That might buy her some time to get an apology together.

The urge to end this separation and be with Houston again overruled her caution and sent her heart fluttering.

"Let me talk to him, Paul."

"Ooh, Honey—I just love the way that works out, bein' your name and all—I can't give him the phone. He's gone."

Whew. "When will he be back?"

"Whenever the season ends I guess. He's on his way to the airport."

"What!"

"Yes, chile. That's why I called. I was hopin' you'd drive on down there before—"

"Oooh!" Honey shouted, slamming the phone down on its base. She'd deal with Paul later. Right now she had an airport to get to.

Chapter 30

A week early. He was leaving a week early. Honey knew. She had the date memorized in her head. They'd briefly talked about spending Thanksgiving together. The air had gone heavy in the middle of that conversation, the words between them dropping like stones. They were treading into dangerous, I-might-be-getting-serious-about-you territory. When neither of them backed down or backed away, it provided another signal that things were moving between them, solidifying. They were becoming a couple.

Honey had been counting down the days, marking them off with digital checkmarks on her electronic calendar. Days leading up to the end of their no-strings-attached liaison. The only problem was they *had* developed strings. Lovely, strong, life-altering strings that made each passing day roll forward like a giant stone of dread.

They'd willingly passed the point of no longer single.

In the cool afternoon, she pushed the speed limit. Past the Governor's Mansion, the Plains Hotel and the Union Pacific depot. Folks in their best crowded the streets, where in some areas it made more sense to ride a bicycle than drive—even a car as small as hers.

Honey didn't even try to rehearse what she was going to say. She had no idea. All she knew was what she felt.

There was no way she could get all of that into a coherent thought. She just hoped—as she parked and dashed through the terminal—that seeing Houston would inspire all the right words.

It didn't, though. She spotted him right away. His fine self queued up to show his ID and boarding pass to the man standing next to a sign that read No Non-Ticketed Persons Beyond This Point.

"Houston!" she called like a crazy fool. She didn't care. She was crazy to take a chance on losing the man who set her life and her love right.

He turned, but didn't see her. She ran forward and called again. "Houston Pace!"

This time he saw her. His frustrated traveler's face melted like movie butter. Replaced by a quirky smile and a jig to get out of line and meet her halfway.

They moved quickly, but stopped short of the boy-gets-girl-back hug.

"What are you doing here?" he asked. The happiness in his voice was obvious and delightful. Some of Honey's distress faded.

"I—I—I love you," Honey answered.

Houston's expression lost some of its brightness. "So you've said."

Honey shook her head and spoke under her breath. "Damn. I should have rehearsed this."

Now all the shine was gone. He was frustrated again, and Honey was losing time. And words. She thought *I love you* would do it. Like Stevie Wonder's song "These Three Words," she thought they would work magic and fix what was broken between them. But Houston was still waiting and Honey's mind was grasping at straws.

"What else are you?"

"What?" Honey asked, then recognized the words as Houston's olive branch. She had to come up with something meaningful or else…

"Sorry!" she blurted. "I'm sorry."

Houston nodded his acceptance of her haphazard apology. "I thought I'd gotten inside you. Like you'd gotten inside me. I thought I was part of you. But—"

"No, no! You are. You have. You did!"

"Then what happened?" he asked. His eyes were full of pain. Pain Honey never noticed that last day. She was so consumed by her own pain that—

"Because I forget that everyone is not out to hurt me. I swear, Houston, some days I wake up and it's like all that stuff that happened when I was a kid is still happening. I start to think that nothing I've ever done or can do will shake it.

"But I don't want to be that person anymore. I can't. Not if it means losing you."

At the end of the concourse, flight attendants called out boarding announcements over loudspeakers. Honey would have sworn she heard Burbank in one of those announcements. But she couldn't be sure. Her mind was preoccupied with Houston's mouth caressing hers so sweetly and the warm wet tongue he slipped between her lips. The arm that pulled her against him. The sigh that came out of his body that she pulled into hers.

"Stay with me this last week. Before you have to go. Spend the holiday with me. And then—"

Houston's mouth came for hers again. His delicious, wet mouth. Hot now, and greedy.

Their distant future was uncertain, but their immediate future seemed set. Only they might not make it to a bed.

Chapter 31

Thanksgiving came in with a slow breeze and a bright sky. The distant sun had chased away a gathering of steel-gray clouds. The crisp cool of winter thinning the air, turning the green to umber shades.

Honey had spent the quiet of the morning awake and in awe. The man she loved held her all night. Loved her all night. For the first time, her heart was full of more love than she thought it could hold.

She had to get up soon, she knew. In addition to Lela and Collen, Brax and Ariana were coming, and there was still all the cooking to do. But the last thing she wanted was to ruin the moment. For a second, she was afraid to blink for fear she'd disturb Houston, he'd wake up and leave. Honey held off a yawn as long as she could, and then released it soundlessly. Houston stirred, pulled her tighter, held her closer, then settled back into sleep. If she could stretch her happiness, extend it, make it grow... She counted each second of bliss. Memorizing it, as she had all her life. Her happiness had been fleeting. She'd never known when an abrupt change would cause her pain. Pretty soon her mind became the great compensator: *Don't get used to anything.*

But last night, she'd made love to Houston without barriers. Without holding anything back. Without her past crawling into bed with her and leaving dirty, pain-stained memories on the sheets.

Could it be over?

By midday, Honey started to believe that maybe it was. A cacophony of voices started at breakfast and increased as the day went on. A conglomeration of constant sound. Because she was so often in her home by herself, the clamor took Honey aback. It took some getting used to.

She'd never had so many people in her kitchen since she bought the place. Every surface in her kitchen was taken up by a dish about to be prepared or in the middle of it. Cupboards squeaked. Drawers gave off raspy sliding sounds. Utensils clanked against bowls and cookware. It was like a soul-food cookfest up in her place.

Joy washed over her in great, soul-stirring waves.

The moment Brax and his family arrived, Honey was relegated to assistant. They wouldn't let her cook a thing. Even Houston pitched in alongside Lela and Collen.

"I'm the host. I have to cook something," she insisted.

"You cooked up the idea," Collen said. "Let us do the rest."

They weren't quite treating her with kid gloves, but they sure weren't letting her do any of the "heavy lifting." So, Honey divided her time between helping Collen outside with the fried turkey, and cleaning up behind the assembly line of cooks in her kitchen. Honey couldn't believe how well everyone worked together.

She inhaled thick, season-infused smells until her mouth vibrated with the comforting aroma of soul food. The air in her home was redolent with smoked ham, baking biscuits, macaroni and cheese and steaming greens. They had all eaten light that morning in anticipation of the evening's meal. As time nudged into the afternoon hours, Honey's stomach rumbled with emptiness and longing to break bread with all those who meant so much to her.

By 4:00 p.m., Honey sat down to Thanksgiving dinner with Houston, Lela, Brax, Ariana, Ariana's little sister Selena and Collen. They sat nearly elbow to elbow at Honey's dining room table. Another first, she thought.

The glad and smiling faces at the table made Honey's heart flutter. A deluge of emotions surged inside of her, all fighting for control and freedom. She opened her mouth to speak, but nothing came out. In her mind, she thanked everyone for coming. She said how much she appreciated their presence, their hands in preparation, their love. And then she started a prayer to bless the food.

In her mind.

In her soul, the onslaught of feelings stole her breath and pulled slow tears from her eyes. Happiness. Joy and gratitude didn't begin to describe what was mixing and mingling inside her and creating new, even more powerful and overwhelming emotions. She reached over to Houston, hands trembling, but she couldn't see him. Tears clouded her vision.

Houston's warm and strong arm came across her shoulders. "Oh, baby…what's the matter?"

"It's…it's…me," she said finally. "It's always been me.

"I thought it was Brax, the way he's so closed most of the time. I…I thought it was Collen, because he never seems to land on anything and stay. And then, when Lela came, I thought…I thought… See that. It's really her. Because she can't see two feet in front of her for looking for our mother. But all the time…"

Houston's reassuring arm tightened around her shoulders. "Baby. It's okay."

"No," Collen said. "Let her talk. Let her get it out."

Honey's pulse pounded in her ears, and a knot constricted her throat. "It's me. I'm the one who's not whole. I'm the one in so much pain that I had to build physical barriers around myself. Clutter as tall as walls so I could hide. If it wasn't for Houston…"

Overwhelmed by the love flowing toward her, Honey noticed how much she had in common with her family. The same intense eyes, the same way of attacking the world, the same cautions. Even their hands—strong, work hands—looked the same.

Houston had cracked open the levee. Placed the perfect stress on it, and now the waters of her purist emotions rushed out of her.

"It's okay, baby," Houston crooned, his voice and hands reassuring.

She raised a shaky hand to her face. Pushed the tears off her skin. Gazed into the eyes of everyone at the table, and said, "I know."

"Shall we bow our heads?" Brax asked. Along with being thankful for her bountiful meal, Honey gave thanks for everything in her life. Everything. Her past gave her a strength and a compassion for others. It made her want to help and make life better for other people. It made her want to be part of the world and make things happen instead of watching what happens.

It gave her a family that appreciated each and every second that they could spend together. And amazingly, in the craziest way ever, it gave her Houston.

"Are you still eating?" Lela asked Collen.

"No," he said, reaching into the roasting pan and pulling away a small chunk of ham.

"Me, either," Lela said, taking one also.

The buzz of conversation had long since tapered off. Replaced by groans, moans, yawns, soft burps and the occasional and labored, "I'm stuffed."

While the men rubbed their stomachs and pretended to be too busy to clean up right away, the women went to work, covering food, putting dishes in the refrigerator and scraping plates for the dishwasher.

A sudden jolt of memory shot through Honey as she spooned Collen's mac and cheese into a storage container. "Oh my gosh. I forgot all about Cliff!"

"Cliff?" Ariana said. Her voice sounded perplexed, with just a pinch of irritation mixed in.

"Yeah. We *always* spent Thanksgiving together. It's our first holiday apart, and he doesn't cook. I'd been thinking that I'd just take him a plate, but I forgot."

Lela rinsed a plate and stacked it in the nearly full Maytag. "He's probably with his own family, right?"

"Cliff's a loner, like…like I used to be," Honey said, and giggled at her change. "He's at home, flipping channels, grumbling because there's no good programming on holidays and waiting for his microwave meal to heat."

Lela frowned and put down the foil she was using to cover the green bean casserole. "That's plain wrong."

"I'll take him a plate," Honey said.

"Him who?" Houston asked, entering the kitchen.

The women in the kitchen stared at Honey. Their sudden all-eyes-on-her reaction made her wonder if she should have been self-conscious. Before she could consider that question, she knew the answer.

Heck, no. She may not know who her father was, but she knew who *her daddy* was. She smiled at the thought. Ariana, Selena and Lela took a conspicuous break and left the kitchen.

"What's up?" Houston asked, striding over to where she stood next to the refrigerator. His stomach puffed out against his belt. He'd put a hurtin' on his meal. All three helpings. Honey wondered if that little paunch was a hint of things to come. A flash of them in their eighties, in rocking chairs, Houston still frisky, trying to push up on her, and his belly getting in the way flickered in her mind. She grinned then.

He slipped his arms around her waist, brought her to that place against his body that she was made for. The place where she fit perfectly. "What?"

"I love you," she said, so happy. So satisfied.

"I love you, lady," he answered back and kissed her on her forehead. "So, who are you taking a plate to?"

"Cliff."

"Thought so."

"I'm sure what he's eating this evening comes from a box that reads, PEEL BACK THE FILM AT ONE CORNER AND MICROWAVE ON HIGH FOR SIX MINUTES STIRRING HALFWAY THROUGH COOK TIME."

"Wow. You've got that down."

"Trust me. Before Tony, I was a microwaving diva."

"Speaking of Tony," Houston said, staring into her eyes.

"I know," she said. She wondered when it was coming. "No more special deliveries."

He gazed at her expectantly with that familiar and-what-else? look.

"And no more landscaping, or home repair."

She feigned a pout, then realized what getting rid of her handymen would really mean. "What am I going to do, Houston? You'll be in California and there are certain things I'm just not about to do."

"So don't do them."

"But what about—"

His eyes grew bright with excitement. "Come to California with me."

"W-What?"

"You wouldn't have to move right away. There's a chance—although it's damn slim—that this thing won't fly. But if it does, I don't want to commute. I want you with me."

Honey swallowed hard, her nerves twittering inside her like tiny birds. "Houston, are you sure?"

"You can run your company from anywhere, right?"

"Well…yeah. But I don't know. This is quick. I'm just starting to get to know Lela."

"And if you hadn't noticed, she's pretty much turned into a cowgirl."

Houston was right. Since their first visit to the Sugar Trail, Lela's other fascination had been Brax's ranch. Honey knew it was only a matter of time, days even, before she'd ask if she could stay there. And she didn't see Brax refusing that request.

"I need to think."

"Stop thinking. Just feel," Houston said, pulling her closer.

He took her hand. Placed it against his chest. Against his heart. The beat was strong. As strong as she'd ever felt.

"I feel…I want…yes! I'll go with you."

Houston's mouth fell upon hers, his lips and tongue possessive and scorching. Her insides caught fire. Their breaths came out ragged. Urgent. She pressed her hands against his chest. His heat flowed into her.

She shivered with the realization that this man was hers and he wanted her in every way possible.

"Take your plate," he said. "But hurry back."

"Okay," Honey said, dazed and hypnotized. If Houston kept kissing her like that, she might not be able to refuse him anything. Ever. His good love made her want to give all her customers a twenty-percent discount, with some free lube thrown in as a surprise gift.

Houston gave her butt a firm, appreciative squeeze, brushed his lips against that sweet spot just behind her ear. His breath made her tremble. Then he strolled out of the kitchen wearing a pride-wide smile.

Honey went to work fixing Cliff a generous plate. She made sure she piled on his favorite…dressing with brown gravy, wrapped the meal in foil and headed next door.

"Who is it?" he asked when she knocked on the door.

"You know who," Honey responded.

Cliff swung the door open. Leaned against the jamb. His face was soft and immobile at the same time, his eyes all-knowing and curious. "Happy Thanksgiving."

"Same to you," she said, standing still and feeling a little awkward.

His eyes dropped to the plate in her hands. "That for me?"

"Yes," Honey said, allowing herself to smile. She handed him the plate. It must have weighed five pounds.

Cliff took it easily. "Thanks."

"No," Honey said. "Thank you." A wave of appreciation crested within her. He'd been a patient, understanding companion. She knew there was a great love in his future. There had to be; he deserved it.

"Thank you for everything, Cliff."

He nodded and his eyes smiled. "You look happy, damn it."

Honey chuckled and held back a little. Every time she thought about how happy she was, she just wanted to giggle herself silly. "I am happy."

Honey was not so self-absorbed that she didn't notice the twinkle in Cliff's eye. "You look happy your darn self."

"Um, let's just say a dude is…satisfied."

"Ooh," Honey said. "Anybody I know?" She thought about their neighbor. They'd make a cool couple.

Cliff stared off in the distance. "Well, I'll be damned. It's you!"

"Me?" she asked, noticing his gaze focusing behind her.

"Yes," he said. "Look."

Honey turned. Her body felt as though it were moving in slow motion. Nervous perspiration popped out on her face. Even before she could see who it was, a nervous lump stuck in the middle of her throat.

Their eyes caught. Their identical eyes that shared mitochondrial DNA. A cab pulled away from the curb, and the woman stood on the sidewalk carrying a long bag in her palms.

Cliff placed a hand on Honey's shoulder. "Is that—"

"Yes," Honey answered. She patted the back of Cliff's hand, then started back toward her house. "Wish me luck."

"Good luck," Cliff said.

Chapter 32

The day was so crisp, brittle branches and twigs weren't the only things breaking off and falling. It seemed to Honey that if she listened closely, the clouds, the sun, the very air around her were snapping in two. And quite possibly, her heart would be the next thing to break.

The woman standing near the curb was as fragile as a twig and appeared just as windblown and dry. The sight drew up her entire body like a tight fist.

Yes. She looks like me. Even after all these years. Honey knew her mother had a remarkable way with drugs. A skill, actually. Taking just enough to get plenty high, but not enough to pass out, foam at the mouth or convulse. Amazing, but that sweaty tightrope must have been what had kept Carnetta above ground and looking

like a woman twenty years her senior instead of an ema-
ciated smack junkie. Fifty degrees outside today, and the
woman actually had some color in her face instead of
that ashen, dry-cheeked complexion Honey recalled.
She was relieved and repulsed at the same time.

The walk back to her home lasted only seconds, but
it took twenty-eight years. Each step a mile long and
a woeful memory wide.

Time travel. It does exist.

With each stride, Honey rolled back the pain-
heavy years.

Her mother actually smiled. She needed the services
of a good dentist, but it did Honey good to see her
mother smile. It was a sight Honey hadn't seen since
she wore kneesocks over her then bony calves.

Neither woman spoke. Just stared and dared to
breathe in the most uncomfortable place either of them
could have been at the moment. Just seeing her mother
and knowing what an ordeal it must have been for her
to come melted the remaining ice that frosted Honey's
heart, but she refused to speak first.

"I brought dessert," Carnetta said. Her voice shook
as if there were an earthquake in her throat. "You used
to like my bread pudding."

Honey stared at the brown paper-wrapped package
in her mother's hands—hands that looked so much
like her own.

"I still do," she said, finally.

Honey's body trembled as she led her mother up the
stairs and into her home.

The buzz had started again. By the tone, folks were

getting their second wind and their second grub on. Well, Carnetta would either increase the buzz or grind it to a halt.

When they entered, every eye in the living room fell on Carnetta. Honey closed the door and moved to her side.

"I'll take that," she offered, reaching for the dessert.

Her mother handed it to her gently, as if she were afraid to give it up. It was the only shield between her and the barrage of emotion building in the room.

"Well, I'll be," Brax said.

Collen crossed his arms. "I don't freakin' believe it."

"I *knew* it!" Lela said. She flew out of her chair, raced over to her mother and threw her arms around her. "I knew you loved us! I knew it. I knew it. I knew it. I knew it."

Honey stepped away from the reunion, not quite ready to rejoice or let her guard down. It was less than a month ago when she'd spoken to her mother on the phone and the woman was high. Honey had half a mind to lock up all her valuables, ask the woman what she'd come to steal and tell her that no one in her house was about to give her one penny for drugs. But it was Thanksgiving, and Carnetta was her mother. And Honey's fragile heart wanted and needed to believe.

Honey moved closer to the kitchen where Brax and Collen stood. Together, Honey imagined they looked like a barrier of unforgiveness and caution.

"I didn't come here to ruin your holiday. I really don't know why I came. But when Lela came to see me, something in me wanted change."

"When did you shoot up last?" asked Collen, his voice flat and unemotional.

"A week ago."

"Surrogate drug?" Brax asked.

"Yeah," she said.

Collen crossed his arms in front of his chest. "You bring it with you? I wouldn't want to stop in the middle a perfectly good Thanksgiving to take you to a hospital."

"Collen!" Lela said.

"Don't trip," he responded, sitting down. "I'm done."

Collen went back to eating his mac and cheese. Brax put his third helping on the table and never touched it.

"Are you hungry, Carnetta?" Ariana asked.

"No," she said, "but the counselor said I should eat anyway."

"Counselor?" Brax, Collen and Honey asked in unison.

"Yes. I can't get clean by myself."

And that's when the script flipped and the tables turned for Honey. The slow dawn of realization rose inside Honey.

If people are blessed to live long enough, she reasoned, life proves that at some point, adult children eventually end up taking care of their parents. The roles reverse. In most cases, it's only fitting. Only Carnetta hadn't earned the cosmic cache or created the karma to deserve being taken care of by her children.

But she was their mother.

She had a disease. One she was—for the first time that Honey could recall—trying to control. And as long as she stayed honest with her effort to change,

Honey would help her. Stand by her. Show her how to give the kind of support Honey wished she'd had when she was growing up.

But if she did that, then she and Houston...

Ariana squeezed past Houston on her way to the kitchen. "I'll fix you a plate. Selena, come help me."

Selena got up without a word and followed her sister away from the tension.

"I don't know how long this clean-and-sober thing will last. I feel like I've been run over by a hundred-car train and ant colonies are growing in the tracks left on my body. Hell, the last time I remember *not* wanting to get high, well, I must have been seventeen years old. Even with the methadone, I keep converting your belongings, damn near everything I see, to street value."

Collen growled. "Ain't this about a—"

"But I'm *trying*. And that's more than I've done since you all were born."

"It sure is," Honey said.

With shaky hands, their mother pulled a pack of Newports and a lighter out of a cigarette bag. "Mind if I smoke?"

"Yes," everyone except Lela said.

Carnetta nodded her head, and Lela stood. "Let's go outside, Mama."

Honey cringed. Mama. Hearing her sister say the word made her skin feel as if some of her mother's imaginary ants had crawled up Honey's back.

"You all right?" Houston asked, right on cue.

"No. I'm angry. I'm frightened. I'm confused."

"They sound like valid emotions to me. You should be all that. And some more on top of it."

"What I want to be is bighearted. I want to take her in my arms like Lela and say all is forgiven."

"I think you're the neutral one around here. Brax hasn't said a word hardly. I know that's typical for him, but this just feels stronger. His jaw is on lock. And Collen…the brother is hostile, to say the least."

"So, is the cup half full or what?" Ariana asked.

"Half full," Honey said without hesitation.

"Half full," Brax said, to the shock of everyone in the room.

Everyone waited for Collen. Houston, Ariana and Selena seemed just as eager to hear from him as his siblings.

He took his time. Finished every crumb and morsel on his plate. Then he pushed the plate away and pushed back from the table. Collen looked up at no one in particular, sucked his teeth for a moment, then said, "There is no cup."

"What do you mean?" Honey asked. She felt as if she were walking in quicksand.

"I mean y'all smokin' something. This woman checked out of each one of our lives, especially Lela's, a long time ago. And Brax, you can act like you didn't go looking for her if you want to, but I know you did. And I know you found her. We all did. And she told each one of us to get to steppin'. And she probably said the same thing to you two that she said to me. 'If Lela comes around, tell her I died.'"

Honey slumped against Houston. She had no idea

they'd all gone looking for her. Her brothers had just shrugged off her questions about that, so Honey assumed she'd been the only one to actually contact their mother. But it made sense. They all found her. They all contacted her. They were all kicked to the curb. Not something you'd share easily and definitely something you would want to prevent a sibling from going through—that is, if you cared about them.

Collen chuckled a little. It sounded cold and thin. "You all can be saints if you want to. Turn the other cheek. Forgive and all that sweet drama. I'm not built that way. Never have been. *Mama* made sure of that. So as far as I'm concerned, Carnetta is right. She is dead."

Honey watched her brother get up. She knew there was no stopping him. He headed upstairs to gather his things.

"Collen," Ariana called out. Brax touched her arm and shook his head no.

Carnetta and Lela came back into the house and joined everyone in the living room. The pungent smell of cigarette smoke followed them in and oozed out of their pores.

"So," their mother said, her voice still choppy and unsteady. Honey wondered if it was withdrawal or nerves. "You all didn't talk about me while I was gone, now did you?" she asked, trying to make a joke. No one laughed and when she scanned the room, her eyes lost their shine. "I see."

She must have noticed that Collen was gone, Honey thought.

"Shoot, y'all. I'm so nervous right now I could,

well, it just wouldn't be pretty. Just being here is stressing me more than I thought. I'm going to go."

"I'm going with her," Lela said.

"What?" Honey responded.

"She needs someone to help her stay clean. I'm going to do it."

Honey stood up then. "Lela, you're not thinking straight. Besides, you wouldn't know the first thing to do."

"So I'll learn."

"She's already doing it. Just talking to me like she did outside. And listening without judgment, well, it meant a lot," their mother said.

That lump Honey had in her throat came back with a vengeance. If their mother ever relapsed, she would break Lela's heart. She'd get high and get angry and turn into the harsh addict she'd been for decades.

No doubt she'd tell Lela the truth—that Lela was the product of rape. Honey knew it, the way she knew her own name.

"Lela—"

"You can't stop me, Honey. I won't change my mind."

"Then I wish you the best, little sister," Brax said. "Now before you go, why don't we heat up some of that bread pudding?"

Chapter 33

Honey Ambrose would forever be in awe of Houston Pace's organization skills. He could find a place for everything. Clothes. Linens. Books. Inventory. He'd even found a place for the things Honey simply couldn't part with, no matter what.

Most especially, he'd found a place for her in his life and him in hers.

Three weeks after Thanksgiving, the movers were in her home, packing her neatly organized items and dollying them onto a moving van. Sixteen hours to Burbank. With all the connections she had to make, she would arrive just an hour ahead of her furnishings. But that was okay. The man of her dreams would be there to greet her at the airport.

Houston sounded funny on the phone the last time

she talked to him. Nervous. He wanted to make sure she had the itinerary right, made her connections and packed something special in her carry-on.

"I want to take you out as soon as you get here," he'd said.

"Can I shower first?"

"No. Just bring something nice and change before you get off the plane."

"Whoa."

"Yeah. This is serious."

"Where are we going?"

"Someplace special. Someplace cozy."

"Someplace romantic?" she interjected.

"Now, now. Don't steal a brother's thunder."

No, no. Never. Not in a million years would Honey want to steal *this* thunder. It was pop-the-question time. Honey knew it. And Houston knew it, too.

It was a beautiful blessing. One that came right on time. In the weeks since Thanksgiving, Honey and her family had been making…adjustments. A new family member was hard to get used to, Lela was no exception to that rule. And now, if she wanted to call her mother and just say, "Hey, Mom, how you doin'?", she could—at least for now. And on those occasions when she did call and her mother answered sober, clean and eager to talk, well, that was another hard adjustment.

So far, Lela was hanging in there. It was as if she'd found her calling. She'd even talked about going to school and getting a degree in clinical dependence counseling so that she could help others besides their mother. The fact that Carnetta had relapsed for three days and then returned to rehab didn't dissuade Lela. She hung in there, attended every family group session and proved that she was up for the challenge.

As for Collen, he'd gone back to running his trucking business. He hadn't called or asked how their mother was doing even once. Honey wondered if he ever would.

"This is the last of it, Ms. Ambrose."

"Thank you," she said, turning around in her now empty house. The closing was set for tomorrow. In the meantime, she was headed to Brax's ranch to spend the night.

She tipped the movers twenty dollars each and smiled at the broad smiles she put on their faces.

"You have a good day!" one of the movers called.

"You, too!" Honey said, and indeed she would.

Honey looked down at the ring finger of her hand, and knew in her heart that there comes a time in every woman's life, when she looks into the eyes of the man she loves and knows that she will move heaven and earth to be with him and to have the happiness in life that she was meant to have. She stepped out of her house in Cheyenne, Wyoming, knowing that Houston Pace was that man. He'd knocked down every wall of protection she had around her heart and made himself comfortable there.

He was the one.

And she was grateful for everything that had happened in her life that led her to him.

Her cell phone rang and she answered before the second ring.

"Yes, I have everything," she assured Houston, whom she identified by a special ring on her phone.

"All I really need is you, baby."

Honey glowed like she was fluorescent.

"You and that Handyman 4000. It's in your carry-on, right?"

"Whatever!" she shouted. "Just have my ring ready!"

"Just have my answer ready," he called back.

"I will," she said.

A tangled web of revenge,
deception and desire…

defenseless

National bestselling author

ADRIANNE
byrd

Beautiful Atlanta ad exec Sonya Walters knows her sister's
marriage is in trouble. But when her brother-in-law is
murdered and her sister is the prime suspect, Sonya
turns to the one man who can help—defense attorney
Dwayne Hamilton. Sonya is determined to keep things
purely professional…but soon finds herself defenseless
against Dwayne's seduction.

"Byrd proves once again that she's a wonderful storyteller."
—*Romantic Times BOOKreviews*
on THE BEAUTIFUL ONES

Coming the first week of April wherever books are sold.

ARABESQUE®

www.kimanipress.com

KPAB0810408

Model
PERFECT
PASSION

National bestselling author
melanie schuster

Billie Phillips dreams of quitting modeling for real
estate, but she needs mogul Jason Wainwright's help.
Jason's willing to play along to lure her into his bed,
but Billie's all business. With persistence, Jason may
win the girl…but lose his heart.

**"Schuster's superb storytelling ability
is exhibited in fine fashion."**
*—Romantic Times BOOKreviews
on Until the End of Time*

Coming the first week of April wherever books are sold.

KIMANI™
ROMANCE

www.kimanipress.com   KPMS0610408

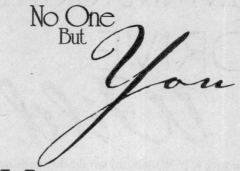

A steamy new novel from *Essence* Bestselling Author

GWYNNE FORSTER

DRIVE ME
Wild

Reporter J. L. Whitehead would do anything for
a story—even pose as a chauffeur to newly made
millionairess Gina Harkness. But when business
turns to mind-blowing pleasure, will Gina believe
that though J. L.'s identity is a lie, their untamed
passion is real?

**"SWEPT AWAY proves that Ms. Forster
is still at the top of the romance game."**
—*Romantic Times BOOKreviews*

Coming the first week of April wherever books are sold.

KIMANI™
ROMANCE

www.kimanipress.com

KPGF0600408

These women are about to discover that every passion
has a price...and some secrets are impossible to keep.

NATIONAL BESTSELLING AUTHOR

ROCHELLE ALERS

After Hours

A deliciously scandalous novel that brings together
three very different women, united by the secret lives
they lead. Adina, Sybil and Karla all lead seemingly
charmed, luxurious lives, yet each also harbors a
surprising secret that is about to spin out of control.

"Alers paints such vivid descriptions that when Jolene
becomes the target of a murderer, you almost feel
as though someone you know is in great danger."
—*Library Journal* on *No Compromise*

Coming the first week of March
wherever books are sold.

sepia™